PRAISE FOR *ALL THEY WILL CALL YOU*

"Tim Z. Hernandez is the real thing. This epic,
and it is in the best possible hands."

—Luis Alberto Urrea, author

"*All They Will Call You* is a heart-wrenching read for anyone who cares, and the names—now etched in stone in a far-off graveyard—have become friends who will travel with me as long as I am walking."

—Arlo Guthrie, musician

"With great compassion and patience, [Tim Z. Hernandez] has immersed himself in a long-forgotten episode of California history and uncovered a multilayered epic of love, injustice, and family fortitude, stretching across generations and borders. This is an intelligent, empathic, and deeply moving work."

—Héctor Tobar, author of *Deep Down Dark: The Untold Stories of 33 Men Buried in a Chilean Mine, and the Miracle That Set Them Free*

"An important and moving book, exploring the theme of identity and loss and disenfranchisement—topics that have never been more urgent than they are now. Hernandez has illuminated the present with this original and riveting examination of the past."

—Susan Orlean, author of *Rin Tin Tin: The Life and the Legend*

"This book is an opportunity to cut through the immigration rhetoric we drown in every day. It's an opportunity to speak about the people behind the abstraction."

—Tucson Weekly

"[*All They Will Call You*] toes the line between journalism, memoir, ethnography and poetry with a rare and invigorating finesse, emerging as the rare piece of art."

—Visalia Times-Delta

"Told with a reporter's eye and a poet's voice, *All They Will Call You* is a great historical piece of work, completing the mission that Woody Guthrie embarked on when he wrote his classic song long ago."

—David Amram, author of *Offbeat: Collaborating with Kerouac*

"Hernandez's loving detail and authentic knowledge of the Valley continue to plant him firmly in Steinbeck and Saroyan country while forging his own path. Part documentary, part thriller, Hernandez's work rings true—nearly breathless with new information and a certain justice now rising like smoke from the wreckage in the canyons of his beloved and mysterious San Joaquin."

—Richard Montoya, Filmmaker and Playwright

"A scrupulous writer and researcher, Hernandez has changed the course of America's musical history, as well as its immigration history."

—Will Kaufman, author of *Woody Guthrie, American Radical*

"This story holds great historical significance as we continue to define ourselves as a nation. . . . Woody would be proud to know that his song played a part as a catalyst for this book, offering overdue closure to the lives of these workers."

—Deana McCloud, Executive Director of the Woody Guthrie Center

"Woody Guthrie must surely be smiling, wherever he is. *All They Will Call You* completes the sad yet compelling story outlined many years ago in his song 'Plane Wreck at Los Gatos (Deportee).' Thanks to Tim Z. Hernandez, the souls of the migrant workers lost in that 1948 plane wreck can now rest peacefully. Required reading for true Guthrie fans."

—Robert Santelli, Executive Director of the GRAMMY Museum

ALL THEY WILL CALL YOU

Camino del Sol

A Latina and Latino Literary Series

ALL THEY WILL CALL YOU

The Telling of the Plane Wreck at Los Gatos Canyon

TIM Z. HERNANDEZ

TUCSON

The University of Arizona Press
www.uapress.arizona.edu

First paperback edition 2018

ISBN-13: 978-0-8165-3484-5 (cloth)
ISBN-13: 978-0-8165-3737-2 (paper)

Cover design by Leigh McDonald

Library of Congress Cataloging-in-Publication data are available at https://lccn.loc.gov/2016027512.

Printed in the United States of America

∞ This paper meets the requirements of ANSI/NISO Z39.48-1992 (Permanence of Paper)

. . . in their rememberings are their truths.

—Studs Terkel, *Hard Times*

Both sides of the river, we died just the same . . .

—Woody Guthrie,
"Plane Wreck at Los Gatos (Deportee)"

El recordar es vivir.

—Don Leovardo Ramírez Lara

For Ayotzinapa, Sri Lanka, Argentina, Ciudad Juárez,
and for the missing everywhere—

CONTENTS

AUTHOR'S NOTE

It began with a job I landed back in 2001. I was hired to travel into the rural parts of the San Joaquin Valley to meet with various communities and listen to their stories. As part of the job my supervisor required I submit weekly write-ups—snapshots of people I'd met, or stories I'd heard along the way. The problem was that I was a terrible notetaker, and by the end of each day I'd heard so many stories that I'd forgotten most of them. I needed a way to remember the details. It was for this reason that I bought a handheld audio recorder.

Around that time, my grandfather, an aged campesino, was admitted into the hospital. Fearing the old man's time was up, I went to visit him that day. When I arrived I found him asleep in a dim, cold room, alone. As he slept, I felt emboldened and got physically close to him in a way I never had before. I leaned in and observed his face, marveling at the toughness of his dark flesh, the way his eyelids appeared like sheets of leather draped above his high cheekbones, and how breath skidded in and out of his slightly parted lips. It was in that moment, while observing my grandfather, that a thought occurred to me. This old man, to whose seed I owed my existence, was the last living grandparent I had. He was the single thread connecting me to my past. I was floored by this realization. Beyond the fact that he was born in Brownsville, Texas, and had been a migrant farmworker since the age of ten, I knew very little. Surely he was more than just the stern-faced Tejano who would criticize us grandchildren for not speaking fluent Spanish. He was living history. And the details of his life were suddenly a matter of urgency. In that moment, alone with my grandfather, I pulled my recorder out and decided I'd wait there until he woke.

Thirty minutes passed before he began to stir. With both eyes shut, he reached for the IV on his wrist and gave it a tug. He scratched at the stubble on his face, and then, as if sensing my presence, opened his eyes. He found me sitting at the edge of his bed. "Mijo," he whispered. His voice was gravelly. I handed him a cup of water. He took a drink. His hand trembled. "Qué haces aqui?" He was surprised to see me. I didn't bother with pleasantries. "I wanna hear about your life, Grandpa," I said. He stared at me with a blank expression, unsure if I was being serious. It was an unusual request. But then he responded, in English, as if he'd been waiting for such an opportunity. "Okay," he said, placing his cup on the bedside table. He scratched at his chin again. "I have some things I want to tell you—"

What followed were not the details of my grandfather that a person would ever find in hospital files, on his birth certificate, or in any hall of records. No, these were the rememberings that by the old campesino's understanding made up the very core of who he was, his DNA in testimony. It was there, in that quiet, dim hospital room, clutching my small audio recorder with its tiny red light on, listening to my grandfather speak, that I went from using the recorder for its practicality to transforming it into a tool for gathering stories. Or rather, as a way to ensure that certain stories were never lost.

It is in this spirit that the telling of the plane wreck at Los Gatos Canyon, and how the song of the same name—which carried its message the world over—has been uncovered after nearly seven decades. While the telling itself is true, its loyalty is not to people of fact but rather to people of memory. Which is to say, all of us. In this way, it's inevitable that some rememberings will contradict other rememberings. If several people witness the same tragedy and offer opposing accounts, whose version is the most accurate? In this case, perception is truth. And how reliable is fact anyway when the "official" documents themselves have been proven incorrect, beginning with the names of the passengers? Officialness too has its inconsistencies. To stumble upon a plane crash is to stumble upon the fragmented and broken shards of stories, and to have faith that from these clues our own glaring humanity offers enough light to fill in the unknown. The facts of what occurred on that day are not, nor have they ever been, the purpose of this book. This telling is not interested in the calculable details, but rather the testimonies themselves, from the people whose lives were touched directly in incalculable ways. How a tragedy and a song had a profound and lasting effect on the people who lived it. And though memory's propeller turns with embellishment, guesswork, and even reimaginings, this telling is rooted in years of investigation and interviews with the surviving families and friends I was successful in locating—a search that required traveling six decades back in time, to numerous cities, ranchos, and barrios, in three countries, three languages, with limited resources, and only a single shred of old newspaper as the clue. In the end, of the thirty-two passengers reported to be on that airplane, I managed to locate the families of seven. But as you'll find, the total number of lives changed on that cold winter morning of January 28, 1948, was far greater.

THE STORY KEEPERS

The Eyewitnesses

Coalinga and Los Gatos Canyon, California

June Gaston, daughter of Happy Gaston and granddaughter of Red Childers
Dolores Crabtree, canyon resident and eyewitness to the crash
Old-Timers, group of local residents and keepers of the canyon's history

Passenger Luis Miranda Cuevas

Jocotepec, Jalisco, Mexico

Casimira Navarro López, the love of Luis's life in 1948
Yréne Miranda Navarro, Luis's niece

Passengers Guadalupe Ramírez Lara and Ramón Paredes González

Charco de Pantoja, Guanajuato, Mexico

Jaime Ramírez, grandson of Ramón and nephew of Guadalupe
Guillermo Ramírez, grandson of Ramón and nephew of Guadalupe
Caritina Paredes Murillo, Ramón's daughter
Don Fermin Ramírez Lara, Guadalupe's son
Don José González Arredondo, close friend of both Ramón and Guadalupe
Olga Cárdenas, Guadalupe's granddaughter

Passenger José Sánchez Valdivia

La Estancia—Nochistlán, Zacatecas, Mexico

Celio Sánchez Valdivia, José's youngest brother
Eliseo Sánchez González, José's friend in 1948
Don Guadalupe Jáuregui, José's friend and cousin by marriage

Pilot Frank Atkinson and Stewardess Bobbie Atkinson

Rochester, New York

Helen Atkinson, Frank's sister and in-law to Bobbie
Mary Lou Atkinson, Frank's sister and in-law to Bobbie
Connie Mart, Frank's niece

Martin Hoffman

Rough Rock, Arizona, Navajo Nation

Sue Edelstein, Martin's girlfriend in 1971
Pete Seeger, musician and friend of Martin's
Lucy Moore, Apache County Coroner on the Navajo reservation in 1971
Margi Hoffman Dunlap, Martin's niece
Dick Barker, Martin's friend and schoolmate at Colorado A&M

ALL THEY WILL CALL YOU

32 ARE KILLED IN CALIFORNIA PLANE CRASH

28 Mexican Deportees, Crew And Guard Victims in Coastal Range Disaster

FRESNO, Calif., Jan. 28 (AP) — A chartered Immigration Service plane crashed and burned in western Fresno county today, killing 28 Mexican deportees, the crew of three, and an immigration guard.

An hour after the airliner appeared to explode over Los Gatos canyon, near Coalinga, shortly after 10:30 a. m., 19 bodies had been recovered from the smouldering wreckage.

Most of those remaining in the plane were jammed into the forepart of the fuselage and mangled almost beyond recognition.

Irving F. Wixon, director of the U. S. Immigration service at San Francisco, said the Mexican Nationals were being flown to the deportation center at El Centro, Calif., for return to Mexico.

Associated Press, January 28, 1948

I

THE WITNESSING

The sky plane caught fire over Los Gatos Canyon . . .

—Woody Guthrie, "Plane Wreck at Los Gatos (Deportee)"

1

WEDNESDAY, JANUARY 28, 1948

10:40 a.m.

As Red ran closer he watched a thread of black smoke unfurl from the mountain pass, where a fragile seam between two worlds had ripped open. His bootheels tore at the earth as he gasped for breath, but even the incline of dirt road wasn't enough to slow him down. His old heart was beating like it hadn't in too long. Everywhere he looked were articles of clothing, papers and documents, life's particulars blown across the canyon. He could smell fire. Rounding the bend, he spotted it. Lodged in the creek bed was the blackened, smoldering ship. He rolled up his shirt cuffs and scrambled down the embankment, but a burning sensation entered his lungs, forcing him to retreat. The tops of trees surrounding the wreckage were aflame. "Anyone hear me?" Red cried out. Only the seething spit of fuselage answered back. A chill ran through him when he discovered that what he first mistook for felled tree limbs weren't trees at all. Even a simple red high heel was strangely out of place among the pinecones and dead grass. At that moment a familiar odor consumed him. He yanked a blue bandana from his back pocket and pressed it to his nose. Wicked utterances whispered in the narrow space between the canyon walls. The echoes of godforsaken screams cast out into the air just seconds ago were still reverberating in Red's ears.

"Red saw seats with people still in 'em being thrown out the hole in the side of the plane," his granddaughter June recalled. "They were screaming until they hit the ground. There was nothing he could do but watch in horror."

Everything was on fire. A bird, flapping embers from its blackened wings, sputtered in the dirt. It was as if Red had suddenly awoken and found himself standing in the gut of a hellish nightmare. For a brief moment he was deafened by it. Something in his mind shut down. "A stillness," he would later describe. And within the stillness he could hear el Diablo's hoofbeats galloping in the mountain pass. At that moment, Red turned and found a stampede of men charging toward him. They were carrying pick-axes and shovels, and they rushed past him, barking orders and tossing dirt at the spreading flames. The men didn't speak, not at first. They were wearing state-issued bonaroos—inmates, all of them, from the nearby Fresno County Road Camp. Warden Wilmurth was among them, along with Deputies George Woodard and Frank Johnson. They tossed Red a shovel, and he too began flinging dirt at the flames, quicker than most, since it was his family's property that was on the verge of incineration.

Red's son-in-law, a man everyone called "Happy" Gaston, had been busing Los Gatos Canyon children to school at that hour when he saw the ball of fire erupt into a black cloud that sailed above the foothills, blanketing all of Coalinga. He floored the gas pedal and sped up the winding dirt road toward his ranch. As he pulled around the bend he could see a crowd of inmates gathered. He spotted Red, shoveling dirt in frenzy. Happy steered the bus to a clearing, slammed on the brakes, and leapt out. He fanned a gust of smoke away from his eyes and ran to help. Schoolchildren who were still on the bus gawked out of windows. A few got off and wanted a closer look. One of them was Happy's own daughter, a tomboyish ten-year-old named Juney. Juney walked closer to where the fire blazed and could feel the heat snaking across her body. She watched as the men, faces hardened in serious masks, pulled out burnt pieces of "cattle." The stench forever imprinting itself on young Juney's mind. For what she witnessed in that moment she could make sense of only by relating it to life on the ranch. The removed expressions on the faces. The silent casualties that were a part of pioneer living. Years later, Juney would vividly recall stepping off the bus and standing before the chaos as if staring through "a window, or a dream."

The remaining schoolchildren filed out of the bus and were scooped up by their parents. Sirens could be heard echoing through the walls of the canyon. A trail of dust approaching in the distance. Voices shouting. Neighbors rubbernecking. Every so often a gasp at the sight of something. A swelling nausea in the stomach. A dry heave. Silence.

And then the guesswork.

"The wing looks like it comes from the exact same mail carrier that Verne Boswell flies for Southwest Airways," someone suggested.

"Do you know Verne? A decent fella."

"It would sure explain the papers all over the place."

"But what about the luggage, the clothes, all them shoes?"

"That's right, Verne's plane is a mail transport *and* passenger service."

"But no logo? If it was Verne's, wouldn't there be a bird logo, or stripes on the wing?"

"Can't see with all this smoke."

A scratch of the head.

"Who are these poor souls?"

A clearing of the throat.

"Don't know."

A short while later the convoy arrived. Vehicles from the Fresno County Sheriff's Department pulled into view. A group of officers, and a few men in suits, emerged and collectively shuffled over to the wreckage.

"Who are the suits?" onlookers would ask one another.

Coroner? Officials?

Yes and yes.

On the warden's order the inmates began quarantining off the site. More onlookers gathered. From all parts of the canyon they came. From the mercury mines in New Idria and Tres Pinos, from the cattle ranches in San Benito, and the oil derricks in Coalinga, they caught wind of something terrible, and they came.

Dolores Crabtree: "I was about twenty-one years old at the time, and was living up in the canyon, about a mile down from where the crash happened. I just happened to be in Coalinga that day, over on Madison Street, at my sister's house. She was giving me a permanent at the time. And her husband comes running in, and he says, there's been a plane crash up in the canyon. I still had rollers in my hair, but we quickly wrapped something around my head and off we went."

A short time later, Deputy Johnson would call out, "Fire's under control!"

"Fire's under control!" the inmates relayed across the hillside.

Red and Happy breathed a sigh of relief.

A gray Cadillac donning a Mexican flag in the front window appeared. It ambled onto the shoulder of the road and stopped in a cloud of dust. People shrugged and looked on curiously. A man stepped out from the vehicle. He was leaning on a cane. He fixed a brown fedora onto his head and made his way to the officials, who were now gathered atop the embankment assessing the wreckage.

Red and Happy handed their shovels to one of the prisoners and gave the officials some room. They were still close enough to overhear the conversation.

"Pleased to meet you, Consul Salazar," said an official, sticking his hand out for the consul to shake. More men in suits approached and greeted the consul.

"Gentlemen," Salazar replied, "thank you for notifying us immediately." His accent was thick. "This is horrendous," he said, his eyes shifting toward the wreckage. The men quieted for a moment. Salazar stood silently, staring across the landscape.

One by one they climbed down into the creek bed. Salazar had to be assisted. He called his associate over, a tall, lanky man named Manuel Gonzales. He braced himself with his cane as Gonzáles helped him down the slope. Stepping toward the wreckage, Salazar removed his fedora, pulled a white handkerchief from his pocket, and pressed it to his nose. The pile of debris was still hissing.

Their eyes could not look away.

"See anything unusual here, Webb?" asked one of the suits.

Deputy Coroner Ray Webb shook his head and jotted something onto his notepad.

They couldn't tell what was what. The stench was penetrating. A few of the suits, including Salazar, found themselves stepping away for a gulp of air.

Webb grabbed a stick and used it to lift a piece of debris. Red and Happy looked on. Webb called one of the officials over to have a peek. The official took one glance and hollered at two inmates standing nearby. The men were ordered to reach into the metal. They didn't hesitate. They took hold of what appeared to be a melted boot and gave it a tug. They tugged and the piece dislodged itself.

"Jesus Christ!" someone gasped.

"Shit," said the warden. "Get the children out of here. Johnson, tell those folks to take their kids home, will ya?"

No one moved.

Johnson gave the warden a confused look.

Los Gatos Canyon *was* their home.

Red and Happy stayed put. The onlookers didn't budge. Even Little Juney didn't so much as move a muscle.

Consul Salazar conferred with Gonzales. Gonzales removed his sunglasses and jotted a few notes down onto a pad. Both men circled the wreckage and observed the details. Though they couldn't make out what was being said, Red and Happy listened as the two discussed the matter in Spanish. It was clear that the consul was making a list. Gonzales wrote it all down:

Maletas
Ropa
Dinero
Papeles
Sobrevivientes—no

12:10 p.m.

The first telling of it would come from the locals. Even before the *Coalinga Record*'s managing editor, F. J. McCollum, arrived on the scene and began taking interviews, the people of Coalinga had already begun the telling. There was a ten-party phone system. "All ya had to do is pick up the receiver and listen in, and you'd get a scoop of the details," said one old-timer. The lines were blazing with first- and secondhand accounts of the crash.

The *Coalinga Record* reported: "Long-distance telephone lines from San Francisco, Los Angeles and elsewhere in the state were overloaded into Coalinga. . . . The first call, within a few seconds after the crash, came from the farmer line to the Prison Camp. As soon as the call came in to Coalinga for the ambulance and the fire equipment, a representative of the *Coalinga Record* and Henry Stuart of the Stuart Photo Shop departed immediately for the scene—"

From the Hernandez Valley, through the canyon, and into downtown Coalinga, the ice-cream parlors, knitting circles, and rowdy crowds on Whiskey Row were recounting the details as they were unfolding. The first reporters were oilmen and cattle ranchers, schoolteachers and farmworkers. Word of mouth was the original broadcast.

12:22 p.m.

And then came the cameras.

The first one on the scene belonged to a man named Henry Stuart, a hired eye for the *Coalinga Record*. Stuart was a Canadian immigrant who'd set up his photo shop in Coalinga. He heard the call come in on the ambulance line and, along with McCollum, was on the scene almost immediately. Stuart photographed the wreckage up close, while the embers were still ascending. Then he went and stood atop the ridge and panned out as far as he could, in an attempt to capture the totality. He did his best to adjust the aperture delicately to document the angle of light just right, so that someone viewing these stills, six decades later, would get an idea, not only of the images, but of the sensory reality whole. But his heart was racing. His hands trembled. The work was compromised. Some of the images are nothing but smoke, as if in a cloud. Photographs taken too close. Strange abstractions. Blobs of black and gray. Empty spaces. Gaps that invite the mind to make their own meaning. If you look close, closer yet, you find shapes, objects amid the shadow and light. Like a Rorschach test, you come to discover the darkest recesses of your own imagination. A scrap of the engine's propeller, at first glance, suggests a human appendage. But no, it's a propeller after all. A skeletal gear. A bone of skyship. Stuart's camera doesn't shy away.

Later that afternoon, before the darkness settled in, Stuart retreated to his office in downtown Coalinga. Alone, he reviewed the details of what his trusty camera captured. And then he made choices. Which ones would go to print that evening. Which would be sent off to the United Press International's San Francisco office. And then, which ones would never, ever see the light of day. It was from these images that F. J. McCollum's article, the first media report of the plane wreck at Los Gatos Canyon, would soon unfold.

But there was still one more eye.

The second camera on the scene was actually not on the scene, per se. It belonged to the *Fresno Bee,* and was partnered with a staff reporter sent from the main office. The *Bee* assigned their ace writer, Joe Smith. While Joe kept his feet firmly planted on Los Gatos Canyon soil, he convinced cameraman Lew Hegg to get a bird's-eye view of the crash. Remarkably, only a few short hours after Los Gatos Canyon had devoured an airplane whole, Lew Hegg went flying over the canyon in an airplane. He boarded with cameras slung around his neck and from only a few hundred feet up he pressed his equipment against the window, adjusted his lens, and fired off round after round.

"There," he pointed to the pilot, "get me over there, lower."

The pilot dipped lower still, tilted the plane, and circled back. Those on the ground kept looking upward, nervous at the sight of yet another skyship making loop-the-loops overhead. The pilot did this maneuver several times, until Lew was satisfied he had gotten all the shots he needed.

"Home," Lew said. "That oughta do 'er."

And from these two cameras, the right and left eye, the images would make way for the media's telling of the story.

12:40 p.m.

F. J. McCollum was the media. A tall, brawny man, he was a robust character, whom locals referred to as Mr. Mac. The grandson of Scottish immigrants, he was a take-charge kind of reporter with the grip strength of a bull rider. It didn't surprise anyone when thirty years before he purchased the *Coalinga Record* and made himself the editor and publisher of the town's only source for news.

Within two hours of the plane crash, Mr. Mac already had a dozen pages of notes in his steno pad. He worked fast and efficiently.

Arriving at the crash site he maneuvered past the prisoners and made his way to a gaunt man with white hair and spectacles. He asked the man his name.

"Red Childers," the man said, cocking his wide-brimmed hat back on his head and resting both hands on his hips. Even though the day was cold, Red was drenched in sweat. Soot gathered in rings around his neck. A thin fog emanated from the wet spot between his shoulder blades. McCollum opened his steno pad and asked Red to tell what he'd witnessed.

Red took off his spectacles and with his blue bandana wiped the inside corner of his left eye. He placed the spectacles back on his face.

"Well," he began, looking up at the sky, "the plane was headed east, oh, about a mile high."

McCollum scribbled down every word that came from Red's mouth. "Go on," he said.

"I was watching it when I noticed a streak of smoke trailing off from the left motor . . ."

"The left you say?" McCollum interrupted. "You certain?"

"As sure as I see you standing there," Red said. "The left wing separated from the body of the plane, and the fuselage and right wing began to spiral down toward the earth."

McCollum jotted the words: "Spiral down. Earth." He asked a few more questions, but then a moment later noticed a group of officers gathering in the creek bed. He paused to observe them. There was a silent ringing in the air. Red continued talking, but McCollum was growing impatient. It was happening fast and he didn't want to miss a beat. He thanked Red and slapped his steno shut, then made his way over to the officers. Warden Wilmurth was telling a few suits what he'd seen:

"I was trying to get phone connections, and I could hear the boys shouting, 'Here it comes, it's gonna land in the yard.' I didn't know whether to crawl under my desk or run. However, I figured from the position of the plane, when I saw it, that it couldn't fall too close, so I kept on with my calls."

McCollum took note.

Wilmurth hesitated. "And what I seen were, uh, nine bodies . . . strewn on the ground. They looked as if they'd fallen from the plane before the crash."

"Nine?" McCollum asked.

Wilmurth counted in his head, "Yes, that's right, nine. I counted 'em. Nine whole bodies. Christ." Wilmurth turned to look at the sky. It was all he could do to contain his emotions.

An hour later, McCollum felt he had everything he needed to write the story in time for the evening edition. He began walking back toward his car, but along the way he noticed a peculiar-looking woman. There wasn't anything special about her appearance, except that she seemed to be standing deliberately away from the fuss. She had a red handkerchief over her mouth, and the skin on her face was pallid. The woman saw him approaching.

"You with the paper?" she asked.

"Yes, ma'am. The *Coalinga Record*." McCollum tipped the brim of his hat forward. "Are you a resident of this canyon?"

"Yes," replied Mabel Johnson. "My husband works at the road camp."

"S'that right?"

"Deputy Frank Johnson," she said, pointing her nose in her husband's direction. McCollum glanced over his shoulder and spotted him.

He could see the woman was shaken. Her eyebrows gathered.

"Mind if I ask you a question or two, Mrs. Johnson?"

"I already told the authorities what I seen."

"So you witnessed how this all came about?"

Mabel waved the handkerchief in front of her face as if shooing away a fly. She was reluctant.

McCollum nudged. "Did you actually see the plane in flight?"

"Yes," Mabel said. "I did." She paused.

"Mind telling me what you saw?"

Mabel averted her eyes from the man. She coughed into her handkerchief. "I'll tell you the same's I told them. Sounded like there was a revvin' of motors, as if the pilot was gunnin' the engines. That's what made me look up." She coughed into her handkerchief. "The plane seemed . . . it was burning in the forward part . . . then, uh, there was a terrific noise . . ."

McCollum jotted down, "terrific noise."

" . . . which I thought was an explosion. The left wing fell off and sort of glided downward. The rest of the plane was in flames, and it, uh, turned over several times and spun to the ground."

"Spun to the ground," McCollum wrote. Mrs. Johnson continued talking, slowly, methodically. She explained to McCollum what she saw. But it was the way in which she spoke that McCollum found most interesting. Her voice was distant, removed. Even as she recounted the details, there was a stillness about her eyes and mouth. It was clear, Mabel Johnson was in shock.

McCollum raced back to his office in downtown Coalinga, contemplating what he'd seen. It was unlike anything he'd ever witnessed in all his sixty-five years of living. Even for an old battle-horse like him, it left a churning in his stomach.

By the time he arrived in his office, sitting there on his desk were the first of Henry Stuart's photos. He picked one up, stared at it a few seconds, and didn't need to see the rest. He reached across his desk and pulled old faithful close to him—a scarred black typewriter labeled *Woodstock*. He flipped through his notes. Placed his fingers on the hard keys. Pictured, once more, what he couldn't forget. His thick fingers began slamming out the first lines:

"Peaceful Los Gatos Canyon was the scene of one of the worst disasters in aviation history . . . broken and charred bodies and an indiscernible heap of debris were all that were left of a government chartered flight from Oakland, which would have taken 28 Mexican Nationals back to their homeland . . ."

5:13 p.m.

The sun was hanging over the canyon walls and sinking beyond the Hernandez Valley. Investigators were still poking around, while a group of locals took it upon themselves to clean up. They worked quietly, gathering thousands of loose papers clinging to the bushes. It was their canyon after all, and they took pride in keeping it as natural as the day they'd come upon it. Happy and Red took part in the operation, obligated since it was their property the whole thing happened on. They shoveled gobs of burntstuffs and clots of whatnot into a pit and covered it with dirt. Minutes went by before a word was shared between them.

"Best get Juney home, don't you think?" Red finally said to his son-in-law. Happy nodded, but didn't reply. He remained hunched over, continuing to gather debris. So proud were the Gastons of their land that they even kept the homestead document signed to them by President William McKinley framed and hanging in their living room. Happy would see to it that all evidence of this gruesome day would be disposed of. At the very least, he'd make an attempt.

Young Juney stood nearby, tired and silent. She couldn't turn her eyes away from the blackened earth. A group of inmates were huddled nearby, along the embankment. They were whispering among themselves. She spotted a few of them pocketing small shards of metal and other loose scraps of wreckage. Sometime later, while ransacking one of the barracks, Deputy Frank Johnson would discover a trove of metal jewelry—rings and bracelets, polished to a shine. The inmates will have made jewelry from the salvaged shards of the skyship to gift to their wives and children visiting on weekends.

One inmate called Juney over. She went to him.

"Look, girl," he whispered, "see here?" He held a crumbled wad of dollar bills in his hand. They were covered in blood. "Go on, girl," he said. "Take it."

The child stuck her hand out and grasped the soiled bills.

"One day these is gonna be worth somethin'," he said.

She looked down at the bills. The smell was pungent.

"Go on," he said, shooing her away.

Juney took the bills and went home, where her mother Iva had been waiting for her. She showed her mother what the inmate had given her. Iva grabbed the bills from her hand and flung them into the garbage.

"That's disgusting," she said. "It's best you stay put here for a while. Nothing to see there no more anyhow." She hauled Juney to the sink and washed her hands twice, and then sat her down and gave her a tall glass of milk.

Iva went over to the front door and stood there for a long time, staring out into the hillside of their ranch property. Juney wondered what her mother was looking for. Eventually, Iva turned back, adjusted her apron, and returned to washing the dishes. As Juney drank her milk, she couldn't shake what she'd seen. In the years to come, she would remember every detail of that cold winter morning.

June: "I had been standing at the kitchen window, like I always did, when I heard Daddy honking the school bus horn. I grabbed my lunch pail and ran down the hill in time to catch it. On ordinary days, the drone of airplanes in the travel corridor above us barely drew anyone's attention. But this time there was a loud noise, and according to our neighbor Mabel, she looked up and saw fire shooting from the plane's engine. The prisoners had been outside, and they watched as the wing ripped off the plane and floated downward, toward the prison yard. Mabel ran, but the wing changed course and lifted up over the mountain toward our house. My mother Iva was in the yard hanging wash on the clothesline, and she heard Mabel screaming at her, 'Iva! Iva!' At the time, my little sister Nancy was behind the woodpile with her pet turtle, when she heard our mother call out for her. Just as she looked up she saw a large silver monster in the sky coming right at her. She left the turtle and started running toward the house. She must've turned directions to get away from it, but when she looked over her shoulder again the thing changed directions and was still coming for her. My mom said she'd never heard any human scream like that, much less Nancy, who was only eight at the time. But Nancy screeched and ran as fast as she could, but each time she'd change directions so would the monster. I guess finally it just disappeared. If you ask me, though, Nancy ran from that monster the rest of her life. She was horrified of airplanes. And my Grandma Nellie, well, she was about sixty-three at the time, but she nearly got the worst of it. Grandma was married to William Childers, who everyone just called Red. He was slender and tall with a strong, handsome face, and he walked with a long stride as though he always had a purpose. Well, when the plane crashed down, Grandma was in the living room working on her punchwork pillows. When the broken wing finally hit the ground, it landed fifteen feet from where Grandma was sitting quietly in her easy chair."

8:30 p.m.

"If it bleeds it leads," goes the newsroom adage. And lead it did.

Before the embers had finally blown out, F. J. McCollum's words were picked up by the United Press International and the Associated Press, making front-page news across the Golden State. The *Berkeley Daily Gazette*, the *San Francisco Chronicle*, the *Long Beach Press Telegram*, the *Oakland Tribune*, and the *San Mateo Times* all ran initial versions of the story. Less than twenty-four hours later the *Fresno Bee* would run a second article. This time, there was an attempt to include the names of the Mexican passengers reported to have been on the airplane. They were listed as Ramon Perez, Jesus Santos, Guadalupe Ramirez, Martin Navarro, Apolonio Placenti, Santiago Elesandro, Salvadore Sandoval, Manuel Calderon, Francisco Duran, Rosalio Estrado, Bernabe Garcia, Severo Lara, Elias Macias, Jose Macias, Tomas Marquez, Louis Medina, Manuel Merino, Luis Mirando, Ygnacio Navarro, Roman Ochoa, Alberto Raygoza, Guadalupe Rodriguez, Mrs. Maria Rodriguez, and Juan Ruiz. And then something most curious, three more names: James A. Guardaho, identified from a driver's license that gave the address of 207 L Street, Sacramento, California; Julio Barron, no information found on his person; and Ramon Portello, no information found on his person. This would be the only mention of James, Julio, and Ramon. Never again would their names appear. Not in print. Not anywhere. Omitted indefinitely.

2

RECONSTRUCTING STORIES (LA HUESERA)

It was clear from the start that in order for investigators to reconstruct what took place, they would have to surrender ideas of exactness. Settle instead for as close a representation as humanly possible. To piece the story together, they would use a method known as "triangulation." A combination of evidence, eyewitness accounts, and good old-fashioned instinct. In the end, no matter the information gathered, some guesswork would also play a role.

For instance, infant garments were discovered among the debris. Investigators noted that "among the Mexican Nationals . . . was a woman with baby clothes beside her. No trace of the baby's body was found, however." Because there was no way to test if either María or Bobbie were pregnant, the investigators—all men—would unanimously decide that the baby clothes belonged to the Mexican passenger, María. Why it was impossible to believe that either Bobbie, or perhaps one of the male passengers, might've been carrying the clothes was never discussed.

But the guesswork didn't stop there.

There was still the task of putting names to the bodies. Because of the total annihilation of everyone aboard, officials were left to piece together the impossible rompecabezas of the human anatomy.

In a photo, taken at the scene of the crash, immigration official J. P. Butler has a notepad in his left hand and a pencil in his right, and he's staring over Coroner Ray Webb's shoulder. Webb is showing him a document of some kind, perhaps a list of names. The caption reads: "J. P. Butler, left, in charge of the Fresno office of the immigration service, conferring with Deputy Coroner Ray Webb on the identification of the bodies."

In the image, Butler's eyes are staring down at Webb's document, and his mouth is slightly open. You can almost hear him asking, "What've you got there?"

"See here," Webb responds, using his middle finger to point at the list. "Four Americans and . . . well, thirty-one, thirty-two . . ."

"I see," Butler says, scribbling names into his notepad.

Moments after this photo was snapped, Webb, Butler, and another colleague named Herman Hannah led a crew that included inmates from the road camp on a thorough search for pieces of human remains. "No matter if it's a single strand of hair, or pile of freckles, we want it." Searchers were instructed to leave any discovery untouched until inspectors had a look first. At which point it would be sealed in a rubber zipper bag, inventoried, and shipped to Yost and Webb Funeral Home in Fresno for further determination.

As the search parties scoured the hillside, one of the inmates, a dark-skinned Californio named Velorio Martínez Martínez, whom everyone called El Indio, remembered a story he'd heard growing up. It was a myth about La Huesera, the Bone Woman. While walking through the dried grass with his fellow inmates, El Indio conveyed to them the story. "She wanders around canyons, just like this, collecting bones of dead animals and people," he reportedly told the other prisoners. "The old woman'll stick her hand right into these snakeholes, and dust off maggots if she's got to—"

"Sounds like my ma," one of the men cut in. "Tough old bitch."

The men chuckled. El Indio went on. "When she finds the bones, she puts the animal, or person, back together."

"Like some kinda resurrection?"

"Shit no, she ain't Jesus."

Again the men chuckled.

"What if she don't got all the bones?"

"She don't need every single bone, man. You can tell a lot by a person's tooth. Just ask any of these suits out here. All they need is one knucklebone, or one good rib, and they can tell you if it's a woman or man, and even tell you if they had chopped liver or mashed potatoes for dinner last night." The men nodded. El Indio pressed on. "So the old woman lights a fire and smokes her tobacco, and puts 'em back together with whatever bones she does have." He paused. "Just like these suits are doing out here right now, scrambling to find bones so's they can piece the story together."

An inmate scoffed. "Well, we sure as hell ain't gonna find everything."

And he was right.

Despite the investigation team's best efforts, in the end, it was a patchwork job. Names were as dismembered as the bodies they belonged to.

Adding an *a* at the end of his first name would turn Tomás Gracia de Aviña into a female—*Tomasa*. Put that arm with this torso. And this foot with that ankle. And now the last name Lara too got a makeover, and the tall stoic caballero, Guadalupe Ramírez Lara, was now Guadalupe *Laura* Ramirez—a female. Ramón Paredes was truncated into *Ramon Perez*. This head with that neck. What about Apolonio Placencia? That finger looks a good fit with this hand, different shade of brown, yes, but close enough. Little did Apolonio know that in death he'd become Italian—*Placenti*. And this was how their names would go down according to official records: Apolonio Placenti, Guadalupe Laura Ramirez, Tomasa Aviña de Gracia. One Italian and two women.

By the morning of January 29, 1948, news of the plane crash had made its way across the country, from California to the New York islands.

> *28 Mexican Deportees, Crew and Guard Victims . . .*
>
> —*Associated Press*
>
> *28 Mexicans Being Deported Meet Death*
>
> —*San Mateo Times*
>
> *28 Deportees en Route to Mexico . . .*
>
> —*Rochester Democrat and Chronicle*

It had the makings of a bad joke. By print, radio, and word of mouth, there wasn't a soul on this continent who hadn't heard the story of the two World War II pilots, an immigration officer, a stewardess, and twenty-eight "deportees," who exploded in an airplane in some unknown California hillside called Los Gatos Canyon.

3

LOS GATOS CANYON

Los Gatos Canyon is furrowed in the foothills just above the oil town of Coalinga, California, near the lower west end of Fresno County. It's part of the agricultural mecca called the San Joaquin Valley, aka the "breadbasket of the world." What the valley produces over 60 percent of the world eats. If it's been grown by God's warm sun, then chances are it comes from this part of the planet, and it'll say so right on the box. What the box won't mention, though, are the people who harvested it. For over a century, families have been coming to this valley for the sole purpose of picking crops. They've come from Oklahoma, South Texas, China, Armenia, Holland, the Philippines, Mexico, Laos, and a dozen other places. They come to work and, in some cases, to live. And for the past one hundred years a few have even put down roots here, and so the valley is their home. Coalinga is their home. Los Gatos Canyon, too, is their home. And the old-timers around these parts love to talk about their home.

"This canyon's just a small piece of the whole Diablo Range. Not sure how it got its name exactly, but way I heard it was anywhere Spanish settlers would spot natives they'd just assume it was where el Diablo lived. But the plane crash ain't the only thing. This whole area's got a history with death. The Mexican bandit Joaquin Murrieta used to hide out here with his gang. He'd visit the brothel on Whiskey Row and sleep off hangovers in the canyon. Just down the road, Cantua Creek's where he was beheaded. This land's seen its share of death, that's for sure. Long time ago, soldiers from the mission in San Juan Bautista massacred a group of Yokut Indians here too. Guess that was pretty common in those days. Gotta be careful where you step around here, never know what you'll come across. The land keeps everything. And it remembers too."

One of its memories would later raise questions about the ancestral pull of the canyon. In 1840, a rancher named Agustín Hernández settled into a small valley tucked at the foot of Los Gatos Canyon and quickly became one of the most prominent ranchers in the area. A few decades later would see two more ranchers, brothers Rafael and Jesús Hernández, of no relation to Agustín, also settle in and leave their impression on the canyon. The Hernandez Valley, as it came to be known, is a six-mile stretch that runs along the western edge of the Los Gatos Canyon corridor and keeps some of the area's most wicked dealings among its fossilized past.

"And this whole area sits right on the San Andreas Fault. That's a million-year-old crack that runs a thousand miles, at least. Yes, this land's alive."

Now and then the tremors rise up. Like a dog trembling to rid itself of fleas, the whole Diablo Range quakes in an attempt to absolve itself from its cursed history. But the records only wedge themselves deeper into the sediment, and in the rings of the black oak trees.

"But times weren't always bad," the old-timers say. "During the oil boom, it was quite a thing to be able to say you were from Coalinga. Especially for anyone who was born and raised here."

The Gaston family were among them. Juney had grown up hearing the stories. "My family first came to California from Oklahoma by wagon train. They were miners before moving to Visalia, and then later Los Gatos Canyon. They were among the first pioneers. We built our house on the hill with prison labor. I'll never forget this one time, Daddy was wanting to put up a fence and had started digging holes for posts. He hit something with his shovel, and it was a human bone of some kind. He tried digging a few more holes and ended up coming across more bones, and even some native jewelry. He realized it must've been a burial ground or something, so he ended up not putting a fence in that location. After our house was built my daddy took up a job at the prison camp as a deputy. He would take the prisoners out on a road crew to bust rocks. He hated this job. He was used to building roads, big crews with heavy equipment and dynamite. Now he was watching over a few guys pushing rocks around with a pick and shovel. He quit and started driving the school bus instead. Nevertheless, we kept ties with the road camp. There were many fires in that dry country, and he always led the prisoners and the men from the nearby firecamp in firefighting. Even as a kid, I sometimes went with Daddy to the road camp. It was always nice and neat, everything painted, cobblestones, bunk rooms, spare but neat, with rows of single cots. The cooks spoiled me with goodies, and I ate there sometimes. I thought the prisoners were my friends. I remember one day we were out with the road crew and Daddy picked out one of the Indians—I was crazy about Indians, being part myself—and he said to 'em,

'Now instead of swinging a pick out in that hot sun, wouldn't you like to sit down in the shade over there and tell little Juney stories about how many white men you've scalped?' I was thrilled, but I had to keep prompting him. The poor guy wasn't much of a storyteller. This is just how it was in the canyon in those days—it was everyday life.

"Sometimes, for fun, Daddy and I would track prisoners who'd escaped from the road camp. Even though it was a relaxed place and the prisoners were on the honor system, occasionally one would get a hankering to leave. They were always caught right away. Except this one guy. He was an old man, probably in his sixties, and nobody looked for him very hard, figuring he would totter out soon enough and they would get him. Daddy and I tracked him over the county line, until Daddy finally said, 'That man probably made it clear out to the border and escaped into Mexico by now. Let him go.'"

II

THE STORIES

Who are these friends all scattered like dry leaves?

—Woody Guthrie, "Plane Wreck at Los Gatos (Deportee)"

LUIS MIRANDA CUEVAS

4

CASIMIRA NAVARRO LÓPEZ

Jocotepec, Jalisco, Mexico
January 22, 2015

For Casimira Navarro López, time would knock on her door sixty-seven years later, almost to the day. Until this moment, she had never been asked to speak about her boyfriend, who was killed in "the worst airplane disaster in California's history."

It was as typical an afternoon as any in Jocotepec, overcast with a light breeze. Still, it was enough to make the eighty-six-year-old's skin cold to the touch. Sitting in her wheelchair, Casimira tugged a knit beanie down over her ears and drew a red knit shawl over her shoulders, before asking her granddaughter to shut the window.

She had no time to prepare for the unexpected visitor, but judging by her enthusiastic greeting, good conversation was hard to come by these days. When I knocked on her door she invited me in, and wasted no time exchanging pleasantries. I apologized for my intrusion and explained to her, as best I could, how I'd found her. I had a contact at the local municipio that fell through. Uncertain of my next move, I wandered into la Casa de la Cultura, over by el jardín, which housed the Biblioteca Pública. When the librarian there asked me if I needed help, I took a chance and told her the story of the plane crash. "It was the librarian who led me to the Miranda Cuevas family," I said, "and they're the ones that led me to you." Casimira gazed at me curiously. I wasn't sure if she was following my story, or if she was trying to discern my poor Spanish. After a few seconds, she inched her wheelchair forward and quickly fell into reminiscing about the early days of Jocotepec, back when it was still unmarred by "the turismo that had taken over."

"In those days life was simple, inocente," she began. "I think to myself, how funny, nowadays there is so much awareness, so much, well, understanding of things. But back then we did not have that kind of understanding. No, we were much shyer, more timid. We didn't have the same kind of communication as today." She paused, and it was clear that she could see herself in her mind as a young woman. The light of her best years had not yet dimmed, despite the eclipse that was January 28, 1948, a time when her only concern was being a young woman in love with a young man. The remembering made it palpable. The mere mention of his name elicited a long silence.

"Luis Miranda Cuevas."

Upon hearing it, Casimira folded her trembling hands across her lap, and the corners of her mouth could not decide whether to lift or hang. They lifted. It was clear she'd been waiting her whole life to speak of him, though at times it must have seemed easier to live out her days without ever thinking back at all. A droplet gathered at the outside corner of her eye. She gingerly pressed the pad of her thumb against the skin to collect it.

"I first met Luis through his brother Antonio," she said, recalling the moment with trepidation, as if she were tiptoeing into a splintery past. "In those years . . . well, we lived across the street from each other, and he was always at the house. So we would talk . . . he and I, and that's how things . . . well, that's how we started." She stopped abruptly and asked her granddaughter to fetch her a cup of water. After taking a sip she continued.

"Luis was a very good man. A young man. I have nothing ill to say of him. He was too good, in fact. He was a mandilón." She chuckled. "He must've been because he did everything I asked of him. Luis wasn't ugly in the least bit. He had a nice way about him. He was very, very handsome. I fell for his personality though, not because he was handsome, or because he did whatever I asked of him. He had so much personality. He was adventurous, and funny. And, well . . . he loved me very much. It was love. Yes. And I loved him. Well, that was a long time ago—" Upon hearing the words "a long time ago" come from her mouth, she hesitated. It felt inaccurate. How could it have been a long time ago if her memory was still so clear, so vivid? She took another sip of water. "Where do I begin?" she asked.

"Continue the story, please." I placed the small handheld recorder with its tiny red light on at the edge of the coffee table.

Casimira tugged on her beanie and leaned back in her wheelchair. The folds around her eyes deepened. "Yes, the story—"

In early fall of 1946, Luis Miranda Cuevas found himself walking eastward up the long, curved Calle Morelos, leading out of his beloved Jocotepec. He'd heard that even though the war was over, trains leaving Guadalajara for los Estados Unidos could still be found, and braceros were still needed.

That morning, as he hurried past Laguna de Chapala, he stopped to take in the sight of what appeared to be a thousand egrets scuttling along the shores, plucking fish and insects peacefully in the cool morning air. He stood there for a moment, gathering his strength for the difficult climb over the mountain pass above the pueblo of Ajijic. At least, this is what he told himself initially. The truth was, before vanishing into the valley of stones, he paused to think of his mother, Isabel. He worried how she would manage without him. A woman of few words, Isabel watched her eldest son take nothing with him but the clothes on his back, a stylish coat passed on by his father, and his shiniest shoes. When he turned back to look at his mother once more, expecting her to say something, preferably something hopeful, all Isabel Cuevas said was, "Cuidate, 'ijo." That was it. Take care, my son.

Luis watched the ice truck hobbling toward him, kicking up dust, on its way to Jocotepec. He stuffed his hands in his coat pockets and continued past Ajijic, and eventually the pueblo of Chapala. By late that afternoon he found himself cresting the top of the mountain pass, where he could stare due north and almost spot the twin peaks of la Catedral de la Asunción de María Santísima in the center of Guadalajara. He caught a ride into the big city in the back of a truck that was loaded with workers all headed to el Norte for the same reason—work. Most of the men had been gathered from the lakeside pueblos of Ocotlan and La Barca. Enganchados, all of them. Hooked on this way of life. Some of them toted small boxes and knapsacks with clothes and food. One enganchado asked Luis where he was headed.

"P'al Norte," Luis said.

"No food for the long trip, compadre?" the man asked.

"I'll be fine," Luis replied.

The men snickered.

Luis pushed his hair away from his eyes. He stared at the men. "You think I'd be foolish enough to make the trip like this, without anything, if I didn't know what was in store?"

The men stared at him.

"I've made this trip too many times to count," he pressed. "In fact, if any of you are going by way of El Paso del Norte, I'll be happy to show you around."

One of the men spoke up. "Not all of us have contracts, compadre," he said. "Some of us go así, contrabando."

A few of the men nodded. Luis looked at those who didn't.

"And you guys?" he asked.

"Pues, contrabando," one replied.

"Contrabando," said another.

Luis remained quiet.

He was alone again, something he had promised himself he wouldn't do. Travel alone. The last time he did this, el Río Bravo nearly swept him downstream and clear out into the Gulf of Mexico. He'd been pulled under by the current, but managed to cling to a loosened mesquite limb to stay afloat. Had it not been for a shallow bend he would've never made it out alive. This much he was sure of. He was too heavy. It wasn't that he was big in size, but really, Luis's body was built less for buoyancy and more for its brute strength. His very stature was proof of it. He was thick-boned. His square chest and large hands were immensities. His neck was the width of a tree trunk—an adequate pedestal for his wide head. All of that framed by two eyebrows that were as thick and defiant as eagle talons. When determination settled in, all of these attributes combined made him an intimidating presence. Even so, traveling such a distance alone, for anyone, was always a bad idea. By now, Luis had crossed the invisible line in the dirt enough times to know better.

As the truck sped up the long, dark stretch of road, he pulled a photograph from his coat pocket and slid his thick fingers over it. It was a glossy, gray image of Casimira. She had given it to him when they said their good-byes.

In the photograph, Casimira is wearing a white blouse with floral print. The blouse is pressed, and a sharp crease runs down her right sleeve. She is angled with her right shoulder toward the camera and her left shoulder receding in the distance. Her head is tilted slightly, and she stares directly into the photographer's lens. Her hair is cropped short, and dark curls hide most of her ear. Her lips are silken, and though the image is colorless, Luis knows her lips are painted a deep rouge. Her skin is fine, satin almost. It glows. But her eyes are the thing. It appears as though someone, maybe Luis, maybe the photographer, had gotten on her last nerve just minutes before the camera shutter snapped. Hers is a serious expression. A scorn, almost. Yet, captured in stillness, it comes across as sultry. Still, Luis can't help but laugh to himself. It's proof, he thinks, why her father's nickname for her is "Cara de Dolorosa"—suffering face.

Casimira rolled her wheelchair forward a few inches, toward me. She reached into a small curios cabinet and pulled the photograph from it. She brought it close to her eyes, but then held it back at arm's length. Her pale hand slightly trembled. When she could not see it clearly, she passed the photograph to me.

"This is the photo Luis had of me, when I was young," she said. "It was taken around the same time that we were together." I studied the image. She continued. "When Luis left, well, it was just one of those things that happens. He was twenty-four years old when he was killed, you see." She paused. "So, we had been boyfriend and girlfriend for three years by then. He would leave to el Norte often, but he would always return. This is just what one had to do in those days."

When Luis arrived in Guadalajara, it was already late at night. He leapt off the truck and headed for the train station, where he waited around with the rest of the men until morning. Huddled there, in the dimly lit railyards, he thought about Casimira and the two promises he had made to her. The first, that he wouldn't go by way of el Río Bravo. Not this time. He would instead wait to take the Juárez-bound train and enter by way of El Paso del Norte. The mere idea was a relief. Just picturing that furious, snaking black river at night was always enough to make him reconsider. On two previous occasions he'd gotten dysentery from crossing el río and had to remain in Laredo for several weeks before he could finally move on to Watsonville, California, his destination. No, this time he would go by train, contratado. Contracted with the same strawberry farm he'd worked for in previous seasons. He knew the mayordomo, and the two got along well.

And then he would remember his second promise to Casimira. It was a simple one. The excitement that appeared on her face when he said it was a moment he replayed in his head. Especially during the hardest of days, when his longing to be with her grew unbearable, painful at times. He could see her clearly. The glow in her eyes the moment he said it. "The next time I return, Casimira, I plan to marry you." And he meant it. The night before he left for el Norte for the last time, they'd stayed up dreaming a ceremony to end all ceremonies. The bougainvillea that stretched around Casimira's house would make an ideal backdrop for a photograph. The church bells gonging against the lush mountains would announce their union to the world. Of course, a mariachi would be hired. He would request a song, just for her. Yes, nothing like a song to mark the occasion: "Eres la gema que Dios convirtiera en mujer para el bien de mi vida / Por eso quiero cantar y gritar que te quiero mujer consentida . . ." All of Jocotepec would be there.

Luis took her hand in his and kissed her fingers. "We're going to get married, mi amor. It will be perfect."

She nodded. She could see it all. "I'll be here, Luis, waiting—"

5

LOS ENGANCHADOS

Early the next morning, while he tortured himself by recalling the scent of Casimira's hair from the night before, Luis quietly departed Jocotepec, eager to take his place among the thousands of enganchados who would be catching the bracero train north.

In early 1942, talks between Mexican president Ávila Camacho and President Roosevelt began. The focus was on how Mexico could be an ally to the United States during its time of need. In a matter of weeks, these discussions resulted in what would come to be known as the Bracero Program. From *brazos*, meaning "arms"—working arms. By March of that first year, a thin stream of cargo trains rumbled from central Mexico into Stockton, California, bringing four thousand men ready to harvest whatever crop the Central Valley yielded. Stockton was to be the testing grounds. Crops were picked ahead of schedule and farmers couldn't be happier. By their own assessment the plan had worked. Without missing a beat, recruiting centers opened up all across Mexico.

By 1944, the numbers had jumped to over sixty thousand workers, who were now shipped in and spread across the United States. Some in factories, others to railroad companies. More than half went to California's fields.

The program would remain for the duration of the war. But by the fall of 1947, when soldiers began trickling home, Mexican labor was once again dispensable. As if anti-Japanese sentiments weren't enough to make all immigrants pray for invisibility, the postwar transition spelled trouble for brown-skinned people. The last of the internment camps had only recently closed, and Nikkei families were returning to life, not as they had known it, but some new, strange version of it. As thousands of Japanese Americans were being bused and trained back into city limits, Mexicans, once again, were being bused and trained out. La migra cast its tightly woven dragnet across the state of California without discretion. The images looked identical to the snapshots taken only two decades prior, when, in 1930, President

Hoover called for a "repatriation of all Mexicans" and rounded up more than six hundred thousand brown-skinned people and shipped them off to Mexico, even though more than half were card-carrying U.S. citizens. But the ousting of Mexican laborers didn't sit well with everyone, including the San Joaquin Valley farmers. Without braceros to pick, the food would rot. And if the food rotted, so would profits. Congressman Alfred J. Elliot, who happened to be from the town of Tulare, in the center of the action, made an appeal in the *Bakersfield Californian*: "If there were sufficient laborers to harvest the agricultural crops of California, I would be the first to ask the removal of the Mexican nationals, giving our own people the employment. But in order to harvest the food crop, and to keep down the cost of living, it is important to keep the Mexican nationals." This from the same congressman who a few years earlier said, "When the war is over, as far as I'm concerned, we should ship every Jap in the United States back to Japan!"

It was clear that, despite the mass deportations, valley farmers were still relying on Mexico's recruiting centers to register braceros, pile them into cargo trains, and inject them into California's fields by the thousands. And as long as recruiting centers were open, there were always infinite lines of men willing to wait as long as it took. And wait they did. With the patience of volcanoes, they waited. Like Luis, most of them came from rural, little-heard-of pueblos, eager to find work in los Estados Unidos.

On the Zacatecas train, they came from Nochistlán, Juanacatic, Jalpa, and La Estancia. They were teenage boys with optimistic eyes, fathers, brothers, and hard-pressed solteros, anxious to hear their names called for the big trip: Juan Ruiz Valenzuela, Wenceslao Ruiz Flores, Salvador Hernández Sandoval, and José Sánchez Valdivia were among them.

José had been traveling with his younger brother, Ramón, and they were on their way to Stockton to meet up with their father, Mateo, who was expecting their arrival. It wouldn't be long before they'd get their chance.

The Aguascalientes track was not nearly as inundated as the one in Guadalajara. Though the roster included dozens of men, farmers mostly, none had been waiting there longer than Francisco Durán Llamas. His ticket north was going on three months now. The little money he had to begin with had long since been depleted. At one point he bartered his father's work hat for a single tortilla. He was now reduced to eating banana peels, and, on two occasions, handfuls of dirt. Francisco had never before so desperately wanted to hear his name called out as he did during those bleak twelve weeks. One immigration guard eventually took pity on Francisco and found a way to get him aboard. When his name was finally called, Francisco plowed through the crowd of men without apology, climbed onto the locomotive, and in the quiet recesses of his mind bade farewell to Mexico once and for all.

On the Guadalajara train, the majority of men had emerged from the quiet yellow hillsides that skirted the northern edge of Jalisco. They rolled in from pueblos named after saints, like San Julian and San Juan, and they climbed down from the mountain village of Manalisco, and over from serene Laguna de Chapala nooks like Jocotepec, Ocotlan, and La Barca. They were young trabajadores who had known little else but life among the adobe dwellings of their world. They waited days, sometimes months, before their names were called.

Luis was among them. When his number did finally come up, he boarded the train without hesitation and didn't even bother sticking his head out a window, like other men did, for there was no one there to bid him farewell. Had Casimira been there, no doubt he would've been dangling from a door, lunging for one last kiss.

Days later, on arriving at the Santa Fe Bridge Receiving Center on the dusty edge of the El Paso–Juárez border, Luis found himself in yet another line. This time he was made to strip naked, carry his belongings in his hands, and wait with the rest of the workers, ass exposed, under the wide glaring eye of the desert sun. If Casimira could see me now, he couldn't help but laugh. Though any chance of lasting modesty would be shattered in the next few minutes, Luis shielded his crotch with his clothes and kept his gaze straight ahead, as did everyone else, until the moment of his evaluation.

The evaluation was a test of degradation. If a worker could endure the test, they most certainly would endure life as a bracero in el Norte.

Luis's upper eyelids were turned inside out and inspected for conjunctivitis. Then his mouth was prodded and examined for sores or abscesses, any signs of declining health. If his body had any scars on it, even just one, he would be turned away and scorned. "We don't want troublemakers here." Next, his testicles were gripped and kneaded by strange fingers. After which, he was made to bend over and spread his cheeks so that his anus could be scrutinized and prodded with a tongue depressor. His hands were then examined for calluses, a sure sign of whether or not a man was capable of hard work. Often, men would cut their hands or work a shovel handle days before their examination just to build up a good callus. No calluses meant no job. Once Luis's physical state was determined, he was then asked to assemble a children's puzzle of Dumbo the Elephant to assess his intellect. Men could not be "too dumb," nor "too smart." It was a "specific kind of worker" they were looking for. One that was "fit enough to perform the necessary duties of a field laborer," while at the same time "would not look to raise trouble." For this reason, Luis Miranda Cuevas would keep his eyes lowered to the ground, so as not to appear threatening. It was one of the many lessons he was taught by some of the more experienced enganchados. Luis would pass his test and eventually be admitted to work in the United States. To officiate the passing, the Bracero Program Welcoming Committee would initiate him with a ritual delousing of dichlorodiphenyltrichloroethane, better known by its abbreviation, DDT. A powerful insecticide sprayed from the top of his black hair, into his ears, across his eyelids, into his nostrils, down over his cold, trembling, naked body, in the creases and folds of his partes nobles, hair follicles, between his fingers and toes, the soles of his feet, and back up again. Before handing Luis back his clothes, they would first be dipped in a bath of Zyklon B, the same chemical agent used to extinguish human lives in the gas chambers of Nazi Germany.

Once a large batch of workers was approved, the enganchados would celebrate by smoking hand-rolled cigarettes while waiting, yet again, for their names to be called. Hours later they'd find themselves standing at the foot of those wide white gates to los Estados Unidos, being waved across, papers in hand. Among them, exhausted, hungry, and excited all at once, stood Luis Miranda Cuevas.

Next stop, Watsonville.

As Luis trudged north, dodging migra checkpoints out of habit, the railroads hummed with trains darting in all directions. He couldn't help but find the whole thing humorous. One second, boxcars flew northbound, hauling a fresh supply of workers into California, while another rocketed southbound, deporting them back to the motherland. On the southbound train were the dour expressions that come from a six-month stint of backbreaking labor, while the northbound train held the wide, curious eyes of optimism. Sparks from both tracks lit up faces that peered out of windows. Hands from both trains waved at one another as they passed. On one side of the tracks, immigration officers were tirelessly dragnetting the entire state. On the other side, farmers were doing all they could to convince policymakers why Mexicans made the best workers. A representative from the Agricultural Labor Bureau of the San Joaquin Valley offered this insight: "We are asking for labor only at certain times of the year, at the peak of our harvest, and the class of labor we want is the kind we can send home when we get through with them." It was clear, the system had become schizophrenic.

Luis was well aware of the talk among los enganchados. "If you're brown, poor, and pick crops for a living, you'll get rounded up sooner or later, compadre." It wasn't a matter of if but when. It was every enganchado's rite of passage. And because the San Joaquin Valley was where the program started, naturally it was where the beginning of the end would also take place. It wasn't unusual that workers would arrive at labor camps that looked and felt more like ghost towns. While one bus was hauling them away, another busload was there to replace them. Entire camps, some with hundreds of workers, were being dissolved within minutes. Cooking fires were still glowing—that's how fast the turnstile was spinning. To add to the circus, la migra was no longer relying solely on buses and trains. It was rumored that they had now found a faster, more efficient way of transporting Mexicans. They had begun taking the C-47 cargo airplane that had been the workhorse of World War II and outfitting it with seats. In an effort to rid the ship of its distinctive war smell—an unmistakable blend of ammunition, sweat, and doom—they had given it a new paint job and renamed it, the Douglas DC-3.

6

THE COURTSHIP OF LUIS AND CASIMIRA

"Luis and I had planned to be married, yes. We spoke about this right before he died. From California he called to tell me that he was returning home, and that he was going to bring me a mariachi. I'll never forget—"

Casimira rolled her wheelchair back a ways, then called for her granddaughter to bring her more water. The young woman emerged from her bedroom and did as her grandmother asked. Casimira fiddled with her red shawl and gazed at me curiously. Her granddaughter handed her the water and she took a long sip. She thanked the girl and continued her train of thought.

"Every memory I have with Luis is a good memory. There are so many. We got along very well. And we did anything we wanted with him . . . well, I did everything I wanted with him." She laughed. "I would make him sew, cook, things like that. Yes, we got along so well. We complemented each other. That I remember clearly." Another memory surfaced. "When we first began, I would make him dress up as a woman and sew with me. Believe it or not, this is what we did! I did this, well, because my father would kill me if he saw us together. And my sisters would help me too. We would all sit side by side, real close, you see, and Luis and I would sit in the middle and talk. And in order for my father to not see him, well, we would have to dress him up as a woman. And Luis would do it. He was adventurous, very much so. A very fun person to be with. And he was willing to dress up like a woman just to get a chance to talk with me, to spend time with me." Casimira's eyes beamed. "And that's how we did it. I will never forget this one time—"

Luis pulled the snug-fitting floral print dress down over his wide chest and tugged it below his thighs. "Luisa," his brother, Antonio, teased. Though no self-respecting macho would ever allow himself to be made fun of in such a way, it didn't faze Luis in the least. Any young man who'd seen Casimira's cinematic allure with his own eyes would've done the same. Antonio understood, but as the older brother it was his duty to shame Luis for going to such lengths for any female. Luis took the dark, curly wig and yanked it onto his thick mat of hair.

"How does it look?" he asked Antonio. His brother laughed. "It doesn't matter," Luis said. "It'll be dark anyway."

"What if her father catches you?"

Luis forced his thick hands into a pair of white lady's gloves. "He won't. Her sisters will be there, and they know."

"They won't be the only ones. All of Jocotepec will know too. I can hear it now: Luisa Miranda dresses in woman's clothes." He paused. "I can't have people thinking that of my own brother. Imagine what they'll think of me."

Luis turned to face Antonio. "What do you think?"

Antonio shook his head. "You realize you'll have to walk and move like a woman too. Of course that'll be impossible with those apelike shoulders."

Luis hadn't thought that far ahead.

"Show me your walk, señorita," Antonio chided.

Luis ignored him.

"You won't make it past the front door."

Luis knew he was right. He would have to at least incorporate a little hip into each step. Maybe fling his locks every so often. He was in over his head.

"Go on," Antonio said, "let's see your walk." He folded his arms and waited for his brother to demonstrate.

Luis thought about it a moment. For all the beautiful women of Jocotepec that he'd had the pleasure of gawking at, he'd never once stopped to pay attention to the subtleties that made them all distinctly female.

"You're as good as dead," his brother said.

"Well, that's exactly what happened. Luis didn't last but a few minutes before my father caught on and chased us. Luis shoved my sisters aside and ran to hide. We all ran and hid. One sister hid in the baby's crib, another sister climbed on top of the bed, and I scrambled under the bed. My father discovered my first sister, the one who was in the crib, and boy did he let her have it. Then he found my other sister in the bed, and he let her have it too. Then he looked under the bed and found me and said, 'Get out of there Cara de Dolorosa!' Whenever my father was upset with me, he would punish me by calling me 'Cara de Dolorosa.' You see, my father called me this because, well, because he loved me very much. He never hit me. I'll tell you why my father never hit me. Because, you see, I was named after his own mother, Casimira. My mother would yell at my father, 'Why don't you hit her too? It's her fault! She's the one with the boy.' And my father would reply, 'I can't hit her because it feels like I'm hitting my own mother!' I know Casimira is an ugly name, but it worked for me because I never got hit. But Luis got away with it. Or at least I don't remember him ever being caught."

When Casimira spoke, it was clear that she wasn't speaking as an eighty-six-year-old matriarch, but instead as a young woman, perhaps no older than twenty. There was a youthfulness about her eyes that was revealed in the remembering. And she remembered everything.

Many evenings, she and Luis would meet at the corner store, or else down by el jardín, where the old men tossed crumbs to the birds and families walked around taking in the sunset. Though they were afraid to hold hands in public, worried that her father would catch them again, or that someone would spot them, they would still find ways to be affectionate. They would stride side by side, rubbing arms, elbows, whatever part of the body just happened to graze the other. Luis was forever talking up plans to go to el Norte and return to Jocotepec, to Casimira, and make good on his word—that they would one day marry, have a family, live there forever, skimming fish off the placid laguna and sucking in the sweet air of Jalisco.

Over the years of their courtship Luis had made the trek to el Norte and, true to his word, returned to Jocotepec, eager to share with Casimira his many adventures and newfound insights. Often he pondered out loud the differences between the two countries.

"Like two worlds," he'd say. "In los Estados, Casimira, the Mexicanos who live there, well, they aren't really Mexicanos, you see? We call them pochos because they were born and raised over there, on that side. And some of them can speak pretty good Spanish, but many of them don't. They've been there too long. They're practically gringos. Even though their own abuelos were born here, in Jalisco, in Zacatecas, all over Mexico, their Spanish is still very, very poor. But they are the ones, los pochos, who help us. If we have errands to run, they'll drive us, or help us find our way around, from place to place."

Casimira would listen to his stories with devoted curiosity.

"That won't happen with our children," Luis assured her. "When I get back from this next trip, you'll see, I'll have enough money that I can give some to my mother and to my brothers and sisters. I'd like to buy them each a bed, you know, so that they no longer have to sleep on sticks. And my poor father. I'll bring him down from the mountains once and for all. He can buy land and work his crops, right here in Jocotepec." Casimira knew he was serious. Though she would never get the opportunity to say this to Luis, there was something unsettling about the tireless ambition in his eyes. That glare of determination worried her. She knew he was capable of going to great lengths to fulfill his promises. She feared that this, more than anything, would be the end of him.

Luis finished his thought. "And the rest of the money we will use for our wedding." He stared directly into her eyes. "And yes, I plan on getting you a mariachi. How does that strike you?"

Casimira liked the sound of it. She kissed Luis, and he pulled her close. She could feel his arms tightening around her shoulders. Their love was a tremor.

Shortly after Luis arrived in Watsonville for the last time, he found himself with both knees planted in the moist dirt, crouched over clusters of the reddest strawberries he'd ever seen. They were so abundant that he wondered if this wasn't what Moses's biblical Red Sea looked like. So big were these particular strawberries that he couldn't fit them into his pocket. If he wanted to eat one he would have to bend over and do so right there, under the cloak of green foliage, out of the mayordomo's sight.

While working he thought of Casimira obsessively. She was his prize at the end of the season. During breaks he would pull her photo from his pocket and fantasize the expression on her face when he would return to her. He would gaze at her image intensely and conjure every memory possible. He pictured her and her sisters and the wild times they all shared, laughing up and down Calle Fortuna, skipping over to el jardín to listen to the musicians. The first time he and Casimira kissed was at night under the bell tower of el Templo del Señor del Monte, right there in the town square. It was during the fiestas. How could he forget? The very photo he was holding in his hand had been taken only days before. Or was it after? Either way, she looked as fresh now as she did then. Staring at her photo, remembering, felt as if he were living each moment all over again. He remembered a dicho he once overheard an old man at el jardín utter: "El recordar es vivir." To remember is to live again. Perhaps no one understood this more than Luis. If he had a favorite pastime, it was nostalgia. It seemed to make the time go by faster. In the soft gaze of Casimira's eyes, months were reduced to weeks. In her supple skin and tender lips, days evaporated in seconds. At this rate, it was reasonable to believe that his beloved Cara de Dolorosa was only a tomorrow away.

GUADALUPE RAMÍREZ LARA AND RAMÓN PAREDES GONZÁLEZ

7

JAIME AND GUILLERMO RAMÍREZ

Fresno, California
April 11, 2013

Jaime Ramírez stands an inch or two below six feet. He's dark complected, with graying hair and a tired shape around his shoulders and eyes. Each morning, he wakes up at 4:30 and showers and gets dressed while running down the day's work in his mind: bills piled on his desk, the health inspector's last visit, the broken air conditioner that needs fixing, and the more than dozen employees whose families count on their paychecks. As the owner of Olé Frijole, a local Mexican buffet, he pours every bit of sweat and muscle into assuring its success. Each morning at the same time he drives the quiet, dark streets from Fresno's west side over to his restaurant on the corner of Blackstone and Shaw, in the heart of the city's dwindling main drag. Always, Jaime is the first to arrive. He rolls up his sleeves and gets busy prepping food for the buffet. He chops vegetables—onions, lettuce, cucumbers—for the salad, puts the beans to boil, then walks into the industrial-sized fridge and hauls out the meats. He preps and washes them, adds his usual spices, and sets them back in the fridge. He sweeps the entryway, counts his register, and makes sure all the chairs are under their tables and that the floors are mopped clean until you can look down and see your own reflection. By the time his employees clock in, the only thing left for them to do is provide good service to all who walk through the front door.

On this day Jaime's prepared to speak of ghosts.

A few days ago he'd reached out to me and we spoke by phone. He'd caught wind that I was looking for information about the plane crash.

The one his uncle, Guadalupe, and his grandfather, Ramón, were both killed in.

"What would you like to know?" Jaime asked, over the phone.

"Everything," I replied.

When I walked through the doors of Olé Frijole it was midmorning, and I found him behind the cash register, polishing the countertop with a wet rag. Though Jaime and I had never met, there was an immediate connection the moment we shook hands. He pulled me into the kitchen and introduced me to his brother, Guillermo. Together, the two brothers led me around the restaurant, introducing me to the rest of the employees. They were dishwashers, cooks, and maintenance—cousins and siblings, all of them related; it was a family operation. Every last one of them descendants of Guadalupe and Ramón. I found myself staring into their eyes, taking note of their gaze and how their faces resembled those of my own family.

When we finally sat down to talk, Jaime pulled two envelopes from a green folder and placed them on the table.

"Tell me about Ramón and Guadalupe," I began. He eyed my recorder.

"Our family is from Charco de Pantoja," he started in, "in the state of Guanajuato. That's where the men were from. From Charco. They were farmers."

"They were hard workers," Guillermo added. "Strong men."

A proud glow shone in their eyes.

Over the next few hours, they told me everything they knew about Ramón and Guadalupe, and about a valley in the center of Mexico they affectionately referred to as El País de las Siete Luminarias. Land of the Seven Lamps.

"My grandpa, Ramón Paredes, worked for the haciendas many years." Jaime said in an earnest tone. "And when they got the land, they made Charco de Pantoja, the little community that is now there. It's a farming community. That's it, just farming. Ramón and Guadalupe both had land there, and that's what they did their whole lives—they farmed. Corn, wheat, frijoles, garbanzos, alfalfa, everything. But to do this, you see, they needed water, a well for irrigation. That's the whole reason they came to the United States in the first place. To raise money for a well. Water is serious business in Charco."

"Yes, very serious," added Guillermo, folding his arms and leaning back in his chair.

Jaime hesitated, wondering if he should share with me the story that'd been passed down for generations in Charco de Pantoja. It was the kind of leyenda that the farmers of Charco kept in the back of their minds as an ominous reminder anytime conversations about water arose. Jaime looked at his brother, before turning his eyes toward me.

"In Charco, everything has to do with water," he began. "Just like anywhere else, you see. If we don't have water, we don't get food. We don't get food, that's it. Well, I don't have to tell you this, you already know. But men have killed each other over water—"

In the seventeenth century, there was a wealthy Spaniard who owned the largest hacienda in el Valle de Santiago, Guanajuato. He sectioned off the land into large plots and envisioned a kind of utopia unrivaled since the Garden of Eden. The idea, an ambitious one, was to irrigate every single plot, alternating one at a time. This would preserve what little water was available, while still maintaining an abundant crop. But the Spaniard soon discovered that whenever he moved from one plot to the next, the previous one would dry up, destroying half of what he planted. Frustrated, he spread word to the townspeople that he was looking to hire the best farmer around, preferably someone who knew a thing or two about water. When word of mouth got back to the Spaniard, it was mutually agreed upon that a humble peasant named Doroteo was the only man for the job.

Later, it would be debated whether Doroteo actually knew anything about water at all. Regardless of his knowledge, the only thing that mattered to Doroteo was that the Spaniard had come from old money and was known to lavish it on anyone who was lucky enough to land themselves in his good graces. And of course, Doroteo, the widower that he was—responsible for three daughters, one of whom was born deaf—saw an opportunity and leapt at the chance to impress the Spaniard.

In their first meeting, Doroteo pointed toward el Rincon de Parangueo, where sat a dormant volcano that was used as a reservoir. The Spaniard scoffed at Doroteo and immediately dismissed him for a lunatic. "Even I know volcano water isn't agua dulce!" He spat at the peasant's feet, insulted.

"Forgive me for asking this, sir, but have you ever actually tasted the water from el Rincon de Parangueo?" asked Doroteo.

"Why would I? Any fool knows volcano water is the fastest way to kill a parcel."

Doroteo stepped closer to the Spaniard's horse. "Sir, have you not seen the mountain lions, crows, ducks, and red foxes scavenging the hillside?"

The Spaniard lifted his chin. "Of course I have; do you think I'm blind?"

"You see, sir, while that is true about the water in most volcanoes, el Rincon de Parangueo is a rarity." He took another step closer and spoke now almost in a whisper. "Only a handful of local farmers know the value of that water, sir, and this is why their crops flourish each year."

"Who knows of this?" asked the Spaniard.

"I cannot tell, sir, respectfully." Doroteo stepped back.

The Spaniard looked up at the volcano. From where he sat he could see the opening of the tunnel near the crown of the mountain. "And you say the water is agua dulce?"

"Most definitely," Doroteo replied. "In fact, sir, that water is better than agua dulce. The few who know about it believe it is agua sagrado."

The Spaniard looked carefully into Doroteo's eyes. "Sacred water, eh?" Doroteo nodded. The Spaniard thought a moment. "I'll tell you what. Take two clay jugs and fill them with that *sacred* water. Haul it off to Mexico City to have it tested. If it proves to be as you claim, then you, my friend, will be rewarded." Doroteo began to express his gratitude, but the Spaniard cut in: "However, if it is not good water, then believe me when I say that I will be forced to kill you for attempting to exploit my generosity and make a fool of me."

"Fair enough," said Doroteo, starting off to fetch the water.

Doroteo began his trek to Mexico City early the next morning. Everything seemed to be going fine, until the halfway point. A storm threatened, and he seized the opportunity to stop and visit friends at a nearby cantina. He placed the jugs outside and went in to greet his compadres. When questioned about the two jugs, Doroteo told them about the deal he'd made with the Spaniard.

"And you've tasted the water in el Rincon de Parangueo?" one of the men pressed.

"Well, not necessarily, but—"

"Not necessarily?" interrupted another. "The Spaniard will kill you—"

Doroteo protested: "I was told by a trusted compadre that the water is agua dulce."

"Compadre or no compadre; what'll your daughters do if you're dead?"

Doroteo sipped his pulque and retreated to his thoughts.

They drank until the next morning, and by then the rain had subsided. As he stepped out into the daylight he reached for the two jugs of water and found they'd been toppled over by the storm. For a second, he contemplated hurrying back to the crater to fetch more water, but knew there wasn't enough time. Desperate, he dipped the jugs into a puddle of rainwater and continued on to Mexico City to have it inspected.

Three days passed before Doroteo finally arrived back at the hacienda, where the Spaniard had been anxiously awaiting his return.

"Well?" the Spaniard said, tapping his trigger finger against his holster. Doroteo proudly showed the Spaniard the official papers, signed *Mexico City*. The Spaniard glared into the peasant's eyes for a full minute before uttering a word. Finally, he lifted his hand and swatted his new foreman on the back. "Excellent," he said. "Tomorrow we begin irrigating." Doroteo breathed a sigh of relief and hurried home to tell his daughters the good news.

But that night he couldn't sleep. He kept hearing the men at the cantina berating him for staking his life on water that he himself had not tested.

Early the next morning, well before the roosters cawed, Doroteo hastened to the volcano to taste the water for himself. He cupped his hand and drew it to his lips for a sip. His face contorted. Just as he feared, it was a salt lick. He slumped to the ground, knowing that if he didn't come up with a plan before sunrise the boars would be gnawing on his eye sockets by noon.

He hurried over to the creek. It was practically dry, but there was still a narrow trickle. Enough for one decent crop, he estimated. At least it would buy him some time.

Months passed, and the Spaniard was more than satisfied with the results of the first crop. It was better than anything he'd been able to produce. The garbanzos flourished, and the entire plot shone like an emerald blanket. Doroteo could breathe, if only for a little longer. True to his word, the Spaniard lavished money on his new foreman. Even with a sack of coins now clenched in his fist, Doroteo was a nervous wreck. He considered taking his daughters and fleeing San José de los Horcones, but life in that part of Mexico was all they knew. As far as a permanent solution, he had nothing. He continued to pull agua dulce from the waning creek for as long as he could, but by the next season, when the creek was finally depleted, he had no choice but to pull water from the volcano.

Come harvest time, the stalks hadn't grown but a few inches, and the corn practically coughed when touched. The Spaniard eyed Doroteo.

The next evening, he invited his foreman to meet with him in the tunnel at the top of the volcano. Worried, Doroteo questioned the Spaniard's intention.

"I want to give you an expression of my gratitude," the Spaniard assured Doroteo. "You've been such a fine partner." Doroteo, albeit hesitantly, obliged.

The two met that afternoon at the top of el Rincon de Parangueo, near the tunnel's entrance. Doroteo arrived a little early to calm his nerves by taking in the sight that was El País de las Siete Luminarias. From the foot of the tunnel it was a breathtaking view of the valley. Lush and dynamic. A panorama befitting of the very name.

When the Spaniard finally arrived, they greeted each other and entered the tunnel.

"Please, you first," said the Spaniard, waving his foreman in. The humble peasant began walking, with the Spaniard following close behind. They were quickly enveloped by the darkness, and though they were a few feet away from each other, only their breath could be heard. When they finally reached the halfway point, Doroteo could see the pinprick of sunlight seeping in from the other side of the tunnel. It was a relief. But then an unsettling chill crept over him. The Spaniard was too quiet. Doroteo kept his gaze on the tunnel's end and continued putting one foot in front of the other. He wondered if he should say something, if only to break the tension.

The Spaniard cleared his throat. "Do you see that light, Doroteo?"

"Yes, sir," Doroteo replied, hurrying his pace.

"Can you tell me, my friend, where exactly that light comes from?"

"The sun, of course, sir."

"Indeed," said the Spaniard. "You are a wise man, Doroteo."

Doroteo could feel the tension starting to dissipate.

"And can you tell me how the sun is able to shine so brilliantly?"

Doroteo held back his laugh at this strange line of questioning. He didn't want to offend his boss. "Forgive my lack of intelligence, but exactly what do you mean, sir?" His voice echoed in the tunnel.

"What is the source of the sun's light, Doroteo?"

Doroteo could hardly believe that the Spaniard, the farmer that he was, didn't know the source of the sun's light. "Well, sir," he said, proud that he himself knew the answer, "fire—"

Doroteo heard the revolver click and that was it. He dropped dead. No parting words or final scorn. The Spaniard dragged the peasant's body from the tunnel and left his warm corpse on the side of the road for the townspeople to see.

Days later, when his daughters laid their father to rest, they said his eyes were still open, and it appeared that a teardrop was solidified in his ducts.

His story was a message for the people of Charco de Pantoja: "El agua es vida."

8

EL PAÍS DE LAS SIETE LUMINARIAS

"It wasn't until after Pancho Villa's revolution that the land was divided into parcelas and given to the people. The parcelas are small plots of good land, with good soil, where families can plant crops and make a living, you see. But the parcelas, back then, were the only means of survival. And this way of life, making sure the farms always had a harvest, was all Guadalupe and Ramón worked for. They weren't looking for trouble; they just wanted to live in peace and have a family. But in those days, there was trouble anyways. You see, for a long time there used to be two haciendas there—el Hacienda de Parangueo and el Hacienda de Pantoja. Later they were named Charco de Pantoja and Charco de Parangueo. But there was always trouble in those times. People tried taking over the small pueblos, and well, they learned it wasn't easy—"

In the earliest days, shortly after the revolution, small outbreaks of conflict continued to plague the rural areas of Mexico. It was a territorial thing, mostly. The stealing of land by vigilantes who were still feeling the sting of the Porfiriato was a common force to be reckoned with. Meanwhile, farmers and peasants everywhere began the process of knocking the dust off their trousers and getting back on their feet, despite the beating their small farms took from Díaz's industrial hammer.

They picked up right where they'd left off a generation prior. Till the hardened land, sow the seeds, make fervent offerings to the Holy Trinity: La Virgen, San Isidro Labrador, and of course Tlaloc, god of fertility and abundance.

"Make sure the offerings are ample, don't skimp," the farmers would remind one another. "Candles, cakes, copal, flowers, cigarillos, anything and everything. Kneel down daily before the altar and pray, pray harder, for water, sun, bread. Come harvest season, pray more!"

Whether it was because the residents of Charco de Pantoja didn't pray hard enough, or because their gratitude lacked conviction, the townspeople awoke one night to the whistle of bullets riddling their bedroom walls.

A posse, backed by the hacienda and formed of thugs from the nearby pueblos of San Antonio, Guarapo, and San Cristobal, had gotten together to take Charco by force. It was a problem that stemmed from the fact that the hardworking farmers of Charco saw themselves as self-reliant and independent and therefore refused to abide by hacienda law, as the others did. Gunshots tore through the quiet air. Men on horseback bullied their way into homes and stables, or started to anyway, but they didn't count on a motley group of steel-toting men, for whom Charco de Pantoja was a birthright.

For Ramón and Guadalupe, as young as they were, their way of life was at stake. Armed with a revolver in each hand, and a satchel filled with enough bullets to permanently slap the grin off the hacienda's face, they took to the streets and lit up the night sky in a hailstorm of bullets, giving the name Land of the Seven Lamps new meaning.

Ramón, a gambler, called upon his homeboys, hard-boiled pistoleros who knew every trapdoor and underground tunnel from Charco to Tenochtitlán, to summon the cavalry, which is to say, the kind of brutos who shoot first and ask questions later.

Meanwhile, Guadalupe stood his post, unloading round after round amid a hot cloud of gunpowder, cursing the malcriados who dare suggest that peaceful Charco was theirs for the taking.

Both men were among the small, ill-equipped army of farmers who fought hard that night, banishing the hacienda's posse back to their side of the valley. It was the stuff of legacy and lore. Like the Chichimeca blood wars that took place on the same terrain centuries before, this too would become a story that their children's children would speak of generations later.

"When that happened," Jaime said, "my grandpa, Ramón, y tambien mi tío Guadalupe, they fought."

Guillermo cut in. "They protected Charco—it was their little town—but they protected it . . . because, well, those guys wanted to burn the whole place down, take over, you know, but they fought them off, with guns, and with their fists too. Guadalupe was well known for being a good fighter. There are many stories in Charco about how good he was, but that's how they fought them off." And so goes the story.

Guadalupe's reputation would hang in the air above Charco for as long as there were mouths to speak of it. His grandson Fidel Ramírez would recall: "Those times were much different, but people here still talk about it. It had been rumored that my grandfather Guadalupe killed a man while defending Charco. When I was kid, growing up, my grandmother Micaela, who was Guadalupe's wife, forbade me to play near the hacienda. Even though my grandfather had been dead for decades already, it didn't matter. Micaela would say, 'Don't go near there, 'ijo. If they know you're a Ramírez they might want to take revenge.'"

9

RAMÓN AND ELISA

By the time the dust had settled and the embers had cooled off, Ramón had found himself a lovely bride. A local beauty named Elisa Murillo Granados.

In the only photo of Elisa ever taken, she's staring directly into the camera. Her left eyebrow is raised, like the curved beak of a hummingbird, and there's a glimmer in the black of her pupils. It appears the light source is placed in front of her, just to the right of where she stands. Her hair is a dark, thick mane, and it's pulled back, away from her face and bound behind her neck, though loose enough so that her curls can be seen below her earlobes. She's light-skinned with a smooth complexion, contrasted by the sternness of her gaze. Her lips are closed. Her jawline square. Her chin defiant. She's standing with her back against a wall. Her shadow blurs the lines between her head and the wall itself. A crease runs across the middle of the photograph, as if it were folded at some point, perhaps stuffed into Ramón's coat pocket during one of his trips to el Norte.

Elisa and Ramón began a family immediately. Six children, one after the other—

Federico, Caritina, Blandina, Guadalupe, Mercedes, and Ramón Jr. Their home was a humble dwelling made of adobe and stones gathered from the creek, and the vigas were cut from abundant mesquite trees that surrounded them. There, they cared for their children and did their best to forge a simple life. If they dreamt at all, it was to have food, a place to call home, and to live long enough to enjoy grandchildren.

During those early years, it was widely known that Ramón had three devotions: his family, the ejido, and gambling. In that order. Of these, the majority of his time was spent working the ejido. Ramón was a pragmatic man. If there were no crops, there was nothing to eat. It was as simple as that. The few goats they owned, a cow, chickens, all possibilities of meat were reliant on what the earth itself could produce.

As Mexico was still struggling to regain its balance in the years following the revolution, the rural pueblos were the last territories on any politico's mind. The families in these parts were left to fend for themselves. This put all the burden on making sure the ejido was thriving. As always, water was the primary concern. The farmers of Charco decided to organize themselves in order to make the most of their combined skills and resources.

The committee, mostly men, though a few women, met in the center of town one afternoon. They haggled a little about process and fairness, and when it came time to select roles, it went smoother than they thought it would. They had grown up with one another and knew who was capable of what. Guadalupe was put in charge of the plowing, for no one could set rows as straight as he could, with his proven technique of using strings and sticks to align points and counterpoints along the way. He would teach his own children, and the other farmers, how to do this with precision. Others were assigned tasks such as sowing and harvesting, and even a president was selected to handle the official matters. Because he was an avid gambler, good with numbers and unafraid of handling money, Ramón was nominated and selected to be the treasurer. It wasn't as difficult a decision as one might think, assigning a gambler the sensitive role of handling the money matters, for Ramón was also an honest man, many would even say, loyal to a fault. Plus, everyone knew Ramón wasn't going anywhere anytime soon. He wasn't much of a wanderer. He took pride in Charco, had put his own life on the line for it. The mere thought of leaving and never returning simply wasn't in his DNA.

He accepted his role as treasurer with pride. Each night he'd come home and share with Elisa the matters of the day. Who was doing their part, pitching in, and who wasn't. How much money would have to go to the purchase of a mule for plowing, and then, how optimistic the forthcoming season looked. Months later, how dreadful the yield was, or dismal the garbanzos. "Practically shriveled into raisins from lack of proper irrigation," he would say. As goes the history of Charco, water was the only conversation. The nearby creek was hardly enough. It was now being siphoned by other ejidos, and by the time it reached Charco it was so depleted it was hardly a teardrop.

Ramón had a conversation with the irrigation boss.

"If we don't do something fast, in a few months' time we'll be eating ground squirrels."

The jefe scratched his beard. "What do you suggest?" he asked.

"The water from the crater?" Ramón said, half-serious.

"That's not agua dulce. It's salt. It'll kill the land, that'll be the end of us."

Ramón looked out across the ejido. It was evening, and he spotted Guadalupe in the distance, cutting furrows. His black Labrador, Lobo, was at his side.

After a short silence the irrigation boss spoke up.

"We need to dig," he said. "A deep well is the only way."

Ramón bent down and grabbed a handful of soil. He sniffed it. "Water below?"

"Of course."

"What will it take?"

The irrigation boss looked at Ramón. He fanned his fingers. "Plata," he replied.

Ramón wiped his brow. As treasurer it was his call.

The next day he brought it to the committee. Within the first few minutes they all agreed. Water was of the utmost importance. A deep well was the only answer. The look of uncertainty on their faces right then was not about whether or not a well *should* be dug, but whether or not a well *could* be dug. It all boiled down to money. Ramón opened the committee purse and a few coins tinkled out. They looked grimly at one another. No one said a word. Ramón felt the weight of their silence. The issue was too grave for words. He knew what he had to do.

Later that night, Ramón found himself in el Valle de Santiago, staring down into a spread of cards, sipping pulque, eyeing a table of red-eyed men, who by the looks of their gaunt faces were more desperate than even he. The idea was not only to win back his money, but perhaps, if he played his cards right, win enough to make the well a reality without having to consider the only alternative, el Norte. He sipped his pulque slowly, so as to remain sharp with his strategy. Each move was a matter of survival. Elisa was counting on him. His children were counting on him. In those tense moments, amid the shuffling of cards and beads of sweat, he had convinced himself that all of Charco de Pantoja was counting on him.

As hours passed he wiped the blur from his eyes and kept track of his opponents' cards. He noticed their quick fingers, their facial tics. Who had a habit of twisting their mustache. Whose profuse sweating gave away their bluff. He'd win a round. Then lose one. It was like that Aztec dance he'd once seen, el baile del colibri, where the woman, adorned in colorful regalia, lunges her body forward a few steps, then drifts back again, as if in flight. Forward and back. This is how Ramón's night went. Win some. Lose some. Ten pesos. Then twenty. Lose fifteen. Win five more.

The sun had been up for a couple of hours, and the men could hardly keep their eyes open. They agreed they needed sleep. They stopped midgame, left their cards on the table, pocketed their winnings, and had themselves a rest. A few hours later they awoke and the game resumed right where they'd left off. As long as Ramón had money he would keep playing.

The second round went late into the night, and again, at some ungodly hour, the men collectively agreed on taking another nap. Lying on the cold hard floor, Ramón fingered the last few coins in his pocket, and the pessimism settled in. The thought of going home a loser made him furious. He took another sip of pulque and passed out.

By that evening, blurry-eyed, drink emanating from his pores, he stumbled in the direction of home. He was a wreck. At least he hadn't lost it all, he consoled himself. He passed the ejido and stood there a moment, taking it in. He spotted Guadalupe's dog, Lobo, in the distance, sniffing around the mud. He whistled the dog over.

Lobo came to Ramón, licked his hand, and plopped himself onto the dirt. Ramón joined him. The whisper of birds in the nearby bushes could be heard. In the perfect silence of the evening, Ramón looked across the ejido and could almost envision the well. He could see the glistening rows of water and hear the infinite trickling of a stream. It was the sound of Charco's success. His own success. He could see the corn growing to unfathomable heights, garbanzos as large as fists. The fertile earth a shade of red, umber, its scent wafting like a sash across his chest. There was only one choice. As much as he hated to admit it, el Norte was the only solution.

"You see, Lobo," he said to the dog, petting the back of its neck. "This might be the ultimate gamble. The only kind that matters. Here in Charco we know the odds, don't we? Only God knows the odds over there, en el otro lado."

Lobo said nothing. He sat there, allowing Ramón to pet him.

"I wonder if los Estados Unidos is everything they say it is."

Lobo licked Ramón's hand.

"Then it's a deal," Ramón said.

And that was it. A pact between man and dog.

After having been gone for three whole days, Ramón entered his house, singing at the top of his lungs—

Una pasión me domina / y es la que me hizo venir

Valentina, Valentina / yo te quisiera decir.

It was the one song that he'd committed to memory. He'd heard many rancheras, but none so impassioned, so dead on about matters of pride, that it vibrated in his core of cores.

One of his children, Blandina, still a baby, would be the first to greet her father. When sung, the lyrics "Valentina, Valentina" sounded so close to her own name that the child would come scrambling out from beneath the bed and cling to his leg. "Blandina, Blandina," he sang, while tickling the child and making her giggle—

Dicen que por tus amores / un mal me van a seguir

no le hace que sean el diablo / yo también me sé morir . . .

Elisa would walk toward him; she could smell the booze in the air. She would kiss him once, and then resume her work. Ramón serenaded her.

Si porque tomo Tequila / mañana tomo jerez

si porque me ven borracho / mañana ya no me ven.

Eventually, Elisa would break into a smile. She couldn't be angry with him. She was aware of what her husband had attempted. She was proud of him for it. When he told her of his meager earnings, she said nothing. Didn't belittle his efforts. In that moment, with a shadow of defeat pulled over his face, her stoic silence was a gust of fresh air.

"Elisa," he said, reaching down to lift Blandina into his arms. "I've made an important decision."

Elisa already knew. Even before he took another breath, she knew.

"Necesito ir pa'l Norte."

She kept her gaze on him. Looked through him, actually. She could see clear across the line in the dirt, to the North of every man's destiny. According to the wives of Charco de Pantoja, el Norte was less a place and more a mistress. The way their husbands and sons would return home, talking of el Norte—a seductress that would have them yearning long after they left. Perhaps this why they referred to one another as enganchados, they would whisper.

"Elisa," Ramón spoke up, "I have to, mi amor. It's the only choice."

She had long been preparing herself for this moment. But with the recent talk about his role in the ejido, and how the weight of the community was on his shoulders, she never suspected it would be anytime soon. Certainly not today.

"Promise me you won't go alone," she found herself saying.

Ramón hesitated. "Of course not." He paused. "I plan to ask my compadre Guadalupe to come along."

"I doubt Micaela will let him out of her sight long enough."

"We'll see," he replied.

She watched her husband tickle the baby's feet playfully. She eyed his face and his thick, wavy hair. There was a sincerity in his gaze.

"Promise me that you'll come back to us."

"Of course, mi vida."

She hesitated. Blandina tugged on her father's mustache. "Well then," Elisa said. "Dinner is almost ready."

He stepped to Elisa and kissed her forehead. He looked Blandina in the eye—

Blandina, Blandina / rendido estoy a tus pies
si me han de matar mañana / que me maten de una vez.

10

EL NORTE

Guadalupe accepted Ramón's invitation. He admitted he'd been considering the same for weeks now, and after many long sleepless nights, that his compadre was also going seemed like auspicious timing.

"Micaela will understand," he said. "She's been wanting to have a family, and that's as good a reason as any."

The week before their departure, Guadalupe had taken to casually riding his horse, Relampago, around the quiet dirt roads of Charco. He wanted to take it all in, to remind himself of the reason he was about to gamble on some unknown place in the faraway north. From atop the horse he would stare out across the tilled rows and admire how perfectly aligned they were, as far as the eye could see. Beneath the shade of the very mesquite tree he himself had planted as a boy, he couldn't help but ponder his failures. After all his efforts cultivating the ejido by hand, not to mention shedding his own blood for Charco, the fact that he needed to leave, to run away, in order to provide for his family, and for the ejido, was a beating to his pride like none he'd ever known. Not even one hundred years had gone by since the line in the dirt had been drawn between Mexico and los Estados Unidos, and he could still hear his grandfather Don Refugio's voice, recalling with great clarity his memory of those times.

"Some laws take years, maybe even generations, before the people begin to abide by them," the old man often said. "Back then, no matter how much they told us there was a line in Sonora that we could not cross, no one believed it. Alta California was still Alta California to us."

As a young man, Guadalupe would work the ejido with Don Refugio, and each day got an earful of the old man's ramblings. Usually, they centered on his disdain for the white man—"los invasores," as he referred to them. And how life before the invasion was idyllic, utopian even, according to his memory. A time when there was no such thing as extinction, and animals were abundant. According to the old man, "In those days there were so many red foxes that all of el Cerro de Peralta appeared as if it were on fire. And if one needed a reminder that we were born from warriors, great fighters, all you had to do was put your hands in the dirt, right here in Charco, and you would find the evidence."

Guadalupe asked the old man if he was referring to the Chichimecan shards that farmers would strike with their plows from time to time.

The old man was appalled that his own grandson didn't know the history. "'Chichimecas' was not their name! That's what los Espanos called them. No, 'ijo, they were Guamari, Zacateco y Guachichiles, these are their real names. They were fierce fighters, so los Espanos called them 'perros rabiosos.' But los indios did not know very much Spanish in those times, so to insult them, los Espanos found out that the word for savage dogs in their own language was 'chichimecas.' That name was meant as an insult."

Guadalupe thought the old man was crazy, and quite possibly wise beyond his understanding. If nothing else, his lessons made the long summer days at the ejido tolerable.

As Guadalupe mentally prepared himself for el Norte, he pondered what he'd been told by the more experienced enganchados, those who'd made the journey their livelihood. He'd heard that in many cases, Mexicans received the warmest of welcomes. It was even rumored that sometimes gringo farmers would host welcoming parties, where they'd butcher meats and spread colorful dishes out on endless tables, feasts fit for pilgrims, all in the name of "good labor relations."

Guadalupe and Micaela had long discussions into the night.

"What choice do we have, Micaela?" Guadalupe pressed. "Without irrigation how do we grow crops? Without food, how do we raise a child?"

Micaela knew he was right. She had to force the words out. "If there is no option—"

"There isn't," Guadalupe interrupted. "You think I haven't considered everything?"

Micaela quieted. Not because she didn't have the words. But because she knew Guadalupe well enough to know that once his mind was made up, that was it.

"Everything depends on the well, mi vida. That's how it is. No water, no bread."

Micaela was aware of the situation. She was sick of hearing about it. All anyone talked about anymore was water. Without it, El País de las Siete

Luminarias was barren. In place of crops, desperation grew. Sending their men off to el Norte was a last resort.

That a small group of farmers from el Valle de Santiago would be traveling together helped ease the worry in Micaela's mind. Guadalupe had a tendency to be alone whenever he found himself in strange places. She'd seen it before. His gruff exterior would be diminished to a humility that made him nearly unrecognizable. This is what worried her most. His emotional state. When he returned from el Norte, would he be the same? His physical well-being was one of her least concerns. She knew if anyone could handle himself, it was Guadalupe. Even before his eighteenth birthday, he'd already established himself as a gallo of the highest pecking order. He was a local boxing champion, also skilled in the art of Greco-Roman wrestling. No one knew how or where he acquired these skills, only that he was good at it, and that no one dared cross him because of it. In the end, Micaela, equally as staunch, knew she had no choice but to set aside her emotions. She longed for a child, a family of her own, and a place where her children could feel at home. It was a small sacrifice, she convinced herself, but the payoff would be worth it.

Days later, while at the ejido, Guadalupe spotted his friend José González Arredondo struggling to plow a section of the land. José was hunched over the dirt attempting to measure furrows. Guadalupe rode his horse over and offered a hand.

"Let me show you the trick," he said, dismounting his horse. He snatched a tule reed from the thicket and snapped it in half over his knee. "You see, to cut the best furrows both sides must be the same. See these two sticks here, José?"

José nodded.

"You must hold them at a ninety-degree angle, like this, so that they point perfectly straight to the stick you have at the other end of the field. From here to there, you see?"

"Yes, I see," said José.

"Now, from here, you need to walk over to the other side and place two more sticks there, in the same ninety-degree angle, so that they point straight back to this one. When you have the mule here, he should dig his hoof as close to this point as possible." Guadalupe wedged the heel of his boot into the earth to mark the spot. "And then it's up to you to guide the mule directly to that other point. If both sides are equal, you will have a straight line."

That afternoon the two men aligned the furrows together, and José González Arredondo was grateful.

When asked about it years later, José would say, "It's true—Don Guadalupe guided me in the knowledge of plowing. He got off of his horse and showed me how, right here at the ejido. He was a busy man, and must've been on his way to who knows where, but he stopped to teach me how to cut furrows. In fact, it was here, at the ejido, where I first began to call Guadalupe Ramírez Lara my good friend. Whenever he was home from los Estados Unidos, he would come by the ejido, and he would always stop and ask how I was doing, and we would talk. We would talk and laugh. We had such good times. Yes, he was a good, good friend."

After he was done teaching José how to cut furrows, Guadalupe mounted his horse and took one long gaze at the ejido. At that moment he informed his friend of his decision to leave with Ramón Paredes to el Norte. At first José said nothing. He rolled a cigarette and offered one to his friend, but Guadalupe respectfully declined. As José took drags from his smoke, he admitted he was surprised to learn that Guadalupe, of all people, would even consider leaving Charco de Pantoja.

"We could certainly use a well," he said, nodding. "But who will manage the ejido?"

"Ramón has made arrangements with the committee," Guadalupe replied. "We won't be gone long, six months, a year maybe."

José walked around his mule and rested his arm on the yoke. "Do you need someone to watch over the dog while you're away?"

Guadalupe shook his head. "Lobo will be fine. Micaela handles him well enough."

A few minutes passed before José dropped his cigarette in the mud. He lifted his hand for Guadalupe to shake and without ceremony bade his friend good-bye. He cocked his hat back on his head and stood among the furrows, watching Guadalupe lead his horse away from the ejido, kicking up dust as he disappeared beyond the fields and past the cemetery.

Those closest to him understood that Guadalupe felt an undeniable connection with his dog, Lobo. Some even suggested the two were spiritual kin. Guadalupe would shrug off this kind of talk. But in the quietest of hours, just before bed, when he and Micaela were alone, he would confide in her.

"Dogs are loyal."

Micaela would simply nod.

"Lobo more than most."

Again, Micaela nodded.

"Take good care of him, amor. He's old, but sturdy."

"Don't worry," she said, "he'll be fine." As she said it, a thought entered her mind. She recalled how, often, whenever Guadalupe hung his soiled work coat on the fence to dry, Lobo would refuse to leave from that spot until Guadalupe returned. The dog was practically the size of a pony, so it made him near impossible to lift. If Guadalupe had business that would require him to be gone for a few days, and he left his coat there to dry, Lobo would lay himself down on that very spot, beneath the fence, and wait. So often did this occur that there was an impression in the ground the shape of Lobo's body. Micaela couldn't count how many times she had tried luring the dog away from the fence with food, but most times even that failed. If the weather was bad, she would have to fetch a neighbor to come help lift the dog and take him inside the house. Lobo awaited his master faithfully.

"He's a good dog," Guadalupe said once more, before blowing out the candle.

"He is," Micaela replied.

That night, on the eve of his first trek to el Norte, after he placed his horse back in the corral and found Lobo promptly awaiting his arrival, Guadalupe leisurely walked the perimeter of his small property contemplating what was to come. His mind replayed stories he'd heard about the journey itself, and how Mexicanos by the trainload were being shipped off to save the harvests of California. It was all he had to go on. He had heard the names of towns, places like Stockton, Woodland, Selma, and at the suggestion of Ramón had even begun to practice these names. "Estockton," he whispered to himself. "Burlan." He repeated, "Burlan." Despite being told about el Valle de San Joaquin, this near-mythical place in the heart of Don Refugio's Alta California, where fruits and vegetables grow everywhere, even right up through the concrete, it was hard for him to imagine any valley more abundant, more beautiful, than El País de las Siete Luminarias. He had not yet taken his first step to el Norte and already he was envisioning his return. The first thing he would do would be to kiss the dark soil of his parcel and vow to San Isidro that he would never leave Charco again.

In that moment, it would've been impossible for Guadalupe to predict what his future held. How could he know that this first trek to el Norte was only the beginning? Had anyone warned him that walking through the golden gates of los Estados Unidos would almost certainly lead to his becoming an enganchado—a courtship that would map out the remaining years of his life—he would've laughed in their faces and perhaps brandished his missing finger. "Nonsense," he might've protested, "Charco holds pieces of me."

11

THE PHOTOGRAPH

Before Guadalupe left for los Estados that first time, Micaela made him take a photograph so that she could look at it while he was away. He was reluctant at first and told her only vain people did such things. Of course, being the farmer that he was, wearing any piece of garment that wasn't soiled or patchworked felt unnatural. Despite his misgivings, Micaela fussed over him that morning, taking all measures to make sure the photograph displayed the sheer handsomeness that was her husband. She even borrowed a hot iron to run over his only nice pair of pants and shirt. When he tried the shirt on that morning, it was obvious it was a size too small. The cuffs stopped short of his wrist bone.

"This is pointless," he said.

Micaela tugged on the sleeve. "I can let it down," she assured him.

Guadalupe shook his head.

It was the same issue with his pants. The cuffs rode up.

"Do you know how long it's been since I've worn such ridiculous things?"

Micaela wasn't having it. "I can let those down too," she said. "Besides, we can ask the photographer to photograph from your knees up. It'll be fine."

Guadalupe huffed.

At six feet tall, with shoulders as wide as a bow yoke, his options were limited. After hemming his clothes, Micaela took some sheers to the front of his hair and cropped the thick mat down to a manageable cowlick.

"What's the point?" Guadalupe remarked. "I'll be wearing my hat anyway."

Micaela glared at him.

"Go on, kiss me," he said, playfully. She swatted his arm and finished cropping his mane. When she was done she split his hairline over the left side of his head and with a comb pulled the cowlick over his right eye.

"There," she said. "You look decent now. Fit enough for a photograph."

Because they owned neither mirror nor silverware, Guadalupe could only take Micaela's word for it. Still, on their way out the door, Guadalupe saw his hat parked on the table, and like any self-respecting campesino would do, he snatched it and crammed it onto his head.

At the studio, posing for the camera, he felt awkward. It was all too much. The shirt he wore made him itchy, and his pants kept riding up. To make matters worse, the photographer hassled with his contraption for an hour before the photo was even snapped. Now and then Guadalupe would shoot Micaela a look, as if any moment he would tear his shirt off and run out the front door. If things weren't bad enough, she forbade him to wear the hat.

"You're not at the ejido," she scolded.

"It's my good hat, Micaela," he spat back. "It was Don Refugio's; I always wear it."

"But you have good hair. And this photograph will last for all time, Lupe."

"Is that thing almost ready?" he pressed the photographer.

"Almost," the man replied.

Guadalupe noticed Micaela smiling up at him, her youthful lips and deep-set eyes. He knew he would stand there for as long as it took.

"Okay," the photographer finally said. "Stand straight, please. You only get one shot at this." He eyed Guadalupe's pant cuffs. "Have you ever taken a photograph before, sir?"

Micaela piped up. "This is his first."

"In that case, let me tell you a few things. You'll want to keep your eyes open, sir. I will count you down from three, and whatever you do, do not close your eyes. Also, do not move a muscle. Any bit of movement and you will come out looking like a ghost. Understand?"

Guadalupe nodded.

Micaela motioned for him to keep his eyes open.

"I shall count you down now, sir. Three, two—"

In the photograph of Guadalupe, there are many things to consider. First, what the photographer's lens captured: Guadalupe is wearing a plain white button-up shirt with long sleeves that are visibly short. The shirt is tucked into his brown pants and bound with a thin leather belt. He is standing next to a table with a floral tablecloth. We know that Micaela won the hat discussion, because his hat is not on his head. It is on the table. Even so, his right hand still rests on it. His cowlick is combed over his right eye and slightly disheveled. The expression on his face is naïve, simple. The line of his mouth is tilted neither up nor down. It is a perfect horizon. There is a large window behind him, to his right, and another light source coming from directly in front. It's very possible too that he moved his shoulders, just slightly, a moment before the photographer pushed the button. For the combined effect of lighting and movement gives Guadalupe's white shirt the appearance of being illuminated. He is staring directly into the camera.

A person looking at this photo, years later, would never know why Guadalupe's hat is there, on the table, or why his hand is placed on it. Perhaps it was a nervous gesture, grasping for something familiar in an unfamiliar space. Or perhaps, in the most subconscious way, to touch the hat that once belonged to Don Refugio was to touch a part of his own past. It is likely Guadalupe hadn't a clue as to why he was reaching for the hat, and perhaps it wasn't that profound at all. It is possible that the photographer simply asked him, "Sir, would you mind placing your hand on your hat?" Still, years later, a person looking at this one-dimensional photo would draw their own conclusions about such details. Make guesses at his age, his state of mind. Going by this photo alone, one might consider Guadalupe a kind of man-about-town—he's dressed that sharp. Not accurate by any means if Guadalupe were to have his say on the matter. Regardless, the photo itself was to serve one purpose and one purpose alone. It was to give Micaela peace in knowing that the image under her pillow, that sweet mannish boy, contained enough light for the darker times to come. And until Guadalupe returned safely from el Norte, this would be the photograph she saw when she rose each morning and went to bed each night—

12

DEAR ELISA

Fresno, California
April 11, 2013

I could see that Jaime and Guillermo were now both visibly tired of speaking. By the third hour, it became obvious to them that my curiosity was insatiable. Guillermo excused himself and made his way to the kitchen. Jaime angled his eyes at me, and I could tell he was searching for words. After nearly a minute, he reached across the table, picked up one of the envelopes, and opened it. "Let me show you something," he said. He pulled out a tattered paper. "I think you will like this. See?"

"What is it?"

"This is the last letter Ramón wrote home to his wife, Elisa, before he was killed in the plane crash—"

On June 21, 1947, after having traversed the entire state of California by car, train, and foot, dodging la migra, and hustling to find even the most menial work, Ramón found himself in a state of complete exhaustion. On the afternoon that he sat down to compose the letter, his work shoes had holes and his feet were so swollen they looked as if they'd been clubbed with a mallet. To make matters worse, he and Guadalupe had parted ways out of sheer necessity, and the solitude of el Norte was beginning to take its toll. It was clear he had reached his end. If only he could see Elisa's supple face, glean a kiss from her, a touch, something to restore the ganas to keep on. The guilt of not being able to satiate his children's hunger was fast eroding his pride. As if that weren't enough, Elisa had been sick recently, and though she refused to tell Ramon what was wrong, the last time they corresponded, she left him with the impression that she was on the verge of losing her mind. How could any man ask his wife to endure such an impossible life? He shook his head at the provider he had turned out to be. He sat down beneath the shade of a tree and wrote his family an overdue letter. With a blue ink pen, he placed a single sheet of paper atop a rickety table and imagined the first few words he should say to her. They would have to be uplifting, hopeful, enough to distract Elisa from the cold whistle of his absence. His tilted his hat back on his head and wrote:

> *Junio 21 de '47*
> *Señora Elisa Murillo, mi estimada y inolvidable esposa. As you hold this letter and as it leaves me in good spirits, it would give me much joy knowing that you are in good health and in the company of all your children, and I hope that you are all better, gracias a Dios. Elisa, after this greeting I will say the following, I have not written you because I wasn't here. We spent about 26 days on the outskirts of where we've always been. I left before getting your letter, and I just got back and found your letter and found out about everything that you tell me. And well on one hand it's fine but on the other it's not because you must have been left without money and not been able to pay for expenses. I'm referring to the household expenses because when I became aware of this I have been very worried about the expenses you had to make and me not being able to help you. In the meantime I started heading up and la migra caught me in Ventura, California. I was held in the can for 15 days and I am without money and without a job and immigration was tough; didn't leave any work; not even the ranchers could hire workers without immigration papers because they'll get fined, therefore I have no hopes in being able to help you at the moment but I'm going to do everything possible. Maybe I can borrow some money and head down and possibly get hired with a landowner in return for a small piece of land to plant a little corn. As long as I can get work with the same owner even for one week it will be enough to go to Baja and secure more work. So if you have any garbanzos left and find yourself in much need, sell them and spend it on whatever you need and it might be able to help you in some way, while I find work or money to help you. I shouldn't be in this position but because I went to where one goes to win more money, I didn't*

win, although it would have been a small amount anyway. Let me also tell you that when we left we stayed at the house of el güero Vicente. We slept there one night and we encountered good luck, except later we met bad luck. If we had known that bad luck would be there, we would have turned around and not even bothered, for it already would have brought us failure to our adventure—and by the way it was in Buena Ventura where we turned around. And in other things, I ask you to tell me if you are in good health, both you and the children, that you are all good and healthy, especially you, the one that sees and cares for the children. You I am most concerned about because you haven't been in your right mind, but I pray to God that you are well and healthy as well as the children. I will also not worry about us being poor. Besides it's not new to us, God doesn't allow us to stop being poor. This will be our fortune. With nothing more to say at this time, say hello to your tía Rosa, and to Domingo, and my compa Enrique and family, and my compa José, and my comadre Maria and family, and your dad, and your tía Juanita, and everyone in general, and give the baby lots of hugs and kisses, and everyone else, and for you, receive the most loyal affection and love from your husband who wishes you good health and happiness.

Tu esposo,
Ramón Paredes

13

GUADALUPE'S CHRONOLOGY

There's nothing like our first journey away from home. Away from the land we know, the faces we're accustomed to, and away from that familiar sense of belonging that exists nowhere else. To travel to a foreign land, particularly if our survival depends on it, is to throw ourselves into the flames of disarray. In order to do this, we have to be willing to let go of control and deal with the paranoia of the unknown. Some friends will tell us, "Over there, they are good people, kind, generous." Other friends will warn, "Over there, they are hustlers, swindlers, devils." In this strange environment every decision we make is a matter of our well-being. Instinct becomes law. What side of the street to walk on. How to ask for help. Who to trust. Regardless of age, the experiences we've accumulated are almost useless in this new dimension. We're practically reduced to children. So we cling to the little familiarities. A dog scampers by and we try and commune with it. The night moon waxes and we greet it as if it were an old friend. Memory too becomes vital when so far away from home. The ability to recall a loved one's voice, or even the warm smell of bread, can mean the difference between alienation and a welcome reminder that we are still human. Our survival depends on it. Alone, far from the touch of a familiar hand, we reflect obsessively on why we are here in the first place, in this strange land, and for whom we are here. Perhaps there was something about love in our decision to have traveled so far. Why else endure any sacrifice? We remind ourselves, constantly, who benefits from our aloneness. Sometimes it's family. Sometimes it's our own tender soul. This becomes our purpose. Central to our existence. And for this, we're willing to leave the comforts of home, time and again, and as many times as necessary. Especially if the survival of those we love depends on it. Especially then.

Only a few months after returning from el Norte that first time, Guadalupe found himself leaving Charco yet again, braving the lonely trail back to

California's fields. And just as he did that first time, he performed the ritual of bending down to kiss the soft earth of his parcel, vowing to make this second trip the very last time. The first trip to los Estados was, without question, necessary. He and Ramón amassed a small savings for the well, and the committee expressed their gratitude. Though it wasn't enough, it was at least a start. They purchased a few supplies and stored them until they could come up with the rest. But now that he and Micaela hoped to start a family, it would take more than a harvest's worth of earnings to feed another mouth. For this reason, a second trip was absolutely as necessary as the first, if not more so.

Guadalupe started off down the same path as before, walking beyond his parcel in the direction of el Valle de Santiago. He had not yet reached the cemetery when already the pale whispers of el Norte began tugging on his ear, suggesting that a third trip might also be in order. He shook the thought from his mind. Ridiculous, he assured himself. Two trips would be plenty. It would have to be. But as any campesino knows, time has a way of changing plans.

"Uno pone y Dios dispone, y llega el Diablo y todo lo descompone." It was a dicho that his compadre Ramón often spouted. Years later, Ramón would utter these very words to Guadalupe while the two spent days inside a holding cell at the San Francisco Immigration Detention Center. It was the only way to make sense of the detours their lives had taken. "One plans, God undoes the plan, and then the Devil arrives and everything goes to hell."

A look at Guadalupe's records from the U.S. Department of Labor illustrates the point. To read them side by side is to glimpse the chronology of one family's survival:

On August 11, 1923, we find Guadalupe at age twenty-one waiting in line at the Laredo bridge crossing in Texas. It's a warm Saturday afternoon, eighty-nine degrees, and he's standing with hundreds of men, all awaiting their turn to cross into el Norte. According to his official documents, Guadalupe has twenty dollars in his pocket and he's accompanied by no one. The papers also show that he's highly adept at reading and writing. When asked if he's ever been to the United States before, he answers, No. When asked his occupation, he replies, Laborer. Purpose for wanting to pass in to the United States? To seek work. Would it be temporary? No. Would it be permanent? Yes. Do you intend to become a U.S. citizen? No. Have you been deported within the last year? No. Health? Good. Sworn to before this day, signed: David P. Simmons.

That fall of 1923 proved to be difficult for Guadalupe. Within a few months' time he's returned back to Charco. There's no evidence as to why, but rumor has it that news of the bombs exploding all around el Valle de Santiago may have had something to do with it. Only a few months after he left Micaela standing at their doorstep, both Mexican and American fighter planes machine-gunned the sacred mountains of El País de las Siete Luminarias in search of three thousand Mexican insurgents. Who could've predicted such a thing, right there, in the quiet serenity of Charco? Whatever Guadalupe's reason for returning, he found himself home again, with his beloved Micaela and his dog, Lobo.

His next attempt would come seven months later. Again we find Guadalupe, now age twenty-two, standing at the same Laredo bridge crossing in Texas. It's a busy Monday on March 24, 1924, and he's in line with hundreds of men, awaiting their turn to cross. The temperature is in the upper forties, and the men are huddled in the cold morning air. When the immigration officer calls his name, he says "Guadalupe Ramírez," omitting his mother's maiden name, Lara. In this case, Guadalupe will leave her name off of the official record. According to his paperwork on file, he has on his person only fifteen dollars. Again he's accompanied by no one. Asked if he'd ever been to the United States before, he replies, No. Occupation? Laborer. Purpose for entering the United States? To seek work. How long do you intend to stay? One year. Do you intend to become a U.S. citizen? No. Have you been deported within the last year? No. Health? Good. Sworn to before this day, signed: David P. Simmons.

This time he finds his way to the fields of California's San Joaquin Valley and works until his contract is up. After which, he returns home, back to Micaela, back to his parcel, and back to his dog, Lobo. Now and then, he will gather the committee and assess the water supply. Whenever Ramón is home from el Norte, the two will consult with the irrigation boss and purchase material to create a channel, in lieu of a ground well. Even with their combined efforts, this is all they can afford. A channel made of impenetrable volcanic stone and wood collected from the hardest trees. A true ground well will have to wait.

Over the next several years, Guadalupe will learn this dance, and learn it well. Back and forth, and back again. He hears some of the men refer to him as an *enganchado,* or when in los Estados, *bracero*. Even though he now falls within either of those categories, he prefers to be called by his name, Guadalupe. He's always found the word *bracero* to be a menacing label. Arms. As if removed from the body. And the label *enganchado* carries a whole other connotation. It suggests that the allure of earning little money, enduring physical labor, not to mention a constant longing for home, is something one comes to rely on, like an addiction. Enganchado or not, Guadalupe returns time and again to los Estados, because if he doesn't then the ejido withers. It's that simple. And if the ejido withers, then so do his plans to make a family with Micaela. Which is to say, everything withers. She's expressed to him on many occasions, "The timing will never be right, Guadalupe."

He knows she has a point. "Just one more trip, mi vida," he assures her.

She ignores his excuses.

Guadalupe is growing tired of her pressure to have a child.

While in Charco, he drinks, rides his horse, and tends to the parcel, until the next trip north. By now, that first trip with his compadre Ramón feels like a lifetime ago. It makes him cringe to think how green he was back then. That he would actually get on his knees and kiss the soft earth of the ejido before heading out makes him laugh. And how he would make promises to his parcel, and to Micaela. So many promises.

Though he's not yet thirty, in recent months, he's begun to think and act like one of the viejitos in Charco, perhaps something closer to Don Refugio. "If I ever hear myself speaking of the good ol' days, as God is my witness, Lobo, I'll shoot myself," he once confided to his friend. Lobo didn't reply. Instead, the dog lay down in the shade of a mesquite tree, lifted his leg, and began vigorously lapping his testicles.

But the chronology of the Ramírez Lara family continues.

According to the Mexican Censo de Poblacion, recorded on May 15, 1930, in el poblado de Charco de Pantoja, Guadalupe included the letter *L* after Ramírez, out of respect for his mother's maiden name, Lara. But that detail isn't as important as what the record also shows. After numerous trips to el Norte, and the perpetual sacrifice of living in two separate worlds, he and Micaela have come together long enough to fulfill a dream years in the making. They finally have a child. A newborn baby girl with hazel eyes like her mother and the dark skin of her father. She's an angel of God, and the records show they've named her Ofelia.

With newfound purpose, Guadalupe decides, once again, that he must return to el Norte; it is now more crucial than ever. The ejido is still without adequate irrigation, and the baby requires constant feeding. He leaves, and he returns. The dance continues. Each time he takes the same route, due north, crosses the same bridge in Laredo, and has his papers stamped by the same David P. Simmons. He wonders if "el Señor Simmons" will ever retire. Of course, nothing in Simmons's face suggests that this'll happen anytime soon. In fact, the opposite.

"I think Simmons is getting younger," Guadalupe jokes with Ramón.

Ramón replies, "Don't be surprised, compadre, if the next time you cross by way of Laredo you'll find Simmons drooling on your papers and crying to suckle from your breast!" The two friends have a good laugh over it.

By the time Ofelia reaches eighteen, Guadalupe will have crossed and re-crossed the line in the dirt so many times he'll have almost single-handedly erased it. He'll have attempted dozens of routes, and along the way come to discover that his favorite entry point is Nuevo Laredo in Tamaulipas. It is the passage that makes the most sense. Due north, as the crow flies. The number of Mexicanos seeking work in los Estados has grown immeasurably. Often the lines in Laredo are so long that crossing el Río Bravo is faster. And of course, urgency is of grand importance. The sooner he secures work, the sooner he makes money. With money comes water. With water, bread. The sooner he crosses, the sooner he returns to what matters most, Micaela and Ofelia. Guadalupe will become such an expert at crossing el río that he'll come to understand the currents of the river according to the season. He knows where the water thins out and where it rises. Others come to rely on his experience.

Jaime: "My uncle was a very tall man, and oftentimes, when he would go, he would cross el Río Bravo, and he would help the women and children cross by carrying them on his back, or on his shoulders. Yes, my uncle did that, and people knew him for that. How he would help people cross."

In late March of 1943, Guadalupe returned home from el Norte to discover his brother Fidel was in a dire situation. Fidel's wife Maria Carmen had fallen ill and was bedridden with pneumonia. The couple had just had a child, a boy they named Fermin. Within a matter of days Maria Carmen had succumbed to her illness, and Fidel was left staring into the face of his cooing infant son without a clue in the world as to what the fragile creature required. Because they were the baby's godparents, Guadalupe and Micaela agreed to raise the boy. At a mere forty days old, Fermin was now, by all definitions, Guadalupe's son. It was a fact that Guadalupe himself wore like a badge for the rest of his days.

Oftentimes, Guadalupe could be seen with the boy perched atop his horse, and together they'd go trotting along the parcel to check on the crops. If they walked anywhere, they walked together. Guadalupe took care of Fermin, kept him close, as he promised his cuñada, Maria Carmen, he would. There was no question in the boy's heart, Guadalupe was his father. His memory was proof of it.

"There is one special thing about my father," Fermin would later recall, "one thing that I will never forget, because it is so vivid in my mind. It was an accident that happened to him. I remember that it happened to him on the first day of January in 1945. It was the new year, and he had been shooting his gun, well, like everyone did in those times. He used to like to shoot his gun, you see. And, well, this one time, on that day, he shot his own finger off. Well, he shot it, and it had to eventually be cut off. I don't remember if it was the left or the right finger, but this is one fact that I remember very clearly, yes. The reason I can remember this fact about my father, you see . . . why it is special to me, well, is because he would hold my hand whenever we walked anywhere. And as a boy, I remember clearly, I would hold his hand too, and I could feel his missing finger. I remember this about my father."

JOSÉ SÁNCHEZ VALDIVIA

14

CELIO SÁNCHEZ VALDIVIA

February 22, 2014

The day Celio received the phone call at his home in San Diego, he'd been recovering from a mild stroke. He spoke dimly over the phone, attempting, as best he could, to answer my questions about his brother José. It was obvious that given his condition, he had little desire to respond to unusual solicitations.

"I didn't know much about my brother," he said. "I was the youngest, and José came to los Estados long before I did. He and my older brother came here, with my father and a cousin."

"Is there someone alive who might've known your brother well?"

Celio coughed into the phone. "Well, yes, my brother's best friend. He is still alive, I believe. He lives in Stockton, the last I heard. He has the same name as my brother, José Sánchez, except he is González. José Sánchez González. But I don't have his phone number. You'll have to find that on your own."

When I arrived at the doorstep of the Sánchez González home in Stockton, California, it was late March. The day was gray, and it had been raining all morning. The family stood in the doorway and welcomed me into their home. The living room was cold and dimly lit, and they were bundled in sweaters. Aside from the weather, there was a sullen mood that loomed.

"Are you José Sánchez González?" I asked the eldest man, extending my hand for him to shake.

"My name is Eliseo," he said, waving me inside. "Pasale. Siéntate." I took a seat on the couch and placed the small audio recorder on my lap. Eliseo started in. "José Sánchez González was my brother. His best friend, the one who died in the plane crash, was José Sánchez Valdivia. He was a friend of mine too. We worked together in the 1940s, up until he died." Eliseo paused to look at his family. "Unfortunately, my brother José passed away on the same night that you contacted us. You just missed him. He would've loved to have spoken with you. But maybe I can fill you in."

"I'm sorry for your loss," I said. "Can you tell me how your brother José was friends with José Sánchez Valdivia?"

"Yes. I can confidently say that my brother José was the best friend of José Sánchez Valdivia. Anyone who knew the two Josés would agree with this. Not that they would ever call each other 'best friends,' but well, that's what they were, compadres who were more like brothers. I knew José too, fairly well. Of course I was the much younger of them, so I didn't spend a lot of time with the older guys. But my brother, I wish you had found us just a few days sooner, he would have told you everything. Anyone who knew one José knew the other. Well, here is what I know. We all came—the Valdivia family and ours—all came from the same place in Mexico, a small rancho named La Estancia, en el estado de Zacatecas. In those days it seemed everyone from La Estancia was here in Stockton. They came as braceros, because there was work here, so it makes sense. But no one called the two Josés by their first names, it gets too confusing. Everyone called them by their last names, González y Valdivia, that's how it went. They were very likable men, the two. Together they picked every crop one can find here in the San Joaquin Valley: onions in Coalinga, cotton in Corcoran, grapes, oranges, lechuga, betabel, everything. We all did. This has been our life. Sometimes we would race to see who could pick the fastest. The farmers loved us younger men, because we weren't afraid to work hard. And yes, my brother and José Valdivia were good, good friends. They were the big boys, and me, well, I was younger, and looked up to them. Especially when they played baseball. They loved to play baseball. But yes, they were hard workers. Every day the same thing. Work, and more work. Every day—"

For the two Josés, an average day looked something like this: Rise before sunup. Splash water on the face, brush teeth, layer clothing, pull on boots. Gather the work tools: tijeras, cuchillo, el cortito, depending on the crop or season. Then meet the others outside, near the truck, for a head count. Peer out across the dark landscape for any sign of la migra. In the fields, picking, bending, slicing, whatever the work calls for, until noon. Lunch break, maybe thirty minutes. Water. Piss break. No sign of la migra. Back at it until sundown. Twelve hours start to finish, typically. Back to the camp, wash, eat, and toss a baseball around until they could hardly lift a hand. Maybe crack a few jokes with their compadres in between, or else scribble a letter to the family back home, before hitting the sack and doing it all over again.

"Here, in los Estados, one never sleeps," Valdivia would write to his mother. "You have to keep one eye open, nothing like La Estancia, where you can sleep peacefully with nothing but the sound of goats or the rustling river nearby."

La Estancia was a small dwelling, even for a pueblo. It sat in the shadow of the nearby town of Nochistlán. Forged from river rock and mesquite trees, and tucked within a bed of yellow rolling hills, it consisted of only two main roads, with a church at the center. No radio stations reached La Estancia because there was no electricity. Kerosene lamps lit the way. During the annual fiesta de el Papaqui, which happened each January in Nochistlán, when they celebrated "el Guerito" San Sebastián, the sizzling fireworks, earthy scent of pinole, and explosions of laughter could be heard all the way in La Estancia. But during the rest of the year it was a village of almost unfathomable silence. If not for the occasional crack of a baseball against a bat, one might think they'd gone deaf in La Estancia, it was that secluded.

15

EL BAMBINO CALLS HIS SHOT

1932–1940

As a young man, growing up with a natural ability for athletics, Valdivia dreamed of playing ball. Whenever the opportunity arose, he would find himself in Nochistlán, gathered at el jardín, listening to an American baseball game with the old-timers. Long before el Norte had come to represent seasonal work, for Valdivia it represented baseball. Babe Ruth had already become a mythical figure in his young life.

On October 1, 1932, while his father, Mateo, was out harvesting their meager yield of corn, José, only ten years old, was huddled over a staticky radio, gnawing his nails, listening to game three of the World Series. He was often at el jardín against his father's wishes.

"Puras ilusiones," his father warned him. "A man cannot eat his illusions, nor will his dreams feed his family."

Even at such an early age, José could see his father's point, but if not for baseball, what else was there for a kid of his natural ability to hope for in a place as desolate as La Estancia? Besides, it was the World Series, better known as el Bambino contra los Cubs, illusions be damned.

As fate often has a way of rearing its head when one least expects, it all came down to a single moment. What happened in game three of the World Series would prompt José to follow his father to los Estados Unidos.

It was the fifth inning with the score tied at four apiece, and through the small radio speakers it sounded as if all fifty thousand fans were attempting to stomp down Chicago's Wrigley Field. The game had built up such intensity that fans had taken to throwing fruits and vegetables at the players. The radio announcer's spitfire talk kept the old men at el jardín, and young José, on their toes.

"What's this?" the announcer blared. "Babe Ruth is pointing his bat at Charley Root!" The old men glanced at one another. The small speakers trembled. They wiped the sweat from their faces. "Here comes the pitch . . . strike!" The roar crescendoed and the radio shook. The men could hardly hear. They hushed one another and leaned in, shoulder to shoulder now. "All of Wrigley is on their feet!" spat the announcer. "Here comes the second pitch . . . strike two!" Again the fans cheered, and now the radio was almost pure static. Young José could hardly stand it. The old men didn't say a word. "Ruth is calling his shot!" howled the announcer. "The Bambino is calling his shot!" "He is pointing his finger toward center field fence! The Bambino is calling his shot!" For a moment the men stood frozen. "Arrogance," mumbled the eldest, shaking his head. A second before the final pitch was hurled there was a silence. "Here's the pitch . . ." The next sound that came through the speakers was perhaps one of José Sánchez Valdivia's most favorite sounds—a leather ball being smashed by a wooden bat. *Crack*. El Bambino had smashed the ball and sent it rocketing over the center field fence, just as he promised. It was unheard of, a predicted home run. The radio swelled with static, and the men at el jardín slapped their foreheads and hooted and jabbed at one another. "El Bambino!" they boasted. "El Bambino," another said, swatting young José on the back and messing up his hair.

José basked in the fervor of the greatest game his ears ever had the privilege of listening to. But this event alone wasn't the moment that changed the course of José's life. No, it was what came next.

The eldest man pulled a blue handkerchief from his back pocket and fanned a fly away from his face. He was unimpressed. When he opened his mouth, what he said made José's ears perk up.

"Luque would have struck el Bambino out."

A couple of men nodded in agreement.

"Luque?" young José asked.

The old man snickered. "Adolfo Domingo de Guzman Luque," he said.

"Luque," another man said, eyeing the kid.

José could only shake his head. He had never heard the name.

"El Orgullo de Cuba," the old man piped up. He coughed into his handkerchief.

José was dumbfounded. Another man proceeded to tell his young friend about a ballplayer nicknamed the Pride of Cuba.

"Los Americanos called him el Dolf," he said. "The best pitcher in the game. First with the Braves, later los Cincinnati Reds."

José could hardly believe what he was hearing. Why had he never heard of Luque? Was it even possible that by some God-given miracle a brown man had actually made it to the major leagues in los Estados? This was the moment that changed everything.

The years draped themselves over the shoulders of La Estancia languidly. The town was old, and felt old, like the men who shuffled each morning from the carnicero with a walking stick in each hand, hardly able to lift their feet against the pull of Earth's gravity. During these years, José, along with his two younger brothers, would tend to the family parcel and care for their mother, Dolores, while their father, Mateo, was lost somewhere in the land of el Bambino, picking fruit.

By the time José was a young man, with little more than peach fuzz adorning his upper lip, his father made a request. Mateo asked his boys to leave La Estancia and join him in a place called Stockton, California, where together they'd pick and earn three times the wages. It didn't take much convincing. José only heard the word *California* and already he was picturing himself on deck, a bat slung over his shoulder and his hip cocked, as he stared out over a field—not of grapes or plums, but the kind of field that yielded home runs. The plan, as Mateo had arranged it, was that José and the second oldest boy, Ramón, would hop a train in Guadalajara and meet up with him in California. Celio, the youngest of the boys, too young still, would have to stay behind. The boys understood. José tried hard to contain his excitement, only for his mother's sake. Dolores was stoic. She could see the wonderment in the eyes of both her sons. Though they were young men now, she could not help but see them as children. Naïve and spirited as the day they had emerged from her womb. She lit candles and prayed for their safety until they reached their father. Perhaps they are still too young? she questioned Diosito. God did not answer back.

When the day came that José and his brother Ramón boarded the train in Guadalajara, José was beside himself. He flung his belongings onto the wooden planks of the boxcar floor and yanked Ramón aboard with him. The two brothers stood side by side, staring out across the hot Mexican landscape as the train began rumbling forward. It gained speed quickly, and in a matter of seconds José had a wall of wind pushing against his face and flapping the tail of his shirt. It was a sensation like none he'd ever known. His arms felt electric, as he stood there, feet shoulder-width apart, hovering over home plate. A smile lit his face, and he couldn't help himself. As the wind forced his eyes shut, José hoisted an invisible bat over his right shoulder. He slit his eyes open and gazed out beyond the rolling yellow hills of the Jalisco highlands. He pictured California, somewhere beyond the horizon. He could see it all clearly in his mind's eye. He lifted his left hand into the air and brazenly pointed his finger in the direction of el Norte.

Ramón took one look at his brother's foolishness and shook his head. "Ilusiones," he said, mocking their father. "Puras ilusiones." The brothers laughed.

16

THE MEXICAN LEAGUE

Stockton, California
1943–1947

José tossed another dirt clot high into the air, then cocked his work hoe back over his shoulder and swung with all the force he had, shattering the imaginary baseball into a cloud of dust.

"Ponte a trabajar, José!" Mateo hollered at his son from across the field of sugar beets.

José lowered the tool to the ground and continued tearing away at the weeds. Now and then, when his father was nowhere to be seen, he would toss a stone into the air and send it sailing across the field with one swing of the hoe. Early on, he used sugar beets, but after the mayordomo threatened to fire him, he resigned himself to dirt clots.

It was clear from the beginning, California was nothing like José had envisioned. It didn't have shiny high-rise buildings, and it wasn't a bustling city with a blue ocean nearby and baseball stadium lights glaring overhead. How was it possible that the California he was now standing in looked and felt more like La Estancia? There were fields and farms, and there were cows. Endless cows. This California was nothing but an immense bowl of cow dung. The stink was inescapable. "It gets in your hair, clothes, and nostrils, and it never comes out," he'd gripe to his brother Ramón. Ramón could only shrug his shoulders. To José the only difference between this California and La Estancia was that this California was noisy. Trucks belched up and down the Golden State Highway at all hours, day or night, hauling off fruit or manure. The campos were filled with people from all parts of Mexico. And if this weren't disappointing enough, he was sure half of La Estancia was also here. The fields were so infinite they seemed to wrap themselves around the entire planet. By the time a picker reached the end of a row, new fruit was already sprouting back at the beginning. No wonder his father never made it back to La Estancia after years of promises. The seasons passed quickly here too. There was no such thing as winter. It went from summer to fall to spring and back to summer. José had been in California only a few months and already he'd seen three baseball seasons come and go. At least it felt this way. His first impression of el Norte was no impression at all. And so it went. His only consolation was batting practice with dirt clots, whenever the ol' man wasn't looking. It was a kind of desperate Mayday, a beacon for any disenchanted soul groveling among the endless fields who possibly shared his passion for the sport. The distress signal, as feeble as it seemed, worked.

José Sánchez González was square-jawed and had shoulders as broad as a backstop. The first meeting between the two young men was uneventful. The way it was told was that one day Valdivia looked up from his row of sugar beets and spotted González across the way, slugging rocks in his direction. A few words were exchanged, and before he knew it, Valdivia had found himself a teammate in González. In the beginning it was just the two of them, tossing a ball around, fielding grounders and shagging fly balls. Eventually, another campesino would join them, and then another. By the following spring the Stockton labor camp had its very own ball club.

They were part of a nascent wave of ball clubs that had sprung up in various campos across the valley. An unlikely wave that called itself the Mexican League.

Teams consisted of campesinos who were from all parts of Mexico. It was a ragtag league, with no real equipment or baseball fields, but it was a league because they said it was. For the most part they were men who, unlike Valdivia, participated as a way to distract themselves from the incessant longing for home. Because none came close to the seriousness with which Valdivia played the game, the players unanimously agreed that he should be the team's captain.

They met each day after work and used the clearing on the perimeter of the campo as their field. Orange crates would be piled and used as a backstop, and bases would be forged from whatever was available—potato sacks, buckets, and on one occasion wilted heads of cabbage. From as early as February until midsummer, they practiced each evening, until they could no longer distinguish the ball sailing through the air from the fruit bats that circled the night sky. Each day, while picking strawberries or shearing onions, the players would gather and strategize about the next game. They went over hand signals and argued about the batting order. A few games into the season, someone brought up the idea of uniforms. "Don't get carried away," Valdivia said, causing the other men to laugh. "But caps, yes, we aren't real ballplayers until we have caps." So they purchased white baseball caps and asked their wives and mothers to embroider a black letter *S* onto them—for *Stockton*. So proud was Valdivia of his cap that regardless of the season, he never took it off. And because he was superstitious, each season he refused to wash the cap, and the material quickly went from white to brown.

During the season, everyone knew that Sunday was the only day that really mattered. After Mass let out, between two and five in the afternoon, families from the surrounding campos would gather to watch sons, uncles, and fathers battle it out for nine innings against teams from rival labor camps. Tortillas would be made, watermelon sliced, beer passed around, and the raucous laughter of children would tangle up with the aromatic ribbon of carne sizzling on makeshift grills. Every Sunday, every spring. A typical season would run twenty games, and the champions would carry that honor, not in some cheap plastic trophy, but in the only way that mattered, on the lips of the people. They would boast, and boast heartily. Even La Estancia would catch wind of the games, and the boasting would carry on back home too, at the molino, the carnicero, and in the town's only church. Had it not been for word of mouth, José's poor mother Dolores might've never known how her boys were doing, or how her son José now wore a constant smile on his face and was getting along fine, way out there, in a place called "Estockton," California.

Just as quickly as they came, the seasons ended. For most, it meant packing up and moving their families on to the next crop.

"La pisca no espera!" they'd holler to one another.

Oregon, Washington, northern Wyoming—wherever harvesting could be found. Players would gather and wave good-bye to their teammates.

"Catch you next season," they'd shout from the backs of rickety trucks.

"Por ahí nos vemos! Hasta la proxima," they'd echo, before rattling away in clouds of dust.

The few who were lucky enough to secure work in Stockton would stay put. The two Josés were often among them. The Valdivias and the Gonzálezes were strong, hardworking families, and their reputation for being such was widely known among the farmers in that part of the valley. Of course, there was always the matter of their work contracts.

When the day came that Mateo's permit expired, much to his frustration, he was told he would have to be "dried out." It was a kind of backdoor renewal. A legal loophole that farmers used to their advantage. The mayordomo confirmed that the only way for Mateo to continue working on this particular farm would be to voluntarily deport himself.

"A small formality," the mayordomo assured him. "In Mexico you'll show them you have work waiting for you here in Stockton, and they'll issue you a new permit. You'll then board a bus or train, as you did the last time, and be returned to this camp."

The first time Mateo heard of this "drying out" business, it sounded like a trick. But he'd since seen men return and was convinced it was purely a systematic movida. He didn't mind doing the bracero shuffle, as long as it meant he could continue working. One day he climbed aboard a migra bus with nothing but a single change of clothes and a nervous expression on his face, waving so long to his boys through a dirty window. José and Ramón stood by the González brothers as they watched their father being hauled away, uncertain whether they'd see him again, or for how long.

It would only be a matter of weeks before they'd know the answer. On the very same route the bus had left, it returned. Just as Mateo had been promised, he was right back in Stockton, embracing both his sons and taking in the pungent aroma of cow dung that had now become the welcomed perfume of the Central Valley. The new season was fast approaching. Life, once again, would return to normal.

FRANK AND BOBBIE ATKINSON

17

MARY LOU AND HELEN ATKINSON

March 17, 2013

It was a Sunday afternoon when I interviewed pilot Frank Atkinson's two younger sisters, Mary Lou and Helen. The four-way phone call was arranged by their niece, Connie, who lived in San Francisco. A few weeks before, Connie had received my e-mail asking questions about "the worst airplane disaster in California's history." She knew instantly what I was referring to. Her reply: "My uncle Frank died the same year I was born and has been a legend in our family. He was dearly loved by all for his great sense of humor and his kindness." But I had more questions. Connie relayed to me that her two aunts were the only ones alive who still carried the stories of Frankie with them. At the time of their brother's death, Mary Lou was fifteen years old and Helen was nineteen.

Uncertain of my intentions at first, the sisters spoke cautiously. The phone connection was poor, and their voices cut in and out.

"I believe Frankie was named after Saint Francis," Mary Lou offered. She was hesitant. "Uh, he was pretty religious. A very loving brother. He took care of us." She paused. "Was more like a dad to us. Wouldn't you say, Helen?"

"Yes, that's right. I would have to agree with that," Helen replied. "When I was still practically a baby . . . how I heard it anyway, Frankie set out to cut railroad ties in order to make a few extra bucks to buy me some milk. I guess I was hungry and times were rough, and he took it upon himself to do something about it. That's just how Frankie was."

A long silence.

"What else can you tell me about Frankie?"

"Well, uh . . . he worked for Kodak back then. Processing film and such. But sometimes it wasn't enough, so he and a friend would go cut railroad ties."

"There was this one time, I guess Frankie and his pal were headed out by the tracks, when all of a sudden he looks down and finds this single dollar bill just sittin' there. Guess the boys got excited 'cause it meant they didn't have to cut ties after all. But Frankie, well, he took it as a sign from God. He was very religious."

"He sure was. But he was quite a character too. A joker. I remember in those days Grandma didn't know how to drive, and it was Frankie who decided to teach her. He took her out in the car, and I guess Grandma had been complainin' about how fast he was going, so Frankie pulls the steering wheel right off and hands it to her, and says, 'Here, you drive.' Of course, Grandma just about had a heart attack."

The sisters chuckled.

Mary Lou continued. "Ever since he was a young man, Frankie had always wanted to be a fighter pilot, but he couldn't 'cause his eyesight was pretty bad. I remember he kept eating carrots, that's all he ate for months just to get his eyesight better. They still wouldn't let him in, not at first. He eventually went on to become a great pilot though."

"Yes. Yes he did," Helen added.

As I listened to them talk, I pictured the two sisters in my mind. Their hair a shock of white and eyes as blue as a clear sky. I thought of my great tía Apolonia Maynes Casillas right then, a staunch woman from New Mexico, whose own Spanish blood swathed her in skin the color of buttermilk, and eyes like two turquoise stones. This is how I pictured the two women. Their phones pressed tenderly to their ears, each sitting in her own living room a thousand miles apart. Even in their silences, especially in their silences, I could tell they were harking back to their distant memory, to the image of their big brother Frankie as a young man. Perhaps, earlier still, to the boy they had grown up hearing stories about from their mother Agnes. They now found themselves relaying, to a perfect stranger, these same stories—

As a boy, Frankie Atkinson had been fascinated with the idea of flight. In 1930, there was one comic book that could be found tucked into the front pocket of every boy's overalls. It was about an airborne wiz named Buck Rogers. A kid couldn't walk down the street without getting an eyeful of the helmeted avenger and his handy Atomic Disintegrator lighting up a gang of villains. He was a hero from the twenty-fifth century, and as the radio broadcast declared, "A one-man army of greased lightning!" On the back cover of one particular issue, Buck gave pointers to young heroes in training. Among them, eat carrots. Lots of them. "You can't rule the skies without good eyes," claimed the dashing hero.

It wasn't too long before that Agnes had taken Frankie to the eye doctor, where it was brought to their attention that the boy's eyesight was just shy of twenty/twenty. He was given three chances at a standard eye exam but couldn't see the last row of letters. Frankie knew Buck's advice was the only remedy. From that moment on, he always had a carrot in hand. Agnes cooked with carrots as often as possible: carrot stew, carrot salad, carrot juice, and for his birthday, what else but carrot cake. It went on this way for nearly a year, until one day his father, John Atkinson, pointed out to his wife, "Is it me or does the boy have an orange hue about him?" Agnes hadn't noticed it. She pulled her son under a lamp and examined his face. She lifted up his shirt and turned him around.

"My word, Francis, what've you gotten yourself into?" Agnes said. The boy's skin tone was no longer the pinkish cream she'd known it to be. "You look like an apricot, Frankie!" The boy felt fine. He laughed about it. Agnes and John fretted.

A quick visit to Doctor Sterling the next day would assure Agnes that nothing was wrong with her son. "Except, perhaps, too much beta-carotene in his diet," said the good doctor. It was clear that from an early age, Frankie was determined that one day he would fly.

18

AN AMERICAN DREAMER

Frankie, age 17

Frankie pressed his back against the measuring tape. "Five feet five inches," announced Coach Mitchell, making note of it on his clipboard. "Now the scale." Frankie stepped onto it while his teammates observed. "One hundred thirty pounds. Good enough," Mitchell said, eyeing his star quarterback. "You've put some meat on. Good thing. Extra padding's not a bad idea, a boy as narrow as you." Frankie didn't respond. He was the team's captain. The more stoic he remained, the tougher he appeared.

Every player on the St. Thomas of Aquinas football team agreed that despite Frankie's size, he was the best athlete for the position. He could outplay any man on the field. "A born-leader type," they'd later say of him.

Even beyond the school grounds, it was widely known that Frankie Atkinson was one of Rochester's finest athletes. When interviewed by the local papers, Coach Mitchell didn't hesitate to refer to his star player as a "terrific athlete and well-mannered boy, but with the ornery streak of an elephant." John and Agnes didn't disagree with the coach. They knew what they had in their son. If someone told the boy it was impossible to start a fire with a toothpick, not only would he build a fire, he'd make it blaze.

"Nothing's impossible," he once told his youngest sister, Mary Lou. "And whoever says so isn't much good to you anyhow. Remember that, sis." And just as her brother suggested, Mary Lou would remember it.

When he wasn't busy doling out advice to his kid sisters, or tossing around the pigskin, he was taking out his best girl, Dorothy Anderson, a local beauty who was the catch of every boy's eye. Though he and Bobbie Kesselring had known each other since they were kids practically, and even went to the movies a few times, Dottie was his true love in those years.

Even when John informed his son that if he was now taking the "Anderson girl" seriously, he would have to earn his own money, Frankie didn't hesitate. He landed a job at the Eastman Kodak Company processing photographs. For someone who was born with bad vision, learning the skill of film processing was a daily exercise regimen for the eyes. The ritual of watching images, people, come into focus from sheets of nothingness was witnessing erasure in reverse, day after day, image after image. The money wasn't great, but it gave him what he needed, and sometimes even a little extra to help his folks with groceries. Frankie knew that managing a house full of children was no easy task for John and Agnes, especially when it seemed that good people everywhere were living in squalor and going to desperate measures to fend off the Depression. For any man or woman, much less a teenager, landing a job took sheer luck. But Frankie, as his mother would often say, "was born with a star on his forehead." On some weekends, if the family needed extra help, like if a birthday was around the corner or the holidays were approaching, Frankie would cut railroad ties for extra cash. The job consisted of hacking trees with an ax all day. A full day's work would yield somewhere in the area of a nickel. He'd save the money and every so often hand his parents a hard-earned dollar. His commitment to his family was undeniable, and though Rochester had its share of hardship, in those days it seemed, at least to Frankie Atkinson, that anything was possible.

Rochester was as typical a town as anywhere in America, the Atkinsons' neighborhood more than most. Life at 496 Clay Street was the American flavor that artist Norman Rockwell depicted in his illustrations for the *Saturday Evening Post*—it was that idyllic. With its unending stretch of Craftsman-style homes, its tree-dappled sidewalks and quaint front porches, its picket fences capped with snow, and somewhere, almost certainly, a calico cat perched in a window, licking its paws. For those who called Clay Street home, it was evidence that an "American Dream" was attainable.

Often, Frankie would sit on his front porch and stare up at the sky in hope of seeing a plane sailing overhead. Once in a while John would pull into the driveway and find his son seated there, a far-off look in his eye. Without uttering a word, he'd take a seat by the boy and wait with him until a skyship would pass, or until Agnes would call them both inside for dinner.

"I'll be up there someday," Frankie often said to Dottie.

Dottie had never known any boy to take himself so serious. "Of course, Frankie," she said. "No one doubts you. Just don't know why anyone would wanna be way up there. Must be awful quiet, I'd imagine." Though she'd never admit it, Frankie's passion for airplanes was a source of resentment. It was an embarrassing fact but a fact nonetheless. Why should any girl be jealous of airplanes? She'd watch how Frankie exercised relentlessly, jogging to and from work each day. Sit-ups, push-ups, pull-ups, it never ended. Had it all been for Dottie, she might've understood, but he'd remind her, "I hafta be ready for when the time comes." His obsession with flying cast a shadow over their relationship.

By their senior year they'd split up for a brief spell. Dottie initiated the break. "Maybe he'll see what he's losing and snap to it," she told her mother over dinner one evening. Her mother replied: "Are you sure it isn't the other way around?" Dottie scoffed and excused herself from the dinner table. It was wrong of her mother to imply such a thing. "What does she know anyway?" she consoled herself.

During their break, Frankie would run across Bobbie from time to time, and they'd catch up on life. The exchanges were friendly, and, once in a while, when it seemed no one was paying attention, it bordered on the flirtatious. But nothing came of it.

By the end of senior year, Dottie and Frankie were back together. Neither could bear the thought of graduating without the other. Except for the recent hiccup, they'd been sweethearts since freshman year. That had to count for something. They would graduate, and life in Rochester would glide past uneventfully.

A year later, while reading the daily paper, John would catch his son scampering through the living room and corner the boy. "What're your plans with Dottie, son?"

Frankie would shrug. "Still lookin' at flight school," he'd reply.

John placed the paper down on his lap and stared into his son's eyes, measuring his seriousness.

"I imagine you've spoken with Dottie about it?"

"Sure, she's fine with it."

John hesitated, then lifted the paper back up to his face.

The push to marry Dottie never scared off Frankie as it would've most young men. He looked forward to having his own family one day, a wife and children. He imagined it all with Dottie. Nothing would've pleased him more. The only thing weighing on him as of recent was that inspiration was growing harder to come by. It used to be that not a day would pass when he didn't think about flight school. It had been over a month now since he'd even sat on the front porch. With each passing day he felt his dream receding to that dusty shelf, where all working-class dreams get filed away.

One afternoon, while walking home from the library, where he'd acquired a dozen books on flight school, he ran across Bobbie.

"How's life treatin' you?" he asked.

"Fine," she replied, folding her arms over her chest. Her mother, Elizabeth, hovered nearby. The woman stood quietly, eyeing the boy. She had a reputation for being something of a hardened soul.

"Hello, Mrs. Kesselring," Frankie said.

Elizabeth lifted her nose at him.

"What've you been up to?" he asked Bobbie.

She tucked her hair behind her ear. "Nothing great." She hesitated. "Bowling mostly."

"How's that comin'?"

"I made the finals again."

"Is that right?" Frankie's blue eyes glistened. "Boy, you're a natural."

Bobbie smiled. Elizabeth grew impatient with her daughter. She cleared her throat to get her attention.

"Maybe you could come out and see me bowl for a trophy next week?"

"Sure," Frankie said. In that instant he remembered their last exchange. While at a high school dance, Bobbie had confessed to him her feelings. "I've always adored you, Frankie, always." He remembered the night clearly, and how Bobbie's words were spoken with conviction. Even back then, there was a likeable sadness about Bobbie. A melancholy he found charming. But that exchange was a year gone. They were adults now. As Bobbie stared at him, waiting for a response, he remembered what he'd said to her back then. It was a callous reply. Just recalling it was embarrassing enough. "I like that you adore me, Bobbie." That was it. I like that you adore me. For the love of God. He wondered if he should just apologize to her then and there.

Elizabeth began walking in the direction of home.

"Well?" Bobbie nudged, "Whadya say? Will you be there?"

"That'd be swell," Frankie replied.

Bobbie chased after her mother.

"Good-bye, Mrs. Kesselring," Frankie hollered. The woman didn't respond.

The following week Bobbie went on to make the final rounds of the Rochester Bowling Annual. Frankie wasn't in her audience. She knew better than to look for him but couldn't help herself. People congratulated her, and while she smiled and shook hands, her eyes glanced over their shoulders. She scanned the bleachers too, but Frankie was nowhere.

The next day her name appeared in the local newspaper. At the bottom of the sports section was a photograph of a group of young women, all hoisting placards. In bold font, the caption read: "Bobbie K." And there was Bobbie, in the lowest row, far left corner. Yellow cropped bangs. Blue eyes and unassuming smile. If she was bothered by the fact that Frankie was a no-show, it was unnoticeable. Her posture gave away nothing.

John Atkinson opened up his paper that morning, and on reading the results of the bowling competition, he folded the paper in half and pointed it out to his son. Frankie leaned in to have a look. As he stared at the photo of Bobbie, a tender guilt settled in his chest. But then he looked at her photograph one last time, and the corners of his mouth lifted, subtly.

19

THE ASSIMILATION OF ELIZABETH LIEBERSBACH

1912

An immense passenger ship set sail from the frigid Baltic Sea, across the green perilous stretch of the North Atlantic, heading straight for Ellis Island. The arrival of this ship would mark the first wave of Polish families fleeing their beloved country for the United States. With Poland unable to feed its people, destitute thousands were forced to leave, sparking an exodus that would come to be known as *za chlebem*—"for bread."

Among the ship's passengers was eleven-year-old Elizabeth Liebersbach. She was accompanied only by her father, Jakob. The three-week passage was uneventful, albeit beautiful in some ways. It was a time during which father and daughter were inseparable. Though Jakob hadn't the slightest clue as to what it took to raise a girl in a new country that was far from anything he'd ever known, his willingness to work himself ragged would be enough to see them through. It would have to be. Throughout the journey he'd point out to young Elizabeth the cloud of seagulls circling overhead, or the sprightly otters that frolicked in the wake of the ship. With the exception of a few morning showers, the sea was mostly calm.

On the day they approached the shores of New York, they spotted, in the distance, an impressive statue towering over the waters. It appeared to be a woman holding a candle. Jakob pointed it out to Elizabeth, and the two marveled as they sailed past. "Wolność," said an old man, who happened to be standing nearby. The man pointed at Lady Liberty. Jakob repeated, "Wolność." A nervous smile lit his face. It was all the assurance he needed. He glanced at his daughter and squatted down to eye level.

"This is home now," he said.

"For how long?" young Elizabeth asked.

Jakob was unsure how to explain to his daughter. He shrugged. "As long as it takes."

The girl stared out again at the fast-approaching skyline. She didn't respond. She watched the statue standing alone, unmoved by the black waves bashing against her feet. The cry of seagulls was like an ominous welcoming.

Their first year in the United States was a test of will. Jakob worked at an ice plant, where the conditions were harsh and the pay meager. To make matters worse, he was ill equipped. His clothes were tattered, and the soles of his shoes had gaping holes. By the end of winter he was suffering a bout of pneumonia. The serum he was given only made him sicker. In a matter of days he was reduced to a gaunt skeleton. His teeth chattered uncontrollably. Not even the sight of his daughter's worried face was enough to will himself better. One cold winter morning, young Elizabeth awoke to find her father dead on his mattress. His hands curled like claws, crossed over his chest. She tried shaking him awake, but his skin was gray and frigid. She alerted the owner of the property and the next morning a large black vehicle arrived. Two burly men hauled Jakob's body away, and that was the last she would ever see of her father. From that day on, she was alone in a strange and unfamiliar place.

As the years passed languidly, Elizabeth worked a string of jobs that paid a pittance but kept her free from probing eyes. She did exactly as her father had always taught her. "Remain invisible." She could still see his serious expression and hear the grave tone with which he instructed her one evening over a meal of boiled potatoes.

"We live by a different set of rules, my daughter," Jakob explained between bites of hardtack. "We are guests in another man's house, and so we must live modestly. Stay indoors as much as possible. We cannot make too much noise or else the neighbors will grow curious. And when in company, don't smile too much, or laugh too loud, or they may think we are taking advantage. Learn how to say 'Thank you.' Practice it and say it often. Try it now: 'Thank you. Thank you.' Yes, see? Here, it is better to say 'Thank you' too much than to not say it enough."

"Thank you," Elizabeth said.

"Yes, that's right. It is good to appear grateful. Be grateful. And when you eat your lunch, especially in public, do not eat too fast. We do not want to come across as hungry, even if that is the case." He bit into his potato. "Beggars are not wanted here. Work harder than everybody else, and never complain. Not to the boss, and not even to those whom you consider friends. And you can't have too many friends. But if you do, do not boast about it. Too many friends can appear as if you are taking advantage. When walking in public, keep your eyes forward, always. Don't stare too long or let your eyes wander, or you will appear meddlesome and immodest. This country relies on our modesty. Listen, Elizabeth. And hear me well. If we want to be happy in this new place, we must stay invisible. As much as possible. If they cannot see us, we cannot disturb them, or their way of life. If they cannot see us, they will leave us be. To be left alone, see, this is the key to our happiness."

At the time, she couldn't have predicted the degree of loneliness that would fester in her father's absence. Still, for a young woman alone in the world, remaining invisible wasn't as easy as one might think. Over the next few years she kept her head down and refused to make eye contact with anyone. If she ever glanced up, it was out of necessity, never curiosity.

But one day she dared. She lifted her gaze long enough to catch her reflection in a window. To her surprise, she no longer looked like the child she remembered. She was much taller, and her face appeared longer. Where once her chest was unnoticeable, now two defiant peaks protruded from her blouse. From then on she began carrying herself differently. Even her father's voice had begun to subside.

By the time she was eighteen, Elizabeth had left the city and secured a small home in Rochester, New York. For the first time since Jakob's death, she was able to step foot again under the open sky and not hear his words guilting her into a hasty retreat. She even began dating men, who for the most part stuck around just long enough to learn her name. They would come and go, leaving no trace in their wake. Except for one. John Koch. Their tryst was brief and rocky. It happened so fast that she wondered if perhaps she dreamed it all up. But there'd be evidence of it. Their relationship would result in her only pregnancy.

She would tell John the news, but on hearing it, he made it clear to Elizabeth that he had no desire to raise a child. In the following days and weeks he became elusive. She cried at first, even considered the alternative, but then one day, while sitting alone at home, she touched her stomach and decided she didn't need a man in her life. Regardless of John's disinterest, the love she felt for what was taking shape inside her was unlike any she'd ever experienced.

The child would be her pride and joy. A first-generation blue-eyed girl born in the free world. Elizabeth even considered naming her Wolność, but knew a name like that would only make life hard on a girl, especially in this new country. She needed something modest, something distinctly American. After much consideration, she settled on Lillian Mary. But she rarely called the child by her birth name. Instead, she addressed her by her nickname, Baby. Except that, with Elizabeth's accent, still as thick as the day she arrived, the moniker sounded more like Bubbie.

John never returned, leaving Elizabeth and Bubbie alone to get on with their lives. It would remain this way until Bubbie's eleventh birthday. While the child had grown accustomed to living alone with her mother, Elizabeth was adamant that her daughter now needed a male figure in the house. Which is to say, Elizabeth Liebersbach was lonely.

Life would drag on. Now and then a faint nostalgia for the Poland she was once able to recall with clarity would settle in. Their old home in Poznań. The familiar voices that populated her young world. It was like a dream that hibernated in the marrow of her bones, only to emerge every few seasons, long enough to stoke the yearning.

According to the U.S. census taken on April 9, 1930, Elizabeth, at age twenty-nine, declared she was from "Poznań, Poland-Germany" and that other than English she spoke fluent German. She was now a "machine operator" for a clothing manufacturer and was still living alone with her daughter Bubbie at 112 Clinton North, Rochester, New York. Their home was situated in the city's immigrant section. Their neighbors were Germans, Italians, Russians, Jews, and Irish, and worked primarily as masons, painters, seamstresses, and factory machine operators. On any given evening, music could be heard echoing out of kitchen windows from staticky radios, in unfamiliar languages. The aromas that wafted down Clinton North, past Main Street, and across the Genesee River were a bouquet of old-world flavors. It wasn't uncommon to catch a wave of rosemary, pickling vinegars, freshly baked bread, and pastries of all sorts hanging in the air. On Friday nights, the Lyric Theater played all the silent films of the day: *Frivolous Wives* starring Rudolph Valentino, *City Lights* starring Charlie Chaplin, or *Mata Hari* featuring Greta Garbo. There was a constant buzz in their section of Rochester, but to Elizabeth it was a party that she could view only from the quiet side of the window. Her father's words still haunted her. She would stare out of her window and find the genuine camaraderie of her neighbors disturbing. Their cheerfulness only enhanced the solitude that had become her life. But things would look up.

A year later she'd meet another man, Oscar Phillip Kesselring. He was a veteran of World War I, and he carried himself with a quiet intensity. Aside from the fact that he was prone to tantrums, she felt that God had allowed for a little light back into her life. Bubbie appreciated Oscar, if for no other reason than that her mother was mostly smiling again. Bubbie even took on the Kesselring name. By now, she had more names than she knew what to do with. Sometimes she'd drop Mary; other times she would simply write *Lillian K.* And still other times she was made to write out her full name, Lillian Mary Koch Kesselring. Still, of all her names, the one she preferred most, which is to say, the one that stuck, was Bubbie. Though, now in grade school, and yearning to fit in, she took it upon herself to bend the accent just so, and her friends knew her as Bobbie.

But their fortune would be short lived. A few years into their marriage, Oscar developed an irascible mental condition, which doctors attributed to the lingering effects of the war. He sought help in the beginning, but the problem quickly impaired his ability to rationalize even the most banal situations. In a matter of months he would be institutionalized indefinitely. Once again, Elizabeth sank into the hole from which she had pulled herself only a few short years before. Bobbie helplessly watched her mother wither. Again the loneliness set in. Nothing helped. If a neighbor happened to swing by, Elizabeth refused to answer the door. Mostly, she sat in complete silence and waited. One day, during a conversation, Bobbie asked her mother what exactly she was waiting for. Elizabeth replied, "Niebo." Heaven. Neither friends or cousins so much as knocked on her door. After Oscar was committed, it was as if Elizabeth had been erased entirely.

Their home was a cave. Bobbie was restless. Her only respite from the doldrums that had become life was bowling. That, and the off chance that Frankie Atkinson would stop by for a visit. It wasn't often, but in the early days of their friendship he would cross the Smith Street bridge and come looking for Bobbie, and together they'd catch a movie down at the Lyric, or else stroll the Genesee, skipping rocks. Even then, Elizabeth chastised her daughter for pining over the boy. "Let him be," she would say, with a look of disgust on her face. Bobbie ignored her mother's comments. "Don't waste your time," she could hear her voice calling from the kitchen. Bobbie chalked up her mother's bitterness as a side effect of her own failed attempts at love. Even so, it was clear to Bobbie that Frankie saw her only as a friend. Maybe he would always see her that way. After all, everyone knew that he and Dottie were an item. Bobbie and Frankie were just friends. Yes, good friends. Perhaps, one day, great friends. Until then, Frankie was just Frankie.

20

FRANKIE GETS HIS CHANCE

"Frankie enlisted in the military the day after Pearl Harbor was bombed," Mary Lou said, proudly. "He went right in and signed himself up. Our other brother, Bob, went to the navy, but Frankie, well, since he'd always wanted to be a pilot he went straight to the air force. Yes, that was the day he finally got his chance—"

The morning of December 7, 1941, would set it off. Radio bulletins blared headlines that the Japanese had attacked Pearl Harbor. They had come by sea and by air, blackening the serenity of the Polynesian islands and exploding everything in their path. Sound clips rattled ears across the globe. They heard it in Canada, and in Europe, and they heard it in Mexico. Every last U.S. soldier was deployed posthaste. Young men, civilians moments before, filed into recruiting offices, gunning at their chance to even the score.

Frankie's official enlistment shows January 19, 1942. He was twenty-four years old. He could hardly contain himself.

"Didn't I tell you?" he said to his father. "I knew it. I knew it would come."

John reminded his son, "We're proud, Francis, but war is serious business."

"Of course," Frankie replied, slapping his brother Bob on the back. "But with us two at the helm, there's no stopping us."

Bob didn't share his brother's expressiveness. He nodded and gave his father a shrug.

What Frankie's enlistment records don't show, however, is that only a few hours after he told Dottie the good news, she was cornered into making a decision of her own.

"Did you even think of me when you went marching into that recruiting office?" she asked. "Of course you didn't," she added, turning her eyes away.

"You sayin' you won't wait for me?"

"Till when, Frankie? Next year? A hundred years?"

Frankie was silent.

"Wars don't got expiration dates, you know. It's in the radio and papers; it's all I hear, young men like you, even better than you, dying every day. If it's what you wanna do, you go right ahead—" She hesitated. Frankie waited for her to finish her thought. When she couldn't, he spoke up.

"I don't get it. I figured of everyone you'd be the proudest."

She pulled his promise ring off her finger.

"It's the war, you understand? I gotta go."

"If you say so, Frankie." She handed him the ring.

Frankie stood confused.

Dottie folded her arms. "It's what you've always wanted anyhow, isn't it? To fly. What do you have to be so sore about?"

"You of all people know this is my only shot, Dottie. If I don't take this—"

"Don't speak another word." She stepped away from him.

"Don't be rash, Dottie. Understand—"

"I understand fine," she said, turning her back on him and walking off.

Frankie waited to see if she'd glance back. When she peered over her shoulder, he wanted to call out, "Tell me you'll write me, Dottie!" Instead, he heard himself saying, "Dottie, it's the war!"

She paused a moment, to look at him once more. She shielded her eyes from the sunlight, then turned and hurried away. He watched her blue skirt flittering behind her and her blonde hair rising and falling. He looked in her direction, until she was no longer in sight. Just like that, Frankie thought to himself, the war had already claimed its first casualty.

21

FLIGHT TRAINING

Southeast Air Corps Training Center
Montgomery, Alabama

From day one, Frankie was aware of the statistics. Even in the years leading up to the war, the odds were against him. In 1939, over eight thousand men applied for Aviation Cadet Training, but only seventeen hundred would make it past the first round of tests. The physical intensity alone would whittle that number down to just shy of five hundred in a few days' time. And then there was the Education Training. Cadets were given nine subjects, among them English grammar, literature, algebra, history. Questions like, "Briefly describe the career of Alexander the Great," were expected to be answered, and done so in "eloquent fashion." Because of the highly selective process, Frankie committed himself to training harder than anyone else. He'd been given his shot and wasn't about to hand it off to some lesser cadet. He watched the instructional films with wide-open eyes, taking in each word that poured from the black-and-white images. He read all the manuals cover to cover. Worked faster. Ran harder. Pushed himself until each night his feet throbbed and his brain ached. By the time he collapsed into his bed, any thoughts of Dottie that threatened to creep in were overridden by exhaustion.

Frankie's only distractions were the letters he'd receive from John and Agnes. "We're proud of you, Frankie, you and your brother Bob." Now and then he'd get a letter from his sisters, Helen or Mary Lou. Dottie sent him nothing.

Tensions around the world increased. On the radio and in the streets, the broadcasts were relentless: "Japanese American families, over 120,000 of them, forced into incarceration in the wake of Pearl Harbor."

War was the only buzz. The cadets spoke of it among themselves.

"MacArthur's evacuating troops from the Philippines."

"We're losing the island."

Another headline: "36,000 U.S. Men Feared Lost in Fall of Bataan."

The cadets of the Southeast Air Corps Training Center wanted nothing more than to get into the sky and give the bad guys a proper ass whooping.

More young men flooded recruiting offices, even in the most rural of places. They dropped their spots on the assembly lines and in packing houses until soon whole communities felt like ghost towns. Soon, new headlines appeared: "Mexican Workers Wanted in October: California has placed orders for 6,000 imported Mexican workers—"

Day after day, Frankie watched the training reels, almost piously, until the instruction was hardwired into his brain and he could recite the entire narration word for word: "The air force has established a number of routine regulations, including such items as the preflight inspection and testing procedures. Of equal importance with these is the daily flight inspection form. Every day, before the first flight, the plane captain inspects his plane according to the inspection form, checking each item as he inspects them. This inspection, which is carried out by the plane captain is the same as the preflight inspection the copilot is expected to make. That is one of the safety precautions, whereby the air force endeavors to make flying more safe for you. You may miss something. He may miss something. Both the captain and copilot are only human."

It was during this time that Frankie would come to forge a bond with one particular airplane, the C-47 skyship. He respected the "Gooneybird" for the tough hunk of machinery that it was. It was practically a big rig of the sky. Its wings, more flexible than most, made it possible to carry heavy cargo. He learned that he could transport tons of food, weapons, and ammo, even small jeeps, and still maneuver the bird with ease. It was a resilient ship. If riddled with bullets, the fabric aluminum made it an easy fix. But its main feature, which Frankie touted more than anything else, were the herculean tires that enabled it to land anywhere there was a patch of dirt. He'd spend hundreds of hours in this airplane, and eventually thousands of hours. He'd memorize the instrument panel the way one memorizes a lover's face. He learned its every button, knob, and dimple until it became muscle memory. A crosswind slightly tugging on the left horizontal stabilizer may as well have been tugging on his earlobe. The C-47 operational manual became his bible, and he heeded its every word, until there was no doubt in his mind that the Gooneybird was a metaphor for his own soul.

By the time Frankie was done with training, spring had arrived. It dawned on him one afternoon while running flight drills. He darted over a wide meadow and spotted a rash of brilliant coral honeysuckles speckling the green grass like an expressionistic painting. "How could it be?" he'd later write to his brother, Bob. "Seems like only yesterday I walked in green as the pastures of Montgomery." Just a few short months after his enlistment, Cadet Atkinson had finally achieved his dream. He had earned his wings. When they handed him his certificate, he did all he could to hold back tears, but one managed to slip anyway.

Southeast Air Corps Training Center

> Upon the recommendation of his Tactical Officer, I do hereby appoint Aviation Cadet ATKINSON, F.C., a CORPORAL in the Air Corps Replacement Training Center to rank as such from the twenty-fifth day of March, 1942. He is therefore carefully and diligently to discharge his duties as Corporal, and all cadets coming under his command are strictly charged and required to be obedient to his orders as such. And he is to observe and follow such orders and direction as he shall receive from his military superiors, according to the rules and discipline of War. Given under my hand at Maxwell Field, Alabama this twenty-third day of April in the year of Our Lord, this one thousand nine hundred and forty two. Signed Mark C. Bane Jr. Captain. Air Corps Commandant of Aviation Cadets.

Within minutes of being handed the document he was given his date for active duty: November 10, 1942. Over the next several months, while awaiting his deployment, he began the work of training new cadets. Despite the long days, he was finally able to carve out time enough to pen a few letters home. John and Agnes were thrilled when they received a postcard from their son. They carted it around and read it to just about anyone who cared to listen. One of the first cards they received from Frankie was an image of fighter planes flying in formation across a clear blue sky. He writes:

Dear Folks, I can't keep up with this pace & still find time to write much, so this is the only way out. Now that it's really hot down here, when evening comes we're licked. I can hardly keep my eyes open but can't go to bed 'til 9:30. I received your letter mom, also Janis & Pete's. I also received the candy from you & aunt Jane, really swell. Thanks a million. We have more than we can eat. I hope you received & liked the pictures. 1 is for Win & Ed, I thought I might as well double up. We've really got our hands full drilling these underclassmen in the hot sun. I'll write as soon as possible.

Loads of love,
Frank

22

FRANKIE GOES TO WAR

1942–1945

On November 10, 1942, Frankie's first day of active duty, Winston Churchill delivered a speech that was broadcast across the country. The base patched it in over the loudspeakers for all to hear: "This is not the end. It is not even the beginning of the end. But it is, perhaps, the end of the beginning—"

Churchill's words would prove prophetic. At its height, the war seemed like it might never end. While he was stationed in India, the next few years of Corporal Atkinson's life would be measured by endless vaults across the "Hump." It was the most dreaded stretch of the Himalayas, where mountains speared to altitudes of twenty-nine thousand feet. Its conditions were straight out of el Diablo's handbook. A wicked terrain of jagged peaks so treacherous that it rendered maps or radio navigation useless. In order to make the vault, a pilot's instincts had to be sharp enough to split the razor's edge. By the time Corporal Atkinson arrived on the scene, the Hump was described like something from Dante's Purgatorio. An in-between realm where the crashed and blown-out carcasses of C-47s went to rot—half-dead, half-alive, never to be heard from again.

It wouldn't take long for Atkinson to learn firsthand that its reputation wasn't mere myth. One afternoon, while braving a lightning storm, the Gooneybird he was flying went down, and despite all attempts, couldn't be located. The territory was neutralized at the time, but for a brief moment Corporal Frank Atkinson was on the verge of taking his spot on a growing list of casualties. But then days later, battered and barely able to walk, Atkinson emerged from the mountain pass. Bruised and disheveled, he was alive. No pilot who went down in the mandibles of the Hump made it out alive. This catapulted his reputation among the most seasoned pilots. By age twenty-six, Corporal Frank Atkinson had sealed his legend.

Over the next two years, Frankie thought of home sparingly. It was the only way to survive the long days and nights. He wondered how his sisters, Helen and Mary Lou, were getting along. No doubt they were navigating the complexities of coming of age in Rochester. Now and then he'd wonder too about Dottie. But over time, with the incessant duties of war, a callus had grown over the wound that came with their split. He'd stopped yearning for her long ago. In fact, these days it was almost impossible to remember her face. If anything, what Frankie missed most were the simple privileges of civilian life. A hamburger. An ice-cream soda. Baseball in April. A long and unhurried walk along the serenity of the Genesee.

One morning, back in Rochester, a headline appeared in the local paper: *Flyer Begs for Burgers.* It read: "The traditional American 'snack' of hamburgers and coffee, ordered one hundred air miles away, was waiting for Lieut. Francis C. Atkinson, 496 Clay Street, at a small Red Cross canteen when he arrived at an airport in the interior of India recently." Accompanying the article was a small photograph of Frankie. His hair a wreck and the weight of war on his face. His gaze, grim and tired.

Viewing the photograph, Agnes worried for her son. So much so that she arranged an opportunity to speak with him.

"How are ya, honey?"

"Just fine, Mom. I'm doin' fine." He could sense her concern. "You ain't gotta worry about me. These boys here got me well taken care of."

Agnes wasn't exactly sure what she wanted to say to her son. "Well, all of Rochester saw the story of you in the papers."

"Is that so?"

"Yes it is. It was quite a thing. Neither your father or I could go to the market without a fuss being made."

"I'll bet."

Agnes sensed something wasn't quite right with Frankie. "We sure are proud of you, honey."

More silence.

"Well, I miss you all. Guess I better get back to my duties. Send my love to Dad, and everyone else, will ya?"

"I sure will, honey."

"So long."

"So long now."

Corporal Atkinson had a difficult time sleeping. The operations he'd grown accustomed to were a far stretch from the skyships that once sailed serenely over his front porch on Clay Street. Some nights he'd wake up under fire, his fists trembling, grasping for an imaginary yoke. Even after three years of solid flying, it seemed the night sweats wouldn't let up. He would stay up late and jot notes down in his small field book. They were more like calculations really. He needed to see for himself the anatomy of his accomplishments, something tangible, a record of his lifelong dream. In his notebook, he wrote:

> Total Military flying hours—2390:55
> Night time—490:20
> Total inst. 192:40
> Actual inst. 85:00
> Twin engine time—1978:40
> Four engine time—89:35
> C-47 Hrs—1883:15 (Air evac & MAT—Military Air Transport)

By that summer, Churchill's words, now three years gone, would seem like a distant memory. Even though the war was in full swing, Frankie could sense that the end was near. Adolf Hitler had committed suicide, and the United States had just dropped the mother of all bombs on Hiroshima. If there was ever a "beginning of the end," he prayed it was just around the corner. His prayers would be answered. A month later the Japanese surrendered, and President Truman broadcasted: "The war to which we have devoted all the resources and all the energy of our country for more than three and a half years has now produced total victory over all our enemies—"

Three long years after walking into the service, it looked, as if with all certainty, that Corporal Atkinson would make it out alive. A decorated soldier. Though he didn't wear it on his face, he was relieved. Riding out the remainder of his service would be a cakewalk. For the first time since stepping foot in that recruiting office, he allowed himself to imagine, once again, a life back home. It seemed easy enough, but in truth the thought of returning back to "good ol' Roch" was almost as nerve-racking as flying over the Hump on one engine. If not more so. What was there for him? Surely Dottie had moved on. He couldn't see himself processing photographs for

Kodak the rest of his life. Maybe he'd live elsewhere. Get a fresh start. He preferred to put Rochester out of his mind.

But the universe has a way of realigning itself.

One evening, while Frankie was busy polishing his shoes, the mail carrier arrived with a small stack of letters. One was from Agnes. She was elated that the war was finally over and that Frankie would be coming home. "Rochester misses you, honey," she wrote.

She updated her son about the goings-on in their small part of the world. The hum of life and the tiny dramas. It was all too real for Frankie to take. He'd put her letter off until later. He shuffled through the envelopes and discovered a postcard. It was dated back in March. He found it curious and pulled it from the stack. The image was of a golden-haired girl dressed in green, tossing a bouquet of clover into the air. Above the girl, it read: *Top o' the mornin' and a Happy St. Patrick's Day to you!* Beneath that was a handwritten note: *Remember me? Love, Bobbie.*

23

DEAR BOBBIE

Over the next two years they carried out a courtship that took place mostly in letters. It was a period during which Frankie and Bobbie would come to believe "a simple truth," as was later conveyed to them by Father Sullivan. Theirs was a love predetermined by the "all powerful hand of God."

It happened quick. The plans were set in motion.

Frankie would be released from active military duty on January 10, 1947. He would work for an outfit called Airline Transport Carriers Inc., a company based in Long Beach, California, where they would live. The job wasn't much to boast about, but it was safe and the pay decent. Mostly he'd be flying between Burbank and Oakland, transporting merchandise and sometimes people. The wedding would take place in May, that time of year when the weather in Southern California reaches the pearl hour. The whole thing would be perfect. They would even fly in Bobbie's mother, Elizabeth, if she'd agree to it. Of course, John and Agnes were ecstatic; they'd known Bobbie for ages and practically watched her grow up with Frankie. At the height of the war, though they dared not speak of it, they had begun preparing themselves, as much as parents can, to receive the most dreaded of phone calls. That they were now making plans to witness one of the greatest days of their son's life filled them with an overwhelming joy. So much so that they would recite special prayers at church over the blessing that was their life.

Three weeks before the ceremony, Frankie returned to Rochester, briefly, to finalize some of the arrangements. From there, he sent his bride-to-be a letter, updating her on how things were going.

Tuesday April 29, 1947

My Darling,
The red tape, plans & necessary arrangements are starting to unravel. I think I'll still be in a spin 'til May 17th and this is

great for a nice quiet wedding! I'm afraid if we had planned a big splash we would have to hire a couple of secretary arrangers, etc. They told me today at the restaurant I have nineteen more shopping days & a few other "ribs" that I am used to receiving. You know hon, Father Kleehammer thinks a lot of you, for him and your many other friends in Rochester. I'm sorry but not too sorry 'cause their loss is my gain, besides I want & need you more than they do & then someday we'll trot back to Roch in all our glory & be able to show the people what a nice looking happy couple we do make & when Cy invites us to his country home, you might tell him he'll only have to have one extra bed. Fact is honey I thought of that at the time of his invite but thought it best at the time to keep it under my blonde curly hair.

I'd give a lot if only you were here with me now and the formalities were all behind us. You see we're alone again tonight, it might be fair to warn you you'd be very apt to catch a cold, it had me down for a couple of days but I think it's about whipped now.

We've got some more business to straighten out. . . . When I presented the paper certificates etc. to Father Sullivan he was pleased that we didn't have any difficulty however he wants two more (1) He said the banns were supposed to be published in your church so can you get a letter from Father Kleehammer saying they were? There are two more Sundays left and that'll be o.k. I think; they were announced out here Sunday. (2) Although he asked for either certificate of Holy Communion or Confirmation, which were produced, he now wants a certificate of your confirmation.

I know it's discouraging honey, I couldn't see all the red tape neither but I think we've just about got it whipped.

Got sneezing so bad I had to quit for awhile, just think honey next week at this time, you'll be on the way then I'll be on edge but you'll just drive during daylight hours won't you?

I wouldn't worry for a minute about you being able to take care of yourself but there's been so much happening lately; it sure is a relief to know Jane will be with you, she's a swell kid isn't she? I hope we can show her a good time out here

& Joe has volunteered to help us; it'll be fun for him too 'cause he hasn't been going out very much.

I'm hoping to receive a letter from you tomorrow with some information on the rings so I can get busy on that. Went down today & shopped around for some material for a suit & finally found what I wanted, then they said it would be impossible to get it before three weeks so I talked fast & told them I had looked all over fruitlessly (get that one), so anyhow they went to a great deal of trouble & effort & agreed to have it by the 15th so that any last minute or minor alterations could be made. Then on Father Sullivan's advice I went to the marriage bureau to see if the physical & blood test you took would hold out here & the lady said the requirements of New York State were the same as those of California however the examination cannot be over 30 days old, so if it is hon why don't you just have the doctor issue a new certificate.

I've got to get mine yet, sure hope I pass. I took a thorough pre flight physical in Jan for the Reserve outfit at the base & passed o.k. but that isn't recent enough. I'm not worried about the physical but don't know if I can spare the blood. Honey I was just thinking, isn't it going to be nice to be able to get up together on the 18th & go to church in Catalina or wherever we are? Incidentally I asked uncle Curtis if he'd give you away & he said he'd have to see you first then maybe he would keep you himself, so I guess we'll have to find someone older (he's only about 55). When we're man & wife do I have to give you change for the collection box or do I put my nickel in & raise two fingers? My eyes are watering & my nose is running so what say we hit the sack for now. I'll write again soon 'til then a big hug & kiss for you & also one for your mom. Goodnight darling.

Yours now & always,
Frank

P.S. Hey Mary! (I didn't know your name was Mary)

On May 17, 1947, the young couple made their vows before a small, close-knit group of family and friends. An intimate ceremony was held at St. Anthony's Church in Long Beach, and Father Sullivan would be flown in to conduct the services. John and Agnes were there. Elizabeth was not. She refused to fly. As much as she'd have given anything to see her Bubbie get married, the thought of flying was almost as petrifying as the thought of leaving the confines of her own house. If she was to ever see her daughter again, it would have to be through other means. Perhaps by train or by bus.

"Maybe for our one-year anniversary," Bobbie suggested to her mother by phone.

"We'll see, Bubbie," replied Elizabeth. "We'll see."

III

THEY'RE FLYIN' 'EM BACK

Goodbye to my Juan, Goodbye Rosalita /
Adios mis amigos, Jesus y Maria . . .

—Woody Guthrie, "Plane Wreck at Los Gatos (Deportee)"

24

CASIMIRA RECALLS THE LAST CONVERSATION

Jocotepec, Jalisco
January 22, 2015

Casimira paused from telling her story to swallow a pill and have a sip of water. She placed the glass on the table and pulled her shawl farther down over her shoulders. She was growing visibly tired now, but she pushed on. "Even before the accident, Luis had already been going to los Estados. Sometimes contratado, as a bracero, and sometimes not. But the last time he went he wasn't contracted. In those days, you see, it was easier to go, pues, así, contrabando. Now it's not the same, it's more difficult. But back then they would just come and go, and the majority would get through with no problem. But it's not like that anymore." She pointed at the television. "Now, you see, so many die while crossing. Everyone dies, it's too dangerous."

She hesitated, and a small silence enveloped the living room. She had now arrived at the point in her story where there was nothing left to share. Nothing but the unavoidable moment. She tugged on her beanie and then glanced over her right shoulder as if distracted by something. "Well, you see, Luis was never able to write or call. Nor did we ever talk much while he was away. But this last time, right before he died, he called me." She nodded her head as if confirming her own memory. "Yes. He called to tell me that he had been picked up by la migra. And, well, it was obvious to me that they had picked up many people, because the plane was full. He said this to me, or something like this. But I remember thinking there was a group of them who had been picked up. He didn't give me the details of where he was picked up exactly, but he told me, 'Casimira, they caught me and they're going to deport us.' That's when I realized there was a lot of them, because he said, they're going to deport *us*. But it was then, in that conversation, I'll never forget, that he told me he was coming home, and that he was returning with a mariachi for me." Casimira's lip trembled. She lowered her eyes to the linoleum floor. "Yes, I could see his love for me. Anyone could see it. It was obvious. Luis loved me. And yes, yes, I did love him—"

25

JANUARY 28, 1948

San Francisco, California
Immigration Detention Center

6:01 a.m.

Before the rippling sun had risen over the bay, Luis Miranda Cuevas was startled awake by the crash of keys. Officer Chaffin slapped them across the bars once more, until the noise stirred everyone awake. Ramón Paredes unfolded his arms and ran his callused hand over his face, then cracked open an eye. He nodded at Luis. By the light of the dimly lit cell, the two men watched as Chaffin poked a finger through the steel bars and began counting bodies. Luis pat his hair down and then stood up to dust himself off. Ramón placed his hat on his head and nudged his compadre, Guadalupe.

"Despiértese, compa," he whispered. "Es hora de volar."

Time to fly. The mere sound of it felt strange coming out of Ramón's mouth. He'd been transported many times by train and bus, but never "en un avión." He hadn't made up his mind how to feel about it. A part of him, perhaps the child inside, appreciated the wonderment. But the rough-hewn campesino in him preferred to be as close to the earth as possible. As a man with a penchant for gambling, it was unlike him to bank on such incalculable odds. Guadalupe, on the other hand, courted adventure. Though it would never be known which of the two men convinced the other that returning to Mexico by airplane was the mother of all opportunities, both Ramón's and Guadalupe's families would later agree that if a choice was to be had, it was more than likely at Guadalupe's urging. The two men stood up, nodding hello to the other warm bodies who were now stretching their backs and massaging awake sleepy limbs. Officer Chaffin said good morning to the group. "Buenos días," a few echoed back. In his best Spanish, Chaffin let them know that the bus would be there in a few minutes. "Prepárense," he said. More bodies rolled off the bunks and began pulling on boots and hats.

The conversations the night before ran into the morning hours. It was the anticipation of the plane ride that kept them abuzz. Even those who willingly agreed to be transported by "avión" were now second-guessing their decision. With the passing of each hour, their minds couldn't fathom the sensation of being aloft, way up among the holy mysteries of the clouds. Was it a sin to find oneself so close to God? It was a question they dared not ask. Their reasoning was practical enough. Efficiency. The sooner they arrived in Mexico, the sooner they'd be home with their families. And how could this be a sin?

"One thing is certain," María began saying. She was the only woman among them, and so the men listened. "It beats the wretched trains that stink like hell of cattle and entrails." Everyone agreed. The trains were filthy and unsanitary. The night before, a group of men had been sharing stories of plane crashes. They were the few who had not been given the choice. Had they been given a choice, they expressed, they would have preferred the "wretched trains any day over el avión."

"Sure, the trains reek to high heaven," one man said, "but at least there is certainty in rails—I should know, I put those tracks together myself." Several men nodded. "Besides, what's a little manure among campesinos?" Everyone chuckled. Everyone except María.

26

THE TELLING OF THE ROUNDUP AT SAN JUAN BAUTISTA

Sometime in late spring, 1948

It first came from the mouth of José Murillo Ramírez. When he arrived back in Charco de Pantoja one warm spring evening, he was certain that the families of both Ramón and Guadalupe had not yet heard, so he prepared himself to be the bearer of bad news. Because Charco de Pantoja had no church, it is likely that José first walked up the steep hill to La Iglesia de Santa Rosa, where he thanked Dios for his safe return. Exhausted and disheveled from the long train ride home, that day he would knock on the door of the house that belonged to his compadre Ramón Paredes to inform his wife, Elisa, and their six children, of the terrible news. When the children first spotted Don José walking up the path toward their home, they leapt with excitement, questioning him, "Donde esta mi papa, Don José?" Believing their father was up to this usual tricks, they glanced up the road, begging Don José to reveal where their father was hiding. José could hardly lift his eyes toward the children. He choked up, but gathered himself. Elisa heard the children outside, their voices chirping excitedly, and she came out expecting to find her husband, Ramón. Instead she found José Murillo Ramírez standing there. The expression on his face said enough. José could not look her in the eye. Elisa began to wail.

It was a telling that would be passed around Charco de Pantoja for generations to come. In the streets, the ejido, the molino, and at gatherings, soon everyone would learn about that fateful roundup of Ramón and Guadalupe in a place called San Juan Bautista, California. Of course, the exact way in which it was told, and the tone in which José spoke it, would be impossible to remember. However, it is collectively agreed that the account he shared with Elisa that day went something like this:

"It was in San Juan Bautista, that town where they have the mission. That's where Guadalupe was staying—he was working there. Ramón lived elsewhere, near San José, I believe, because he was working at a different location, but not too far anyway. I was working there, too, in the same place as Guadalupe. We were picking pears. We had been visiting, and waiting for Ramón to show up. It was during a time where work wasn't happening, so he came to visit with me and Guadalupe. We weren't sure he was going to make it, because, well, you see, he had to ask a ride from someone. Those of us from Mexico did not have cars, but a few men did, los pochos, and we would ask rides from them. Ramón showed up, and he was feeling bad for taking so long. We didn't mind because, well, we understood. It was already getting dark, and so I told the men I would run out to get some things to cook a meal, and so I went. I wasn't long, you see, the store wasn't far away, so I wasn't far from the campo. Well, I went for the supplies, and then I started to walk back. Some guys had been saying that things were heating up, and that la migra had been making the rounds, but there was always talk. When I got back to the campo . . . well, when I was arriving, I could see that la migra was already there. They had shown up while I was away. There were several buses. It was dark by then, but I could see that some men were being taken. I couldn't see very well, but I could see enough. I hid behind a big truck that was parked down the road. It was the kind of truck they use for hauling fruit. It was just there, so I went under it and waited. I tried to spot Guadalupe or Ramón, but it was too dark. So, well, after the buses left, I waited there awhile longer. When they left I returned to the campo and could see everyone had been taken. A few men came out from their hiding places, and I asked if they had seen Guadalupe or Ramón, but they hadn't. I knew then they were picked up. There was nothing I could do. I went to Guadalupe's place, and some of his things were still there. His leather jacket. I brought it with me, and a few of his other things. That is exactly how it happened. And from there, I heard they were supposed to take them to a deportation center in El Centro—"

27

EL CENTRO DEPORTATION CENTER

August 8, 2014

Guillermo Ramírez: "I remember the first time I was sent to El Centro. When you first get to the deportation center, they take you to a room to check in. You have to take your clothes off, everything, and they check you real good. They put your things you have in a bag and give you a uniform with a color. Different colors for different groups. Each room has maybe two hundred people. And they have maybe ten or twelve of these giant rooms with two rooms in each one. And they are all filled with people waiting to be deported. There is a lot of bad people in there. A lot of good people too, but a lot of bad people. You have good people mixed in with drug dealers, cartels, and stuff like that. There are two large rooms. Well, it's one long room, but it has a fence down the middle, so it's two rooms. And then you have a door at the end of each long room. In both rooms you have rows of bunk beds. If a bed is empty you can take it. There they can keep you just a few days, but sometimes weeks, or even months. Maybe more.

"How I came to los Estados Unidos was different from my brother, Jaime. The first time I came it was me and two friends, and they caught us as we were walking through the desert. We started walking toward the highway, but we thought we were smart, so we got some bushes and erased our footprints so they couldn't see which way we were going. It was a long walk, and they knew we were there, they just didn't know which way we went. There were three of us. We had to get to the other side of these orange fields where there was somebody waiting for us already. There was a prison nearby, and we had to go past it. Our mistake was, when we got close to the prison fence one of us touched it. That's how they found out we were there. It must've had sensors. We finally saw the orange fields that we were supposed to get to. So we said, there it is, let's start running, and we ran. But one of the men with us was close to sixty years in age, and he couldn't make it. We started running and he said to us, 'Just go for it, I'm not gonna make it.' And I said, 'No, no, we aren't gonna leave you here.' I heard the noise of the jeeps coming, and I said to myself, 'shit,' and I saw one, two, three of them. One on each side and one in the middle. So they got us. We were one hundred meters from our goal. One of the migra jeeps got a flat tire and the officer was pissed off. He said, 'See what you did? Because of you now I have a flat tire. You made me run, but I got you.' And then he said, 'So, which one of you is the coyote?' I said, 'We don't have no coyote.' He goes, 'Really?' 'No,' I said. He couldn't believe it. I said, 'We are just us three friends. There's no coyote.' So then he just put us in the back of the truck.

"A lot of the officers are nice people. Some of them are bad too, but there's a lot of good ones. I've been to the deportation center in El Centro three times. The last time I was there, my brothers had to bail me out, and then I had to go to court. Inside the deportation center there was this one officer. He was nice, and he started telling me I have a good chance to stay in the United States. I said, 'Oh yeah?' He told me how to do it. He liked me. We talked, and he knew I was a good guy and that I was a hard worker. So he told me how to do it, and when it was time for me to go to court, I defended myself. The judge said to me, 'Where's your attorney?' I said, 'No, sir. I don't got none.' He said, 'You're gonna defend yourself?' I said, 'Yes, sir, that's right.' He said, 'Are you sure?' I said, 'Yes, sir.' And so I did. We talked, well, he asked me a few questions. He could see that I had no record of doing anything bad here, and that I worked here before, many, many times. I even had a work permit before. He asked me what I had planned to do here. I said, 'Just work, that's it.' He said, 'Yes, but your wife is still in Mexico, so how are you going to do it?' I said to him, 'I can do it, your honor. I've been doing it for a long time.' He stared at me and said, 'Okay, you do everything right, Mr. Ramírez, and you will be able to stay here and work.' But then he said I need money to make the bail. He said, 'What do you think?' I said, 'I can pay one hundred dollars, your honor.' He said, 'Oh no, no, no, that's not gonna work. You have to pay fifteen hundred dollars.' He said, 'Call whoever you have to.' So I called my brothers, and they got the money together. That's how I ended up getting to stay here in the United States. I've been here for twenty-six years now. I became a U.S. citizen just last November."

28

UN NUEVO AMANECER

7:20 a.m.

Most of them had been detained for several days, but some of them had been there for weeks. Their necks were sore and their spines tender from sleeping on the concrete floors of the holding cells. There were a few wooden bunks, which they took turns occupying, but it wasn't enough to accommodate everyone. Yesterday, Officer Chaffin had greeted them with rolls of bread and some lukewarm beans. It was good while it lasted. Their belongings had also been returned to them, and in the evening they were given a chance to bathe. Because they shared the only facility available, the men turned their backs so that María could wash with some bit of modesty. She splashed water on the parts that mattered, then rinsed her mouth out and tied her hair back with a rubber band.

Today was another day. A new day. Un nuevo amanecer. At least it felt this way to Luis. Casimira would be awaiting his arrival. He'd spoken with her on the phone, and her voice was as tender as he'd remembered it. "I'll be here, Luis, waiting—" He pulled her photograph from his pocket. *Cara de Dolorosa.* He stared at it for a moment. In a matter of weeks they would be married. He would arrive with Jocotepec's finest mariachi in tow, making a spectacle of their love. An excitement fell over him.

It was forty-one degrees in downtown San Francisco that morning. A few voices, those who knew each other, whispered while they wiped the sleep from their eyes and ambled out into the crisp morning air. They lined up in single file, clutching their belongings as they waited to board the bus. It was early still, and San Francisco's downtown buildings were glowing against the rising sun.

Moments later, the bus belched, dragging them through the quiet city streets and across the Bay Bridge toward Oakland. The sun had risen to just above the ridge of the Berkeley Hills, forcing the driver to steer with one hand and shield the glare with the other. The passengers looked out across the glittering waters and could see the immense barges in the distance, busily importing and exporting, like steady waves crashing to and fro the industrial lip of the East Bay.

Thirty minutes later they found themselves at the Oakland Municipal Airport. As the bus entered through a metal security gate, they spotted the tall, silver skyship parked in the distance. The wings seemed to stretch for miles on either side, and the nose of the ship pointed up, regal-like.

When the bus came to a halt, Officer Chaffin stood up and addressed the passengers. "Formen una sola linea, por favor."

Just as Chaffin instructed, they deboarded, one by one, and in single file followed him to where several other officers stood. A light gust of wind blew José Sánchez Valdivia's baseball cap off his head, and he scooped it up before it had a chance to go skipping down the tarmac. They stopped several yards away from the airplane, where they were made to wait for the crew. It would be another hour before the pilots and stewardess would arrive.

Everyone made small talk to pass the time. Chaffin with his colleagues. The passengers among themselves. The air was frigid still, and María huddled against her husband, Lupe. Ramón and Guadalupe spoke of plans for the ejido, and how it would be nice to return home again, to Charco, and see everyone. The youngest of the passengers was a light-skinned kid named Tomás Márquez Padilla. He couldn't have been a day older than twenty. He looked frightened and didn't bother speaking to anyone. Even when Luis tried addressing him, the kid simply nodded. It was clear he wanted to be left alone.

From the building two pilots emerged, with a blonde woman following close behind. They were wearing dark blue uniforms with brass buttons that gleamed. The woman's red high heels drew attention as they clicked against the gray asphalt. She appeared friendly, light. The pilots tipped their cap at the officers as they strode past, before opening the hatch at the rear of the plane. The passengers watched as the small door unfolded open and a ladder descended from it. The crew quickly climbed aboard. Officer Chaffin stood at the foot of the plane and motioned for the passengers to come closer. Clutching their belongings they stepped forward. Except for the shuffling of their feet, they were mostly silent. They stared at the ship in awe. It was an impressive piece of machinery. They'd only ever seen one from afar. For the first time in their lives, they found themselves standing in the colossal shadow of a Douglas DC-3 skyplane.

Registration: NC-36480
Route: Oakland Municipal Airport to Imperial County Airport in El Centro, California
Role/Function: Nonscheduled carrier transporting Mexican passengers
Contracted by: United States Immigration and Naturalization Service
Owned and operated by: Airline Transport Carriers Inc.
Manufacturer: Douglas Aircraft Corporation
Power: (2) 1,200 horsepower Pratt & Whitney, R–1830–90 radial engines
Engine operation: (Left) 836 total hours, (Right) 309 total hours
Maximum Legal Capacity: 3 cabin crew and 26 passengers (29 total)
Passengers officially reported: 3 cabin crew and 29 passengers (32 total)
Weight: Aircraft 67 pounds in excess of maximum allowable
Routine Maintenance: Overdue 9 hrs. 44 mins. beyond 100 hr. period at time of takeoff

29

JOSÉ SÁNCHEZ VALDIVIA GETS CAUGHT

Stockton, California
March 30, 2014

Eliseo Sánchez González lifted his baseball cap and scratched his hair. The rain was coming down hard now, and it pattered against the swamp cooler that protruded from the living room window. He folded his hands over his stomach and thought for a moment. "Yes," he finally said, responding to my question. "I do remember how they got caught. I remember that well. José Valdivia's father, el señor Mateo, he was pretty upset about it, I remember. His son, José Valdivia, was with my brother, José. They'd been at the billiards all afternoon. This was something they liked to do whenever they had time off. They were always competing at one thing or another. Well, as I recall, after they had been at the billiards all day, my brother José told Valdivia, 'Let's go, it's getting late.' But Valdivia wanted to stay a little bit longer. He wasn't ready to leave. I guess he was winning some money or something, playing some guys there. He was always winning guys at pool. He was just a good athlete, no matter what he played. So my brother came back to the camp that night and left Valdivia there. He left him there with his primo, I believe. A cousin named Amado. That was the last time my brother, or any of us, ever saw José Valdivia—"

When baseball season was over, José Valdivia was always left with an empty feeling in his gut. He yearned for competition. "If it were up to me," he often said to González, "I'd prefer going to sleep for eight months and waking up just when spring was rolling around again."

To quell their boredom they took to hanging out at Shorty's Pool Hall on Church Street. There, they'd order rounds of beer, and after a few warm-up shots, they'd gamble their earnings with just about anyone who was willing. It was their only distraction.

Despite Mateo's disapproval of his son's penchant for throwing money away, Valdivia took his chances. "Be smart, José. It's going to be a thin season," Mateo warned. What else could he do? The boy now towered over him, and in every aspect of his life he conducted himself as a man. Valdivia shrugged off his father's concern and, with his cousin Amado and his best friend González, set out for the pool hall.

What Mateo failed to tell his son was that he'd heard rumors. The need for Mexican workers was no longer critical now that the war was over.

"Work now," a few enganchados had warned. "And work fast. It's only a matter of time."

It could be said that what happened next was predetermined by "la mano poderosa de Dios" and rooted in José's passion for America's favorite pastime. Of course, José Sánchez Valdivia himself would have never suggested as much. Anything that threatened to tarnish the image of the sport he loved was a threat to him personally. If he could've died with a baseball bat slung over his shoulder and his white cap with the embroidered letter *S* cocked slightly on his head, he would've considered it an honor of the highest order.

When they arrived at Shorty's Pool Hall that afternoon it was not yet one o'clock. Valdivia bought the men a round of beer and proceeded to rack the balls. He pulled a cue stick from the wall and challenged his cousin Amado to a game.

"No, thank you," Amado replied. "I'll have my beer while you men throw your money away."

González accepted the challenge.

And so it went.

Over the next couple of hours, the two Josés sank ball after ball, trading wins and losses, one always outdoing the other. Amado sat back and poked fun at the men while he drank his beer. Time passed, and by three o'clock the crowd at Shorty's had thickened. A few men were standing nearby, eyeing the pool table.

"Valdivia," González said, nodding toward the men, "care to go the first round, or should I?"

"I'll play," Valdivia said, waving the men over.

A gaunt white man stepped forward, and within minutes became the first to reluctantly hand his money over to Valdivia. Just as quickly, another man came and went. It was that fast. So efficient were Valdivia's shots that no game lasted more than a few minutes. It was all in fun, at first. More men gathered to watch. Others would step up only to walk off, mumbling under their breath. A tension began mounting. To quell the fires, González would step up and defeat his friend, and this would ease the men off long enough to take a piss break, grab another beer, and replenish their pride.

By six o'clock Amado had stopped drinking. He urged his cousin to do the same. "We have to be up with the roosters," Amado reminded him.

"Don't be such a viejo," Valdivia chided. "You of all people, Amado, so young and already tired. Have another!"

Amado shook his head.

It was now dark out, and after noticing a group of gringos staring at them, González got an unsettled feeling in his stomach and decided to call it quits.

"What do you say we head back to the campo? I don't think my pockets can fit any more money," he joked with Amado and Valdivia. The men laughed.

"I think I have room for a few more," Valdivia said, swilling his beer. Amado yawned. "Maybe you should take this old man back to the campo with you," Valdivia added, "before he falls asleep right here in the pool hall."

Amado ignored his cousin's remark.

"Primo," Valdivia said, "you'll get all the sleep you need when you're dead." Amado shrugged. "You two go ahead. I think I'm going to stick around a little longer." Valdivia eyed a woman who was standing alone at the bar.

"I'm heading back," González said. "The only thing I hate worse than getting up at four in the morning is getting up at four with a hangover."

Valdivia again eyed the woman. He polished off his beer. "Well, compadre, you handle your business and I'll handle mine." He began making his way over to the bar.

Amado sat quietly. He watched his cousin approach the woman.

"And you?" González asked Amado.

Amado looked up from his seat. "Go on ahead," he said. "I better make sure he gets back to the campo or my uncle Mateo will let me have it."

"Good enough," said González. "See you boys at the campo." And with that, González made his way out of the pool hall and into the warm valley night.

It would be another two hours before Amado could convince his cousin José that it was time to leave. "The last bus rolls through at nine o'clock," he said.

Valdivia raised his glassy eyes at Amado. "Fine. All right then," He slurred. He turned to wave good-bye to the woman, but she was already being wooed by another man. Valdivia sneered.

Together, the two stumbled out into the dimly lit streets of downtown Stockton. They walked a few blocks up Church Street, yapping about the great time they'd had. Amado could see that his cousin's green eyes were now red and glassy. He wondered what he would tell his uncle Mateo, who was by now expecting them. They turned a corner and made their way to the bus stop, where they sat down on a bench and waited. It was a clear night and the Big Dipper hovered overhead brightly. José attempted to whistle a song. Amado sat staring up at the stars. He wondered if González had made it back okay, whether he too had taken a bus, or if he had decided to walk the several miles back to the campo. At that moment, Amado spotted the bus approaching.

He helped his cousin to his feet. "Don't be foolish, José. Your dad will be waiting for us when we get back."

"I'm fine," José mumbled, his body swaying.

The bus pulled to the curb and the men climbed aboard. Though all the seats were empty, José followed Amado to the last row. The door slammed shut and the bus lunged forward. José propped his head against the window and shut his eyes, while Amado leaned back in his seat, folded his arms, and rested. Once again, he thought about the excuse he'd give his uncle.

Not a minute had passed when the driver hit the brakes and the bus jerked to a standstill. Amado opened his eyes. He watched as two immigration officers came aboard. He shook his cousin awake. José was slow to respond.

"What's the problem?" he mumbled.

"La migra," Amado whispered.

José opened his eyes and sat up. He watched the two officers address the bus driver. They turned their gaze to the back of the bus. The tips of their fingers tickled their holsters as they began walking toward the men. Amado looked at his cousin and then out the window. In that moment, José Sánchez Valdivia knew there was nowhere to run.

30

PREPARE THE CABIN

8:40 a.m.

Captain Frank Atkinson and copilot Marion Ewing took their seats in the cockpit. Atkinson removed the gear pins, and began going down the checklist: parking brake, door hatches, control locks, and a few other matters were checked. He fired up the engines. Ewing got busy with his duties, testing the oil and hydraulic pressure, the radio, smoke detectors, and transponders.

Atkinson looked back at his wife, Bobbie, as she hung up her coat in the narrow closet behind his seat. He handed her a small card with instructions for preparing the passengers: secure seat belts, place the loose items beneath seats, check cabin temperature.

Minutes later, Chaffin entered the ship. A tall man, he ducked in through the door hatch and claimed a seat nearby. He didn't actually sit down; rather, he stood watch over the operation. Though he was generally a pleasant man, Chaffin was sour about being assigned an aerial transport, and he wore the discontent on his face. At age sixty-three, he felt his seniority alone should've afforded him an option. "Leave these tasks to the young fellas," he griped to his wife, Mary, earlier that morning.

"You'll be retired soon enough, Frank; just hang in there."

"That's exactly my point," he said.

"Well, no use in rocking the boat now, darling."

He thought about Mary's words as he stood inside the ship, arms crossed, counting each passenger as they boarded.

Before lifting a foot onto the ladder the passengers said their name aloud and were checked off a list, and then they made their way into the ship's cabin. María was the only woman, so she was the first to board. Her husband, Lupe, followed closely behind. Chaffin pointed them to their seats. The tail of the ship slanted downward at a forty-five-degree angle, and María lost her balance, nearly falling back. "Oh, dear," Bobbie said, offering her a hand. The two women chuckled. María and Lupe took their seats in the second row, near the front of the cabin. Luis Miranda Cuevas was next. He sat in a window seat on the right side of the plane, opposite María and Lupe. After him, José Sánchez Valdivia climbed aboard. He took a seat directly above the left wing, where he had a perfect view of the propeller. He sat down and took off his baseball cap and placed it on his lap. Behind him, the kid, Tomás Márquez Padilla, walked up the aisle and plopped himself down in the seat next to Luis. As they filed in, each passenger was greeted by Chaffin. Ramón and Guadalupe were the last to board.

Several pieces of luggage didn't fit in the compartment and had to be piled in the aisle, toward the rear. The Civil Aeronautics Board accident investigation report would confirm: *Three pieces of unsecured luggage were in the aisle at the time of take-off, and it is probable that three passengers were seated on this luggage.*

Ramón and Guadalupe were instructed by Officer Chaffin to sit on the luggage. The men didn't complain. They made themselves cozy. They'd been in worse situations after all. In the bed of trucks hauling down long dark highways in freezing winters, making do with potato sacks or sodden tarps. One time, while still young men, they rode horses through one of the fiercest storms that Guanajuato had ever known. Back home, their resilience was the stuff of lore. To sit in an airplane atop mounds of luggage, no wind or hard slashes of rain whipping your face raw, Guadalupe might've called it a luxury.

When the passengers were finally accounted for, Bobbie checked to make sure they were buckled properly. At the rear, she yanked the door shut and bolted it, exactly as Frankie had instructed her. She walked back up the aisle and took her spot behind the cockpit, in the crew seat. She buckled herself and called out to Frankie, "All clear back here." Because her seat was facing the tail of the ship, she glanced down the length of the cabin and saw endless rows of brown faces staring back at her. Their expressions held a seriousness. Bobbie could feel her stomach turn. A nausea crept in. She couldn't help but recall the newspaper articles she'd read just a few weeks ago. Had she listened to Frankie and avoided them, perhaps she'd be feeling at ease right now. It was a "puddle jump" after all. She noticed the passengers' eyes all aimed at her. She forced a smile. It was all she could do to ignore the trembling in her chest. In the far back, seated near the lavatory, was Officer Chaffin. She watched him remove his hat and place it on his lap. There was a quiet intensity about him. He fixed his eyes out the window. The cabin fell silent.

31

PERHAPS SYNCHRONICITY

Four weeks earlier . . .

It seemed like everyone in the airplane business was talking about it. Especially if the plane you were flying happened to be manufactured by the Douglas Aircraft Company. It was unprecedented, the recall of every single Douglas DC-6 airplane that had ever been built. In the past three months two had crashed. On October 25, 1947, the *Los Angeles Times* reported that a plane came down in Bryce Canyon, Utah, killing all fifty-two passengers aboard. The story haunted Bobbie. Regardless of how many times Frankie urged her not to read the papers, she couldn't help herself. As Bobbie read the long list of names and the accompanying stories of the Utah passengers, she discovered that one of the pilots was from Balboa, just a stone's throw away from her own front porch. As if that weren't enough to put a hole in her stomach, one month later another Douglas DC-6 caught fire and crash-landed in Gallup, New Mexico.

All this talk of plane crashes made her nervous. Her only consolation was that Frankie would be retiring on February 2, just a few weeks away.

While discussing the matter with friends one afternoon, Bobbie made a curious comment. It was the kind of comment that, in the moment, came across as natural as any. Had Bobbie known it would go on to become the most prophetic utterance of her life, she may have thought twice before saying it.

"If something were to ever happen to Frankie, I'd wanna be with him." Those were her exact words. "I'd wanna be with him."

It was one of those rare instances where, in the quiet hours before sunrise, the synchronicity would begin to unfold with a single phone call—

4:22 a.m.

The call comes in eight minutes before Frankie's alarm is set to go off. He picks up the receiver, half-asleep. "Hello, Frank here." Bobbie's eyes are shut, but she can hear a woman's muffled voice on the other end. Frankie responds. "Yes, I see." He hangs up.

"Who was that, hon?"

"The stewardess is a no-show," he replies, rolling out of bed.

He goes to wash his face. Silence follows. Bobbie is curious.

"What happens now?"

"Gotta call ATC and find out," Frankie replies, with toothpaste in his mouth.

More silence.

He slides into his pants and buttons up his uniform shirt. Bobbie crawls out of bed and finds her robe. "I'm gonna put a pot of coffee on."

Frankie picks up the phone receiver and dials a number. Bobbie leaves the room. By the time she returns he's already off the phone.

"They're getting on the line with another woman. Maybe she can fill in," he says. Bobbie nods and hands him his coffee.

Seconds later the phone rings again. This time he's on the call no more than a minute before he hangs up.

Helen: "The way we heard it was the two stewardesses who were employed by the company couldn't make it that day. One had a wedding to be at, or something or other, and the other was badly hungover from a party the night before. They had both called in that day. Of course, the airline company needed a stewardess, so they asked Frankie if his wife would be willing to go along, and you know, they'd pay her and such, and so that's how Bobbie ended up going—"

Frankie approaches Bobbie and kisses her cheek tenderly.

"Honey," he says, "neither of them ladies can make it today. We need a stewardess though. Regulations, I guess. They asked me if I thought, well, maybe, you wouldn't mind coming along?" He hesitates. "They'd pay, of course."

Bobbie considers it. "Honey—" she begins to say, uncertain.

"We'd be together, hon," he assures her. "Least this way I won't spend half the day away from you. We'll be home by supper."

"Where to?"

"From Burbank we fly to Oakland, pick up some folks, then fly them over to San Diego. After that, it's right back to Burbank."

Bobbie is hesitant.

"What do you say, hon? Besides, you don't have to do much, just greet the folks as they board, make sure they're comfortable. We'll handle the rest."

She stares into Frankie's face and ponders it another second.

"Whaddya say? Besides, we could sure use the extra money." He glances at her stomach. Bobbie peers into his blue eyes.

"They need to know right now though, hon. Can I tell them you're on board?"

And this is how the early morning of January 28, 1948, begins for Frankie and Bobbie Atkinson.

Moments later, they find themselves heading out the front door of their home at 1242 Raymond Avenue in Long Beach. Walking to the car, Bobbie touches her stomach affectionately and remembers something Dr. Stern said, about the test results and the details of what she could expect over the next several months. Frankie notices the worry on her face and takes her hand. Since her last checkup, her mind's been playing scenarios of what life will be like come fall. Frankie'll make a good father, she's sure of it. He's a perfect combination of sensitivity and strength. Tender when the moment calls for it, but stoic just the same. He sees the crease between her eyes.

"It's only a puddle jump, hon."

She trusts him.

"Think I'll make a good mother, Frankie?"

"Of course you will."

She can't help but think of her own mother, Elizabeth. It's been nearly two months since they last spoke. She can't bear to think of her withering in that dismal house in Rochester, alone. "Maybe after this we can see about getting my mother out here to visit?"

"Sounds like a swell idea," Frankie says, opening the car door for her.

On their way to the Lockheed Air Terminal in Burbank, the two are mostly quiet. It's still early. The sun has yet to rise. While in the passenger's seat she ponders how her family will react to the news of her pregnancy.

"You didn't tell anyone, did you, honey?"

Frankie puts his hand on her lap. "Course not."

"I just want it to be a surprise is all."

"No tellin' how long we can hold 'em off, but I'm with you on that."

She fiddles with the opal stone on her wedding ring. "You think your folks have a clue?"

"We told 'em two more weeks before we'd even find out, didn't we?"

"Parents have a scary way of knowing things."

Frankie thinks about Rochester right then, in a way he hadn't in a long time. He remembers Bobbie as a teenager, her short golden curls, the innocence in her eyes. He thinks about what it means to be a father and how far they've both come. All those years away, off to war. How Bobbie waited, stuck around for him, even when he wasn't sure if he'd ever return. She was the real deal—the war revealed that. One thing was certain, the day Dottie Anderson decided to break it off was probably the luckiest day of his life. He grips Bobbie's hand tight and thinks about what he might get her for their first anniversary, just on the horizon. It has to be something special. Maybe he'll buy her mother Elizabeth a train ticket to California. Yes, he thinks to himself. Perfect.

When they arrive in Burbank, all Frankie has to do is nod at the security guard and he's allowed to pass. Bobbie's proud of her husband. She runs her hand over her stomach again as Frankie pulls toward the main gate.

On the tarmac, Bobbie stares up at the belly of the airplane. Frankie can see she's still nervous. "Nothing to worry about, hon. Each week these babies make forty-eight trips from San Francisco to San Diego. No ship I'd rather be in than the Gooneybird. Trust me." He cocks his pilot's cap back on his head and slaps the left flank of the ship, then climbs aboard. He looks back at his beautiful wife, the morning wind blowing her yellow hair into a mess.

"You comin'?"

Bobbie's hesitant. She smooths the lapel on her blue dinner coat and then notices the strap of her red high heel has come undone. She bends down and fastens it. She glances up the short ladder that leads into the ship and begins to board. Before she enters, she stands for a moment and looks out over the tarmac. A light breeze pushes against her face and this calms her.

32

THE TAKEOFF

9:15 a.m.

Bobbie could hear Frankie calling out instructions to copilot Ewing. "Raise the RPM." The propellers hummed. Passengers could feel the vibration in their bodies. None had ever experienced such a thing. The noise was worrisome. María's hands grew clammy. She grasped Lupe's forearm.

"Don't worry, mi amor," he said. "We'll be fine." María didn't reply. She stared at the curtains. They were a thick material. Dirty yellow with diamond embroidery and ruffles. She pulled them slightly back and looked out the window. She began to think of home.

Officer Chaffin had a stone look on his face. He thought about how much he hated flying. He pondered his approaching retirement. That, and the image of his wife, Mary. He remembered what she had said to him that morning, just as he was headed out the front door. Standing on the other side of the rose garden, she recognized the tired look on her husband's face and said, "Last rodeo, cowboy." He smiled at the thought of her round cheeks and blue eyes, standing beside the roses in those predawn hours. It settled him. The thought of home.

Every last window curtain was pushed aside now, and all eyes were fixed on the long tarmac. They couldn't ignore how much the plane rumbled. Bobbie kept a smile on her face. It was a frail smile. But perhaps if she smiled, this would put everyone at ease. And perhaps their ease would bring on her own. The cockpit curtain was drawn back, and those who had aisle seats could see the right hand of Captain Atkinson and the left hand of copilot Ewing working the instrument panel, flicking switches and valves.

In the cockpit of a Douglas DC-3, there are six small rectangular windows to look out of. Between the pilots sits a large black comm radio, used to communicate with the tower. From their seats, both men could still see the outline of the moon hanging in the morning sky. A waning gibbous, it was gone one second and there the next. Of course, the only thing Captain Atkinson cared about was that it meant clear skies.

"Hydraulic gauges?" Atkinson called out.

"Affirm," Ewing replied.

"Flaps and controls?"

"Affirm."

"Boost pumps?"

"Affirm."

Bobbie could hear Frankie's loud voice coming from the cockpit.

"Temps and pressures?"

"Affirm," Ewing hollered back.

"Cowls?"

"Affirm."

Captain Atkinson called for Bobbie to close the cockpit curtain. She did as requested, then sat back down and buckled in. She looked up at the passengers once more and could feel the tension.

"It'll be a few hours before you're all home," she said, timidly. She felt silly then, realizing it was likely only a few passengers spoke English. From the back, Officer Chaffin translated, "En pocos horas estarán todos en Mexico con sus familias."

María leaned her head on Lupe's shoulder and tightened her grip on his hand. The engines revved. The passengers gazed out the window and watched as the tarmac moved past. The ship began to pick up speed, but then, suddenly, slowed to a halt.

Captain Atkinson poked his head out from the cockpit and mumbled a few words to Bobbie. She turned to face the passengers.

"We're about to take flight now." It was all the officialness she could muster.

With one word, Chaffin translated: "Prepárense."

Control Tower radioed, "Douglas N-36480 clear for takeoff, runway 2-6. Over."

"Roger," Atkinson replied.

A second before the plane lunged forward, control tower radioed the cockpit one last time.

The Civil Aeronautics Board accident investigation report would record, *Before leaving the Oakland tower frequency, Captain Atkinson received a message from his company, relayed through the tower, that he was to return directly to Burbank. His acknowledgement of this message was the last communication received from the flight. Takeoff was accomplished at approximately 9:30 am.*

9:30 a.m.

The ship gained speed. This time it shook and grew louder with each flashing second. Ramón and Guadalupe braced themselves against each other and gripped whatever they could find. María turned her gaze away from the window. The tarmac and distant trees blurred past. The ship trembled.

Ewing eyed the manifold pressure, while Atkinson brought the power up on both the right and left throttle gracefully. The engine's buzz grew louder. Ewing placed his left hand on the throttle to help Atkinson fine-tune the power. The ship was in full stride now. Ewing called out, "V-1!"

At that moment the front end of the ship tilted skyward, and the passengers gripped their armrests. They could feel the hand of gravity pressing their spines against their seatbacks. Luis Miranda couldn't help himself. He looked out the window and could see the ground fall away quickly. He pointed it out to Tomás. Seconds later a loud bang came from beneath the floorboard and startled everyone. At 9:31 a.m. the landing gear of the Douglas DC-3 retracted into the wheel well, and the ship was airborne. A gust of coastal wind blew in right then, and the plane shifted right to left, dipping its wings alternately, working to gain its balance. The engines were throttled back and adjusted for the climb. Those who sat starboard were staring down at the peninsula, surrounded by the vast shimmering of the east bay. They could see the barges, now the size of matchboxes, and the people on the streets became insects scuttling. Higher still, the tops of buildings blended in with the gray concrete of Oakland. Roads became intricate patterns, and trees were blotches of green. Luis pressed his forehead against the window. A second later he leaned back so that the kid, Tomás, could have a look. They glared nervously at the strange magic of it all. For those who sat portside, the view from their window was a blast of light. José Sánchez Valdivia stared at the tip of the left wing, which was now pointing slightly downward. He placed his baseball cap on his head and pushed his hair aside to get a good view of it. María peered out the window and this time saw that the whole planet was tilted sideways. She felt her stomach float. She looked forward, directly at Bobbie. The engines revved and the cabin shook for a few more seconds before, finally, easing off.

9:33 a.m.

In those first few minutes of flight, they couldn't tear their eyes away from what they were witnessing. To see los Estados Unidos from this angle, on the shoulders of California, the footstool of el Norte, was like staring at the anatomy of all their wins and losses. Mountains rolled infinitely into the distance. Patches of land—green, then brown, greener still—appeared quiltlike across the horizon. Soon, an immense canopy of foliage swallowed up the man-made structures entirely. And then there was the shimmering mirror of the ocean reflecting back the sky. Who knew that clouds, when viewed from this high, resembled a vast rolling field of cotton? How could one have guessed that from this far off the ground you could see where the end of the horizon begins to curve back toward itself as if all of life was consumed by a giant circle? Proof that the earth really is, as José Alfredo Jiménez sings, "Un mundo raro!" They might as well have been orbiting space, it was so far from anything they could've imagined. One thing was made clear. From way up here, it was undeniable, Mother Earth was the ruler of all.

The sun glinted off the wing and poked at their eyes. For María, who had always considered herself a practical woman, the whole thing was too surreal. No one had warned her that the miracle of flight was accompanied by a blunt stabbing in the gut. Yes, she preferred el avión over the "wretched trains," but still, the idea that the only thing keeping them aloft, thousands of feet in the air, practically at God's toes, was a thin invention called aluminum was beyond comprehension. Beyond miracle, even. She wondered if it wasn't downright ungodly. Every time the plane shifted in one direction or another, she could feel the blood rush to the soles of her feet and go racing to the tips of her fingers. Her only distraction was prayer. And the thought of home.

A mass of white mist sprayed their windows and they could see nothing. Clouds had swallowed them up and spat them out the other side. Pockets of air made the wings dance. Off and on the plane would tremble, and then release, and then tremble again. It went on like this for several minutes, until the Gooneybird cruised at nine thousand feet.

When the turbulence subsided, Captain Atkinson set the power and then peeled open the curtains again and called for Bobbie. She unbuckled herself and stuck her head in the cockpit. She turned and gazed back at the passengers. She was instructed to say something. Something pleasant. She wasn't sure what.

"Sure is pretty isn't it?" she muttered in María's direction.

María was expressionless. She knew Bobbie was making small talk. She figured it wasn't important because Officer Chaffin didn't bother to translate.

Luis leaned his head back and conjured the image of Casimira.

Ramón and Guadalupe made themselves cozy atop the luggage and braced themselves against each other. They folded their arms and tried falling asleep like that. By the time they awoke they would be a few miles away from their beloved Mexico.

9:47 a.m.

For a short period of time there was silence. Except for the drone of the propellers, no one spoke. Luis had thought to strike up a conversation with Tomás, but the kid now seemed to be half-asleep. What he didn't know was that Tomás was wide awake. He kept his eyes intentionally closed as a way of avoiding conversation. Of all the passengers, he was likely the most reluctant to be returning home.

The reason Tomás had left San Julian, Jalisco, in the first place was not something he cared to discuss with anyone. In fact, he was explicitly ordered not to by his family. If it were up to him, he wouldn't be returning to San Julian, or any part of Mexico for that matter. He'd begun strategizing a way to get back to los Estados the first chance he got. He was sure that if his eyes were open, someone, maybe Luis, would consider this an invitation to pry. For this reason, he kept them closed and tried his best to remain invisible.

Bobbie glanced across the heads of the passengers and could see Chaffin in the far back. He was staring at the passenger next to him. Chaffin leaned over and struck up a conversation.

"What's your name?" he asked the man.

Juan could hardly hear him over the airplane's engines. Chaffin leaned in closer.

"Como te llamas?"

"Juan Ruiz Valenzuela," Juan replied.

Officer Chaffin thought Juan looked familiar. Juan sat motionless. He put up a shallow smile. In Spanish, Chaffin asked him, "Have you ever been on a plane before?" Juan shook his head no. Chaffin asked him if he had family waiting for him back home. Juan nodded. Chaffin looked down at Juan's boots. They were caked with dried mud. He glanced past him and could see his brother, Wenceslao, who was sleeping with his head against the window. The two men looked like boys to him. There was a simple, tired sag about their faces. Chaffin couldn't help himself. He stared at Juan's clothing. Patches were sewn onto the knees of his pants. His red flannel shirt, two sizes too large. The skin on Juan's face, as young as he appeared, was leathery and sun-worn. In that moment, even while confined to the most intimate of spaces, Officer Chaffin felt a world away from Juan Ruiz Valenzuela.

33

A GENEALOGICAL BREAKDOWN OF THE CHAFFIN NAME

What Officer Chaffin didn't know in that moment was that he had more in common with passenger Juan Ruiz Valenzuela than he could've ever guessed.

There were many instances in which he'd been told stories of his family's history, but the truth of the matter was, it was always in passing. The telling of family lore took idled time, which was a rare thing to come by, and it usually only happened at weddings or funerals. Of course, had Chaffin engaged in those conversations, as his wife Mary had urged him, he might've recalled, somewhere in the fuzzy recesses of his memory, that his very own bloodline contained a similar Juan, one who also knew a thing or two about passages. In the vast blue of Chaffin's own eyes the records of an epic migration story had been kept, even without his remembering.

It was the year 1620, and times were tumultuous in the old country. A young man by the name of John Howland was desperate to leave his quaint village of Huntingdonshire, England. He'd heard rumors that in a matter of days a ship would be departing for the New World. An impoverished farmhand from the sticks, young John offered himself as an indentured servant in exchange for a seat on what would become the mother of all ships, the Mayflower. Because of his good looks and mild charisma, he was pigeonholed as a "lusty young man." Needless to say, he was guarded closely. But John would prove himself resilient. Days into the transport, he was flung into the boiling sea amid a hellish storm, and by some miracle of God he managed the impossible. He endured the jagged waves and clung to the topsail halyards, which dangled off the side of the ship. Battered by the sea, he held on long enough to be rescued. No one in the history of migrations had ever survived such a thing. It was the telling of this story that would seal his legacy.

In the years following his arrival to the New World, young John sought to become a freeman, and so he labored manually every chance he got. But in the earliest of days, life was dismal for the newcomers. Howland and his fellow pilgrims found themselves dying of starvation. He seized the opportunity to prove his worth. He sought help from the indigenous peoples, who agreed to teach him how to plant his own crops. With both hands entrenched in New World soil, by plow and spade, by seed and harvest, season after season, young John soon proved himself a vital contributor. It was enough to secure his dream of becoming a freeman. Geography aside, John Howland was the Juan Ruiz Valenzuela of his time.

At that very moment, while Officer Chaffin sat staring down at Juan's muddy boots, little did he know that, in the very eyes through which he had the privilege of looking, the evidence of the Howland DNA had long since been filed away. The name CHAFFIN that was carved onto the shiny brass nameplate he proudly pinned to his uniform each morning was only the latest incarnation.

In his later years, the pilgrim John Howland had a daughter whom he named Hope—a reflection of his optimism. She would go on to marry a Chipman. The name Chipman would remain until the birth of Howland's first grandson. For reasons unknown, the child's name would go down in the books as Chaffin. This would remain the family name seven generations later.

Officer Chaffin looked at his watch. They'd been airborne now for almost an hour. A few passengers were whispering. Bobbie fiddled with the strap on her high heel. Others were still sleeping, or else hypnotized by the view. The nervous look on their faces was no more.

34

CRUISING ALTITUDE

10:27 a.m.

No longer could the glittering Pacific Ocean be seen. They were farther inland now, crossing over the western rim of the Diablo Range. Somewhere in the approaching distance, the town of San Juan Bautista was southwest, while the expanse of California's great Central Valley was eastward. Everyone was quiet. Calm.

10:32 a.m.

The body of the plane gently tilted, angling left, in the direction of the morning sun, which was now in full view. The cabin temperature was slowly rising. Bobbie fanned herself with her handkerchief. Chaffin loosened his tie. Moments before someone had used the lavatory, and the warmth kept the smell lingering. Ramón and Guadalupe had it the worst, since they were seated near the rear of the plane. Earlier, they'd buried themselves amid the luggage and struck up a conversation. They too were now quiet.

10:35 a.m.

Ramón sat up to look out the window. It was nothing but a wrinkle of brown hills below. He didn't know he was staring down at the foothills of

San Juan Bautista, where he and Guadalupe had been rounded up just days before. He thought they resembled the mountains of El País de las Siete Luminarias. Somewhere, he was certain, beyond that infinite horizon, Elisa and the children were anxiously awaiting his return. He wondered how the ejido was doing. It was easy to get lost in the idea of home. He whispered a few lines from his favorite song: "Dicen que por tus amores / un mal me van a seguir / no le hace que sean el diablo / yo tambien me se morir . . . Valentina, Valentina . . ." Before he could sing another word, he quieted. He couldn't ignore the overwhelming sense of failure that had set in since being caught. Once again, the irrigation well would be put on hold. He nudged Guadalupe. Guadalupe angled his face toward his compadre. The two men stared at each other, but said nothing.

35

ILUSIONES

Celio Sánchez Valdivia: "Here is all I know. Amado was a cousin of ours. He had been caught by la migra with José, and it was Amado who was supposed to have been on that airplane, not my brother. Amado didn't like airplanes. José didn't mind—to him it was all the same. I'm not sure how they did it, but as I was told, somehow José traded his spot on the bus with our cousin Amado. I was too young to really get to know my brother, but from what I remember of him, and what people say, is that José was like that, a very generous man. So then, Amado got to return to Mexico by bus, and José ended up going by airplane. And that's why José was on that plane. Had he not been so generous . . . well, maybe things would be different—"

10:37 a.m.

José Sánchez Valdivia pulled his baseball cap down over his eyes. He was deep in thought. Had he left with his best friend González that night at the billiards, none of this would've happened. Perhaps his father, Mateo, was right. "Ilusiones." He could hear the old man's scorn. He thought of his cousin Amado too. Amado, as weak-stomached as he was, preferred the bus. José agreed to trade with him only because it meant the sooner he was in Mexico, the sooner he'd return to Stockton. Still, he couldn't shake the miserable idea of having to start all over again. It wasn't so much the work but baseball. The season would start without him. And aside from letting his team down, his father and his brother Ramón would have to make do without him. They'd been earning good money too, the three of them working together. Mateo was furious. He couldn't speak to José, except to send him home with two messages. One for his wife, Dolores: "Tell your mother things are good here, and that we're healthy." The other message was for Celio, José's youngest brother: "Tell Celio that when you return to Stockton, he is to come back with you."

José thought of his little brother Celio right then. Wondered how big he'd gotten since the last time they were together. Little Celio who chased after him through the cornfields of La Estancia. Little Celio with the muddy feet and runny nose. He'd forgotten the sound of his brother's voice. The thought of Celio put a light feeling in his chest. Perhaps returning to La Estancia this time of year was a good omen. By now, he guessed, all of Nochistlán was celebrating la fiesta de el Papaqui. Surely, statues of El Güerito San Sebastián were being hoisted all over town, and the earthy scent of pinole was in the air. He could almost see the confetti being tossed and hear the fireworks and gun blasts whistling and exploding in the night sky.

The plane shook.

José thought the noise he heard was in his head. Bobbie and Officer Chaffin glanced at each other. María pushed the curtain aside for a look. White mist covered the windows of the ship. There was a subtle odor. It was the stink of burnt rubber. "Smell that?" Luis asked Tomás. The sun poked through the windows. "Yes," the kid replied. The ship cruised over the western ridge of the Diablo Range and sailed over the Hernandez Valley.

"Frankie?" Bobbie called out.

"Sit tight, hon—"

"What was that?"

Captain Atkinson didn't answer his wife at that moment. The passengers sat upright and peered out windows. "Stay put, please," Bobbie ordered.

Captain Atkinson paid close attention to the feel of the control yoke in all ten fingers. With both ears, and the ear deep inside his solar plexus, he listened to the hum of the engines closely. A sound as familiar as the whispering of his own breath. There was a slight skipping. A tug so subtle that only someone of his instinct would notice. He glanced at the small fire warning light, waiting to see if it would come on. A second passed and nothing. The smell grew stronger. There it was. The warning light. It flashed. A bolt of adrenaline shot through Atkinson's extremities, but he remained calm. It wasn't the first time he'd seen that light go off.

During the war, he was assigned to transport a cargo load of fine china to the U.S. base in India. At seventeen thousand feet, the right engine of the

Gooneybird had cut out. Atkinson flew the ship on a single prop, guiding it back to base for a near-perfect landing. But landing the plane on a single propeller wasn't what furthered his reputation. It was the discovery that, of the entire cargo load of fine china, not a single dish had been broken.

Atkinson barked at Ewing. "Left engine's out. Run single-engine emergency checklist." His tone was hurried but sure. Ewing didn't hesitate. He, too, remembered flight training. The instructor's exact words: "The tires on the C-47 are immensities. If they catch fire, you can tuck your head between your legs and kiss yer ass good-bye. When an engine catches fire, landing gear's the first thing down."

The passengers heard a grinding sound beneath the floorboard as the tires of the DC-3 unfastened from the wheel well.

"Firewall shutoff closed!" Atkinson ordered.

Bobbie could hear the urgency in Frankie's voice. She wanted to call to him.

Atkinson glanced up at the large red button labeled number 1. He slammed his hand down on it and feathered the left prop to eliminate drag. Between sheets of white smoke, José Sánchez Valdivia saw the propeller on the left wing slow to a standstill. María witnessed it too. "It stopped spinning," she said to Lupe. She pointed out her window.

"Fuel, oil, all down?" Atkinson's voice blared.

"Affirm," Ewing hollered.

Atkinson's eyes darted across the jagged hills of Los Gatos Canyon. He could see the valley floor, the small buildings, and what looked to be oil derricks. It was the town of Coalinga approaching on the horizon. It was too far off. He searched for a strip of land, a clearing, any clearing would do. Seconds ago they'd crossed over the Hernandez Valley reservoir, but it was too late to turn back.

"There," he pointed.

"Where?" Ewing asked.

He pointed to a thread of road below. Ewing wondered if Atkinson had lost his mind.

The ship bucked and arms flung to the ceiling.

"Son of a bitch!" spat Chaffin.

Smoke filled the cabin. The stink of fuel. Bobbie pressed her hand to her mouth to catch a burp of vomit. Luis gripped the armrests, but the plane bucked again, and again arms vaulted. He cursed, repeatedly.

Chaffin ordered everyone to calm down.

Through a window Ramón could see mountains approaching. They were close. Too close. Luis and Tomás noticed them too. José noticed them. Everyone noticed them.

One hour and thirty-five minutes after takeoff the aircraft was observed over the vicinity of Coalinga, California, cruising at an estimated altitude of 5,000 feet above the ground. At this time a trail of white vapor or smoke 150 to 200 feet long was observed streaming from the left engine of the aircraft.

The cabin was dense, breathing impossible. From where José Sánchez Valdivia sat, he had full view of the left engine. He spotted flames licking the propeller.

"Fire!" he cried.

"Frankie!" Bobbie could hear him barking orders at Ewing. His voice was distant. "Frankie!" she screeched. Her words felt as if they came from a mouth not her own.

María gripped Lupe's hand. She turned once more to face the window. She wished she hadn't. A flame spat at her. A red flash. Then black. María's eyes met Lupe's.

Flames were seen flowing from the left engine over the wing . . . a dull explosion was heard, and the left wing and left engine dropped free from the rest of the aircraft—

José

Bobbie

Sánchez

Valdivia

Atkinson

Luis

Miranda

Tomás

Cuevas

Frank

Márquez

Padilla

María

Lupe

Hernández

Santana

Rodríguez

Chaffin

Martín Razo

Navarro

Ramón

Paredes

González

Guadalupe

Ramírez

Lara

When Luis Miranda Cuevas watched his left leg tear away from his body, more than likely he was unable to comprehend it was *his* left leg. His mouth was agape and gasping for air, while his eyes snapped photos methodically as he tumbled in a freefall. Even the sky wasn't real. Maybe it appeared like a still puddle of water, or the warm surface of Lake Chapala, where as a child he spent his days fishing beneath the glaring sun.

There's a small part of the brain where memory is stored called the hippocampus. In moments of intense trauma, this specific node of brain goes into shock. Any number of memories haphazardly flash, as quick as a camera bulb. The string of blood that poured from Luis's own torn leg could have very well been the bougainvillea crawling across Casimira's bedroom window in Jocotepec. *Mi Cara de Dolorosa.*

The sensation of falling at terminal velocity, where a flailing body can reach speeds of up to 124 miles per hour, may as well have been the sensation of birth. No longer were their souls inside their skin sack. They were between worlds. Dead and alive at the same time. Screams for Diosito, if ever they came, had done so from disembodied mouths.

The ship rolled once, then twice, shook loose another body. Out spilled young Tomás Márquez. Strapped to his seat. Intact but aflame. Somersaulting across the morning sky. Because of the weight of the seat it's likely he reached a terminal velocity of 150 miles per hour. A fireball of lightning.

In the explosion, in the spray of molten metal, passengers were disintegrated, turned ash. Perhaps one of the brothers was first, Juan Ruiz. Ash. Then Officer Chaffin. Ash. Perhaps the gun on Chaffin's hip fired its only round. *An explosion was heard, yet, no evidence of an explosion was ever found.* Row after row, those who were still strapped to their seats, witnesses to their own end, could only make a final gesture. An attempt to cross oneself. A blink of an eye. Flinch.

At the same moment that Red Childers stood looking up at the spiraling ship, one hundred inmates were gathered in the main yard at the road camp. Rudy Larson, the cook, spotted the smoke first. He hollered and pointed up as the left wing exploded and ripped free. The sonic boom echoed down the length of the canyon, forcing the men onto the ground. A ball of fire meteored just east of the Gaston house. The wing sailed down like a shimmering leaf, rocking back and forth across the sky. There was a brief silence, broken by a scream. "It's headed this way!" The ship spiraled in their direction, and they took cover. Warden Wilmurth followed it with his eyes. "My God!" he said, to no one in particular. He scrambled to his office.

Wilmurth: "While I was trying to get phone connections, I could hear the boys shouting, 'Here it comes, it's going to land in the yard.' I didn't know whether to crawl under my desk or run."

As the ship dove toward earth, Red could see through the cockpit window a ghostly face staring back at him. The skin on that face was white, almost angelic.

Of all the passengers, Frankie Atkinson was the only one who saw it coming. Unconscious, Ewing's limp body was pinned against the gears. When Frankie could no longer distinguish the spinning of the horizon line from the plane's propeller, he knew there was nothing left to do. In that moment, Captain Frank Atkinson—*a one-man army of greased lightning!* with more than two thousand hours flying over the most hostile territories known to man—took a deep breath and let go the control yoke. He watched the sky spinning. Felt his skin catch fire. And the mountainside appeared close. Closer. Closer still. Maybe he shut his eyes. Maybe he didn't. Maybe he thought of his unborn child inside Bobbie's womb. Again, the hippocampus triggered. It's a crapshoot. Whatever blip of memory surfaces is the final impression of our lives. For Frankie, it may have been the memory of the last photograph he took with his parents. The three of them standing in the front yard on Clay Street. The proud look on their faces. He'd been home on leave. It was a pleasant day. The smell of rose bushes. Or perhaps it was the image of his namesake, Saint Francis, who courted poverty, conversed with creatures and birds, who preached, "Lord make me an instrument of your peace . . . where there is hatred, let me sow love." Who knows why or how the hippocampus makes its choice. By now it was cooking inside Frankie's skull.

Red shielded his eyes from the sun. When he looked again, he could see undergarments drifting down. A pair of pants kited overhead and sailed out of sight. The closer the ship got, the more clear it became to Red that the bodies spilling out were still alive. By the piercing shrill of their death call, almost whistling so fast were they falling, he watched arms and legs swim desperately against the blue sky, and could hear their bodies, one by one, cracking through tree limbs and thudding down to hard earth.

When the wing broke off, it sailed over the Gaston Ranch house, where young Nancy was playing near the creek bed. The snapping of tree branches caused her to look up. In that instant she saw a metallic feather bouncing along a breeze. As it approached it grew in size. She tried moving away from it, but the thing followed her. She ran but couldn't escape it. She zagged back and forth, several times, but the monster was hell-bent on making her its target. She ran screaming onto the porch of her house, and when she looked back, it vanished. A second later it crashed down thirty feet away. With the wing came a rain unlike any little Nancy had ever seen. It rained:

Paper
Ladies garments
Unexplainable number of shoes
Baby clothes
A fifty-cent piece, burnt black
Torn wool coat
A finger with wedding band still on it
Driver's license in pants pocket, address of L Street in Sacramento
Red flannel work shirt
Baseball cap
Battered suitcase
Handwritten letter addressed to Folsom, California
Photograph of unknown woman
A Mexican blanket or serape
Laundry Workers Union card
A red high heel with foot inside

The left engine was the first to hit.

The engine struck a hillside 600 feet above the main wreckage and rolled down the hill, coming to rest 150 feet below the wreckage.

The propeller was next. It hacked tree limbs and tore into the embankment of the creek, rocketing a hundred yards away. The nose of the ship exploded against the gravelly embankment. Right wing, fuselage, empennage, entrails, hinges, bolts, bone, muscle, and tooth came collapsing in, diced through the sieve of gears and shredded metal until all flesh was minced and packed into a fiery grave. No human spared, not one. Not the pilots, not the immigration officer, not the stewardess, and not the workers. Every body and soul rendered into one clump. Liquefied metal hissed on a nearby digger pine, and the tree went up in flames. Chrome lava spilt down the sides of it and pooled in the embankment.

Wilmurth's voice was the first to call out. "Johnson, shovels! Pickaxes!"

Wilmurth opened the gates, and every inmate went bursting onto the dirt road, carrying tools. They said nothing. Kept their mouths shut and did as ordered. Deputy Johnson hollered, "Hurry fellas!"

In their haste, some toppled others. The sound of their boots galloping down the dirt road was a stampede of wild horses. A cloud of dust arose in their wake. In a mob they flew past the Gaston ranch and tore around the bend. They counted one leg, a hand, three truncated torsos. A face with eyes wide open. The skin on that face brown, angelic.

When they arrived at the clearing, they saw Red Childers standing in a black cloud, paralyzed. "Red!" Wilmurth cried out. The old man didn't respond.

"As I watched I could see bodies separating from the wreckage," Red would later say. "I began running at once to get to the main wreckage and to help anybody who might be alive. I encountered four badly mangled bodies before reaching the debris, which was burning fiercely."

"Red!" Wilmurth called to him once more.

Red came to. He turned and saw the stampede of men rumbling toward him. One tossed him a shovel. Red clutched the shovel and darted for the creek bed. The men began throwing dirt on the fire. There were several fires. The grass was yellow but damp. Still it burned. In the treetops and across the hillside, it burned. It burned and burned, and in that moment it seemed as if the fires would never go out.

June: "By the time I got there the prisoners were pulling bodies out of the creek. The first one I saw was . . . they had exploded because it was . . . well, I thought it looked like a butchered cow, you know. I was a kid, and being raised on a ranch, uh . . . where you're exposed to that kind of stuff . . . well, the arms and legs were off. It was just the torso, and it was open in the front, like it'd been butchered. And not only that, there were parts of people all over the place . . . innards and such. And, um . . . I stumbled over a lady's high heel. It was a red high heel strap shoe and . . . there was a foot in it. Another man who'd been thrown out of the plane landed near a bush and his brains had splattered all over this bush . . . I mean, like it was decorated with brain. And that body had been removed before I got there . . . but I saw the brains, you know . . . in the bush. And um . . . uh, then I saw another place where there was kind of an indentation . . . and one of the deputies there was showing us around, and he said there was a large man on the plane and he made this indentation in the ground. And the smell of all the burning flesh . . . I remember seeing those particular things. And, uh . . . a couple of years later a girlfriend and I were running our horses across that field and my horse kicked a skull. So, they never did find all the parts you know, it was just too difficult. Everything was scattered. Just like the song goes, 'scattered like dry leaves.'"

36

DRY LEAVES

Mary Lou Atkinson

"The neighbor had heard about it first. Guess it was on the radio or something. Helen, Earl, and baby Jim were at the house. Neighbor asked Earl to come over, so Earl went over. I remember Helen looking out the window to see what the men were up to. After a while she could tell something was wrong, so she went outside, and that's when they told Helen what had happened. I was looking through the window at 'em. I saw Helen sit down, and the look on her face . . . I just knew something was wrong. I thought it mighta been Mama 'cause her health was never that good. Never thought it woulda been Frankie."

Helen Atkinson

"We didn't tell Mama until she came home. It was just terrible. Our mother stayed in bed for a long time, she was sick. Just a bad time for everyone. Remember, Mary Lou, they had brought the caskets to the house? I remember the hearse pulling up and them bringing the coffins into the middle of the living room. We tried opening them, but they creaked so loud we got startled and ran off. Their bodies were in black rubber bags. What was left of 'em. Remember that, Mary Lou?"

Caritina Paredes Murillo

"My mother was Elisa Murillo Granados. When my father, Ramón Paredes died, she finished raising us by herself. (Pause) Does it matter if I cry now? I'm sorry. (Pause) The day I found out what had happened I was ten years old. I was getting masa at the molino here, just down the road, and a friend of mine saw me and blurted out, 'Caritina, they say your father died!' Can you imagine? So then, after hearing my friend say that, I ran home and found my mother crying. She was holding a newspaper that a cousin of hers had taken to her, and I read it. I already knew how to read by then. I read it and I saw the pictures of the coffins. I read that the plane caught fire when they were up in the air. And I read that my father, Ramón Paredes, and my uncle, Guadalupe Ramírez, they let themselves fall. They didn't burn. They hit the ground on their last breath, and so they gave their names. And my father said his name was Ramón Paredes González, and el señor Guadalupe said his name was Guadalupe Ramírez Lara. And that is all I know. But yes, when I arrived my mother was already crying, and since I already knew, I didn't ask her. I just took down the bucket with the masa in it, and I don't remember who came to help us make tortillas, because, well, after such news we just didn't have the strength to continue."

Olga Cárdenas

"We were told that when my grandfather, Guadalupe, saw that the plane was about to crash, well, the plane was already on fire, that he let himself fall. He was alive, and they took him to the hospital but I don't remember the name of the hospital . . . but they say he gave his name because he didn't have any identification."

Don Guadalupe Jáuregui

"I was there in Stockton, at the campo, when the crash happened. We heard them say the names on the radio, and that's when we heard José Valdivia's name called. And the radio said, no one knows who these men were, and we said, that's not true, we know who they are, I knew José. (Pause) José was . . . well, he was a good guy, and well, he loved baseball."

Eliseo Sánchez González

"When José's father, Mateo, heard the news that his son died, well, he was very distraught, just terribly sad. It ruined him. He left Stockton right away and returned back to La Estancia. His family, was . . . well, they never recovered from their son's death. It was painful, very painful."

Gilberta Márquez

"Tomás was the youngest in the family. We called him Masito. When we found out he died, his brother Salvador stopped at our house before going to his mother's house. He came to ask my father to go with him to tell his mother the news. I saw my father holding him. I was around twelve years old at that time. And Salvador, he held my father, well, they held each other, and I remember them crying, painfully crying. And then they were talking, but whispering, you know, and I wanted to know what was happening, why they were crying. They were very emotional. They went out the back door and left to tell my aunt, Masito's mother. Later on, us kids also went to my aunt's house, and all the adults were gathered there, and they were all crying, crying very hard. It was just so . . . just horrible. And of course, all of us little kids, well, we began crying too, because we saw the adults crying. It was very a painful time. That we know of they never found Masito."

Casimira Navarro López

"That morning I was at the corner store, and we had all been listening to the radio. The radio announcer said that a plane had crashed, somewhere in California. That it had burned and many people were killed. It was on the news that I heard it. We were all there, my sisters and I . . . and we had this tiny radio on, just listening to it. They began announcing the names of all those killed in a plane crash. We never thought one of those names would be Luis. But we heard them say, Luis Miranda Cuevas. (Pause) There is something curious about me, see. Whenever I feel pain I start to laugh. I don't cry. I laugh, and I don't know why. So I began to laugh. It was terrible. There were a lot of names, everyone who was killed. It was right then that I thought of our phone call, when Luis had contacted me just a few days before. I could still hear his voice in my ear. Strange that before that, he had gone to los Estados many, many times, and never once had he called me before. But this time he did. It was the only time he contacted me, to tell me that he was returning to Jocotepec, and to say that we were going to get married, and that he was bringing me a mariachi."

Yrene Miranda Navarro

"My father, who was Luis's brother, would tell me, well, that they were very poor in those days, very poor. They used to sleep on a single mattress made of twigs. And my grandfather, he would go up to the mountains, stay there for two months at a time, and he would bring back tomatoes, or whatever it is he farmed, and that's what they ate because they were so poor. My father would often say, 'When my brother Luis died, our life changed.' You see, they had given our family, well, Luis's family, money for the accident. And my father said, 'The first thing my mother did was buy us some beds with that money. Beds with real mattresses. Because of Luis, his sacrifice, we slept very well from then on.' They also bought some land and a couple of homes, so I believe it was a good chunk of money. Either that or the cost of living was so low. Still, the money had to be pretty good. My father said that is when things got better for the family, well, financially speaking. But Luis had to die for this to happen. Shortly after he died, Luis's mother got sick from her heart. Their lives changed for the better, but her health declined and she got very sick. It was all just so painful. I had grown up hearing the stories of the plane crash, and had always been afraid to fly in a plane. Just this past November, at sixty-five years old, I finally had the nerve to get on a plane. It was for a nephew's wedding, which was held in Watsonville. The place where Luis was working, picking strawberries, when he got picked up."

Don Fermin Ramírez Lara

"After the accident happened, when my father Guadalupe went missing . . . you see, his dog Lobo was still alive. And well, my mother and I both remember this clearly, that at the hour when the mules would come home from work. You know, back then they used mules in the fields, you see. Well, with the sound of the carriages, the dog would get so excited, he would jump up and yelp and he would run to the gate, like crazy, thinking it was my father returning home. But then, once the dog realized it wasn't him, he would turn back quietly. The dog was sad too. At night he would howl and howl. A year after my father died, his dog, Lobo, died too."

Connie Ann Mart

"One year we were vacationing at Thousand Islands on the St. Lawrence River and someone had this little handmade record. Guess Uncle Frank had made a recording when he was overseas in the air force. And they played it, Mom, Dad, my aunts and uncles, and I. And on the recording he was sayin' hello, and how much he missed everyone . . . I think he was speaking to my grandma. And then he sang a song. I'll never forget, it goes something like 'My buddy, my buddy, miss your voice, the touch . . .' And I remember Grandma really, just really falling to pieces listening to that. All of the adults did."

Mary Lou Atkinson

"Bobbie had a hard life. I remember one Christmas she was sittin' around our house and just marvelin' at our tree, going on about how pretty it was, all the decorations it had 'cause she never had that sorta thing growing up. She had it pretty rough, from what I remember. Was in something of an abusive family, or her father . . . I can't recall, but I know she wasn't happy about her situation. She loved Frankie because he treated her good. They never did anything apart from one another. Two weeks before the accident she'd taken a pregnancy test, and was supposed to find out the results or something. I recall we were all pretty excited about that—"

"Did you know that a set of baby clothes was found at the scene of the crash?"

Silence.

"No. No I didn't."

37

FUNERAL SERVICES FOR THE CREW

There was no absolute certainty when it came to identifying the bodies. La Huesera blew her tobacco smoke over the fragments. A portion of Frank Atkinson's torso was identified by the burnt fifty-cent piece he had on his person. It was his lucky coin. Bobbie was identified by the ring on her finger. The opal stone had fallen out, but the design was clearly Bobbie's. Frankie's brother Bob knew this much. It was he who would make the identification of her finger. How much of her body was actually retrieved is unknown. Days after the crash, Bob would be flown from Rochester to California by the same company that employed his brother, Airline Transport Carriers Inc. If that wasn't bad enough, it would be on a Douglas DC-3. By the time Bob landed in California it felt as if his jaw had been used as a punching bag; it was so sore from clenching his teeth the entire flight. Of that nine-hour flight, Bob would tell his family, "That plane was so ratty, everything shook. Hell if I didn't think it was gonna fall apart with me in it too." Copilot Marion Ewing was recognized by the buttons on his shirt and the fillings in his teeth. It was his father who drove in from Long Beach to make the identification of his son's remains. As for Frank Chaffin, the patch on his government-issued uniform labeled "Immigration and Naturalization Service" made him easy to identify.

Within a week's time, the charred and fragmented remains of all four crew members were collected and returned to their families. Frankie and Bobbie got shipped by train three thousand miles back to 496 Clay Street in Rochester, New York. Their deaths appeared in all the local papers, three hundred friends and family were notified, a police escort led the procession behind two hearses, and wreaths of red, white, and blue carnations adorned their coffins.

As for Officer Frank Chaffin, his remains would be shipped to Berkeley, where his wife, Mary, his two grown sons, William and Robert, and grandchildren, Joanne and little Billy, would receive him and have his body cremated as per his wishes. The U.S. Immigration and Naturalization Service would give him a proper burial.

Marion Ewing's body was eventually shipped back to Long Beach, though not before his wife, Dorothy, with infant son in tow, filed a lawsuit against the deputy coroner for not allowing them to see Marion's body until three days after the crash. She demanded to know why but was only given the cold shoulder. A trial ensued, and a year later the *Berkeley Daily Gazette* would report that Mrs. Ewing argued that "the plane was in imperfect condition," and that she believed it was "overloaded with passengers." The article goes on to report there were actually thirty-nine Mexican passengers aboard, rather than the twenty-eight officially reported. Mrs. Ewing's arguments were swept under the rug. Was it possible that she too had known about the other three names that never appeared again? James A. Guardaho, Julio Barron, and Ramón Portello? Were there more Mexican passengers unaccounted for? Regardless of the trial's outcome, her husband was still dead. Nothing would change that.

Dorothy and her young son would have a proper burial ceremony, with traditional military honors, at the Ivy Lawn Cemetery in Ventura, California. A bugler would be employed to belt out "Taps," while two honor guards conducted the thirteen-fold ceremony of the American flag. As Mrs. Ewing held her little boy and trembled at the sight of Marion's coffin, the honor guards maintained their stoic gazes, while their pristine white gloves went about the ritual of folding and tucking. In her husband's absence, the precision and patience with which they did this felt meaningless to Mrs. Ewing. Whether or not she was made aware of the significance of each fold is unknown. What is known is that it reads like poetry:

> Fold 1, symbolic of life itself
> Fold 2, a belief in life eternal
> Fold 3, in honor and remembrance of the departing veteran who gave his or her own life in defense of this country, and in effort to attain peace around the world
> Fold 4, symbolic of our weaker nature
> Fold 5, right or wrong, this is still our country
> Fold 6, our collective beating hearts
> Fold 7, a tribute to our armed forces in all parts of the world, then and now

Fold 8, in honor of our mothers
Fold 9, a tribute to womanhood
Fold 10, a tribute to our fathers
Fold 11, for our Hebrew citizens
Fold 12, for our Christian citizens, the Father, Son, and the Holy Ghost
Fold 13, the stars outward and exposed, reminding us, "In God We Trust"

Once Old Glory was properly folded and tucked into a perfect triangle, they would approach Mrs. Ewing and present it to her. Copilot Ewing's son would reach up and tug on a corner. Ewing's widow would take it in both hands and stare blankly at it for a moment. Red, white, and blue. Purity. Justice. Blood. A triangular symbol of her husband's duty to his country. Marion Ewing in thirteen folds.

38

FUNERAL SERVICES FOR THE PASSENGERS

"Air transport is never *forced* upon a deportee," an official with the Justice Department in Washington, D.C., stated during a media interview. "If the person objects to traveling by air, other means of transportation are provided."

Consul Salazar was left scratching his head. "I am trying to learn just what action will be taken," he said to the *Fresno Bee*. Salazar did not yet know "whether our government will demand indemnification for the loss of lives." He concluded the interview by stating, "I must await instructions from Mexico City. One of the difficulties is that many of those killed have not been identified."

Of the twenty-eight Mexican passengers reported to be aboard, the exact number of bodies positively identified would be disputed. Some reports claimed only twelve. Others said nineteen. Other numbers even more dismal. Years later, when asked why the bodies were not returned to their homeland, the Mexican consulate would attempt to explain: "It's likely it would have been too expensive. Also, there was no way of knowing for sure who was who."

This response would raise questions by families of the deceased—

"Did God only spare the four Americans from being completely dismantled? What was sent home in *their* caskets?"

As to the question of cost, between 1947 and 1948, an estimated four hundred thousand Mexicans were deported by train back to Mexico. This would prompt the families to wonder—

"Would it have been impossible to squeeze in twenty-eight more bodies?"

The U.S. Justice Department offered no explanation, except to say, "No liability attaches to the government in connection with the Coalinga accident."

On January 31, 1948, just three days after the accident, services were conducted. It would go down in the books as the largest mass grave funeral in the history of California's Central Valley. Campesinos would catch wind of it and spread the news around the labor camps, from the grapevines of Fresno over to Stockton's sugar beets, and back down to the cotton sprawls of Bakersfield. Church circles that cropped up every Sunday morning along the campos and backroads took a knee and said a prayer for the departed compañeros who were scattered in some forgotten part of el Norte. Those in the surrounding towns—Cutler, Orosi, Selma, Dinuba, Fowler, Reedley, Madera, Huron, and Coalinga—dressed in their only Sunday clothes, donned a tie and hat, spat on the scuffed tips of their shiny shoes, primped their hair, and piled into cars and trucks and caravaned up the Golden State Highway uniformly, heading straight toward Holy Cross Cemetery. Along the way, wide-eyed children asked their parents, "Who died?" And their parents replied, "Nuestros compañeros." Their children looked confused. "Who?" they pressed. Their parents looked at one another. "Just be respectful," they said. The line of cars jammed up starting at Highway 99 and trailed west on Belmont Avenue, out to where the open fields of dirt lay untilled. Vehicles lined the shoulder of the road, pulled onto patches of flat dirt wherever they found it, and squeezed their cars into narrow spaces between other cars. Adults holding the hands of their children scampered across Belmont and hurried to where the services were set to begin. Of course, the cameras were already there, vulturing the perimeter and snapping photos randomly.

The crowd gathered around the caskets. Twenty-eight of them. What was inside each casket would never be seen. By anyone. Mismatched or not, the severed arms, fingers, torsos, and heads of Ramón, Guadalupe, Juan, Luis, young Tomás, María, and the rest of the passengers were gathered up and stuffed into black plastic bags and placed inside the caskets. Because there weren't nearly enough body parts to fill all twenty-eight caskets, some of them would remain completely empty. Empty caskets interred before the crowd. The twenty-eight boxes a mere representation of twenty-eight lives. As a way to identify the caskets, they would be labeled A to Z. The human beings, however, would go unidentified for sixty-five more years.

According to a newsletter issued by the Fresno diocese, "Several hundred of Fresno's Mexican Colony were present to join in the final prayers for their fellow countrymen. Twenty-eight gray caskets were surrounded by floral tributes from Mexican societies in the valley. The mass grave is eighty-four feet long and seven feet wide, with a depth of five feet, allowing for the bodies of the twenty-seven men and one woman to be buried side by side."

The *Fresno Bee* reported that those who attended the services "wept openly as Monsignor John Galvin of the St. John's Cathedral and Rev. José de Galarreta, pastor of Our Lady of Mount Carmel parish, intoned prayers for the dead."

Standing before a crowd of hundreds of mourners, Monsignor José de Galarreta opened the Good Book to Genesis 3:19 and cleared his throat: "Con el sudor de tu rostro comerás el pan, hasta que vuelvas á la tierra; porque de ella fuiste tomado: pues polvo eres, y al polvo serás tornado."

The *Fresno Bee* went on to report: "The priests were flanked by altar boys bearing the aspersorium, or holy water sprinkler and censers, and by representatives of Mexico and the United States. Both the Mexican and American flags were flown in unison for the occasion. Floral tributes to the unknown dead were presented by: Lodge No. 30, Alianza Hispano-Americana, Our Lady of Guadalupe Association, Fresno Mexican Patriotic Committee, the Fresno Mexican colony, Unidad Mexicana Inc., Club Gaona, both branches of the Morelos Societe, Logia Hispano America Candelario B. Cedillo, the Mexican Consulate, 21 Mexican Boys, International Society of Mutual Benefits No. 17, Club No. 13, Mexican Chamber of Commerce of the San Joaquin Valley, Joaquin Maciel of Madera, Juan Mercado, and Mrs. Mary Rios." Together, the attendees solemnly "awaited the consignment of the farm workers to the very soil they had spent their last years cultivating."

Despite the unprecedented turnout from the local Mexican community, not a single family member of any of the deceased Mexican passengers was notified of the service, much less invited to attend. Had they been notified, it's likely they, too, would have requested the return of their loved ones' bodies. Had that happened, they would've conducted their own services. Certainly, Fermin Ramírez Lara would have taken part in the honoring of his father, Guadalupe, in traditional customs befitting of one of Charco de Pantoja's sons.

"Had my father's body been given back to us, we would have prepared food for the family that would have come a long way to be here. That first night there would have been café de olla, or té de canela, with bread, and we would have recited the rosary. This would have been followed by singing alabanzas until sunrise. The next day, when his body was being interred, there would have been flowers at the cemetery—everyone in Charco would have brought flowers—and we would continue to recite the rosary with family and friends. It would go on for nine days, the recitation. Each day at the same hour. On the last day we would raise the cross and light four candles. We would say a special prayer for each side of the cross, the four directions. And then, just before they lowered my father's body into the earth, each person would place a single flower, or maybe a handful of dirt, on top of his coffin and, well, everyone would have said their good-byes to my father. He was a very loved man. I loved him very much. And we never had the chance. I never got to say good-bye to my father."

Because there were so many caskets that it would've taken two days to lower all twenty-eight into the ground and shovel dirt over them, on the day of the funeral the Fresno diocese lowered only a few caskets into the earth as a symbolic gesture. For the crowds that gathered. For the officials. For the cameras.

On March 1, four weeks after the ceremony, the independent Spanish-language newspaper *El Faro* released its own account of the event: "Tears and prayers! A beautiful tribute! A deserved honor for our fellow humble countrymen who yearned for a better life and immigrated to this big place without ever thinking their bodies would rest eternally on this foreign land. It was a tribute that all honorable souls deserve—that which gives warmth to a life among hope, but damn the holy demands of livelihood! Poor countrymen! Your bodies were not charred by the flames but by the ardent desire of doing what's right as a husband, as a father, as sons, and as Mexicans. You were charred not by the fire but by the hope of providing your loved ones a better livelihood, of giving your loved ones the delights of abundance and well-being, conquered by your ability and amassed with the sweat of your brow. You were loyal examples of the biblical sentence: 'Con el sudor de tu rostro comerás el pan . . . rest in peace.'"

When all was said and done, and the immense mound of dirt finally settled over the mass grave, grass would eventually return to that part of Holy Cross Cemetery to form a sprawling green blanket the width and length of three passenger vans. But without a granite marker to acknowledge it was a burial site, it appeared like nothing more than a wide row of empty plots available for purchase. No doubt whole families inquired about buying plots in that section—it was so serene and idyllic. The cemetery would have to turn them away, explaining that that section of the cemetery was, in fact, a "mass unmarked grave," and therefore unavailable for purchase. Not that they'd actually use those words. They'd simply refer to the eighty-four-foot-long plot as "Unavailable."

Years later, though there is no official record of it, an anonymous person would donate a small bronze placard for the mass gravesite. Although an act of generosity, the gesture was lackluster at best. The text on it told nothing of the souls who were buried there, and it didn't specify where they were actually buried. It was an ambiguous marker, oddly placed. Anyone walking across that vast section of lawn would see the placard and find it curious.

28 MEXICAN CITIZENS
WHO DIED IN AN AIRPLANE
ACCIDENT NEAR COALINGA
CALIFORNIA ON JAN. 28 1948.

R.I.P.

39

THE TELLING OF MARÍA DE JESÚS'S WORST NIGHTMARE

Three years later . . .

It is said that on the day it happened, reports of the crash made their way across La Estancia by word of mouth. Someone, a neighbor, heard news of it on the radio in Nochistlán. A list of the dead was announced, and the name José Sánchez Valdivia was broadcast from the barrio of San Sebastián over to the quiet benches where the viejitos sat listening to the radio in el jardín. By the end of that day, the name José Sánchez Valdivia had been passed on down the line, until five or six months later, over in La Estancia, it was reduced simply to José Sánchez. As luck would have it, it would be the family of the other José—José Sánchez Gonzalez—that the news reached first.

When they caught wind of it, José's mother, María de Jesús, went into hysterics. She had sensed something was wrong, since it was unlike her son José to be gone for so long. Typically he returned from el Norte at least once a year. And if it was longer he always made sure to write. But it had been too long since they'd last heard from him, and anxieties were high. Life in La Estancia was difficult, and the idea that her eldest son was off in el Norte, earning money, was the only sliver of light that kept María de Jesús rising morning after impossible morning. The poor woman. Had she been told the victim's full name, she would've learned it wasn't her son at all but his best friend who had been killed. And then an even more frightening thought consumed her. If José had been killed in a plane crash while being deported, was it possible that his younger brother, Refugio, was also with him? Had the radio simply neglected to mention Refugio? María de Jesús backtracked to the very mouth that first relayed the news, but the mouth couldn't recall whether or not the name Refugio was ever mentioned. "I'm sorry, señora," was all the mouth could reply. "I only heard that José Sánchez from La Estancia was killed in a plane crash." All the family could do was wait.

Time was a curse.

María de Jesús waited for the news, some bit of formality from the powers that be confirming her son's death. Until then she could eat nothing. She bought a radio and placed it in the center of the house and kept it on full volume at all hours. At first, it took some getting used to, sleeping with it on. But eventually, it was the only way she could sleep. In the blue hours of dusk, before the roosters crowed, she lay awake listening to the news, worried that if she let up, even for one second, she might miss the announcement of her son's name. After a few months her eyes began to sag, and her hair was unkempt. Now and then a neighbor would stop by to try coaxing María de Jesús to eat something. "How will you have the strength to receive your son when he comes home?" they would ask. María de Jesús would gesture solemnly and agree to a cup of broth. Each passing day that her family didn't receive news about either son, José or Refugio, a slow darkening ate at their spirits. Before long, a year had come and gone, and then another, and still no word was given on either of them. María de Jesús alternated between anger and depression. One day she would curse el Norte at the top of her lungs, and the very next day her children would find her slumped over the kitchen table with her face in her hands. She would find the strength to whisper to whoever was around: "Why no telegram from the officials in Mexico City? As if José and Refugio never existed, as if they just disappeared. What heartless animals! Have they no mothers?" At times, she wondered if perhaps she was going crazy. She'd stare catatonically at her other children and ask, "I do have sons named José and Refugio, don't I?" Her children would nod, caress her face, and say, "Yes, of course, 'ama, and they will be home soon."

She would go on like this until the third year. And then one day María de Jesús suddenly found her legs again. She stood up straight, pulled her hair back, and in an angry gesture shut the radio off and flung the contraption out the window. The absence of its staticky voice made her children feel uneasy as they watched their mother pick up right where she'd left off three years before. It was clear María de Jesús had had enough. Her heart could stand no more. From then on she no longer spoke another word of either José or Refugio. If there was any chance that she was harboring one scrap of hope, it would be veiled beneath her silent exterior.

One cold December evening, while María de Jesús was sweeping the hard dirt pathway in front of their house, she saw a figure hovering in the middle of the road. At first she ignored it, assuming it was a neighbor. As she continued with her sweeping, her aged body shuddering in the frigid air, she heard the footsteps of the stranger approaching. In her periphery, she noticed that the figure had stopped at the foot of her walkway, near the fence, and was now staring at her.

"'Ama," the voice said.

She tilted her head up to see where the voice was coming from. She felt a cold finger trace the arch of her spine. Had she lost her mind? It was impossible. There, standing a few feet away, was the ghost of her son José.

"'Ama," he said again, placing his bags on the ground.

María stood petrified. She trembled.

"Soy yo, 'ama, José." He stepped to her and touched her elbow.

The touch unraveled her. In that instant, María wondered if the last drop of sanity she'd been clinging to since the news of her son's death had finally dried up. José placed both arms around his mother and clenched her tightly, and just then María let out a deep wail. Her children came running out of the house to see what was wrong. They saw the ghost of their brother standing there, but before they could reach him María collapsed onto the cold ground.

"'Ama!" José cried.

María struggled to catch her breath. José glanced at his siblings, and they ran to him and embraced him. José lifted his frail mother up and held her hard against his body.

"Forgive me," he pleaded. "I've been gone so long, 'ama, forgive me." Tears trickled from his eyes as he held his family. Ghost or not, they clung to their brother and wept. "Forgive me, 'ama, for never writing, it's inexcusable—" José apologized profusely, but in that moment María de Jesús could not hear a word her son was saying. That he was here in the flesh felt like a dream. It made her nauseous, and all she could do to keep from fainting was to press her face into his wide chest and inhale him. Then and only then, when she was positive that this was her son, José, and not some sinister dream that she'd wake from in a few seconds, she wept uncontrollably—a storm three years in the making.

"That's exactly how it happened," Eliseo would later recall. "My brother first went to the United States contracted as a bracero. He would come and go. But then my mother didn't hear from him for three years. One of my brothers even came to the United States looking for him, but couldn't find him. Then they heard the news of the plane crash in La Estancia, and his name came out, José Sánchez, and so everybody thought he was dead. And then, maybe three years after the crash, he finally appeared over there, just like that, without notice. In those years, well, they had no way of knowing except word of mouth. The whole time they had thought it was him who died. My poor mother."

40

JAIME RAMÍREZ

Fresno, California
April 11, 2013

"I have one last thing I want to show you," Jaime said, pulling the second envelope from his file. He reached in and took out a tattered sepia newspaper. "Maybe you want this?" he asked. "It's the Spanish newspaper they sent my family when our relatives died in the crash, *El Faro*. We saved it all these years. Do you already have the list of names?"

"I do. But the one I have is inaccurate."

"Oh. Well, this paper has a list too. Look?" Jaime turned the paper over and pointed to a narrow column on the right-hand side. The caption read: "The Families of the Dead Braceros in the United States." Beneath it: "In relation to the accident that occurred in Coalinga, California, in which 28 Mexicans were being deported by American authorities, the Mexican Consulate in San Francisco communicated with the Secretary of Foreign Affairs the names of the dead countrymen, their towns of origin, and the names of their closest living relatives. Here is the list—"

I was riveted by what he was showing me. I took the newspaper gently in my fingers and began filing down the list of names. While I whispered them to myself, Jaime spoke.

"That newspaper was one of the first things I brought with me, back in 1974, when I first came to the United States."

"Is this how you found the gravesite?"

"No. I found the gravesite on my own."

"How?"

Long anticipating this very question, Jaime told me the story of how he came to find the unmarked grave where his relatives were buried. "I was living in Pasadena with my father, where I had been working since the day I got here. But then I was transferred to Salinas; so when I got out of the LA area, that's when I first heard about the Diablo mountain range, you know, where it was and all that. I said to myself, this has to be it, it has to be the same place where my relatives were killed. So when I was in Salinas, I had the idea in my head, but I never really thought I would . . . well, I mean I came to this country, no English, no car, not even knowing my way around, nothing. I came in the trunk of a 1964 Mustang, yes. My father paid three hundred dollars to bring me here. I was seventeen years old and never left my little pueblito of Charco de Pantoja. I was so scared. Well, when I was a kid, growing up, my mother used to tell us stories of her father, Ramón, and how he would always go to los Estados to work. And when he would return he would sing a song to her, 'La Valentina.' My mother would always tell us these stories. So when I got older I asked her, 'What happened to my grandfather?' And she would tell us the story of the plane crash. But she never knew anything about where it happened, nothing, nada, just somewhere in the Diablo mountains, that's it. So when I came to work in Salinas, I asked my supervisor for one day off, and I told him I had to go to Fresno to see about something. So he gave me the day off, and, well, it was on October 25, 1989. That's the day I went to the Fresno County Hall of Records and I got their death certificates. And from the certificate is how I found the cemetery. It says on there, Holy Cross Cemetery. So, I looked at the phone book and found it. I went there and I asked one of the workers, 'Have you seen a big grave with a lot of Mexicans?' The man working there said, 'Well, there is one that says something about Mexicans.' And then we walked across the cemetery and there they were. I just . . . I just . . . I couldn't say anything. I just stayed quiet, as if, well, as if I couldn't believe what I was seeing. Because back in Mexico we didn't know anything about where, or how, not even the name of the city. Nothing. For forty-one years my grandfather Fidel had no idea where his brother, Guadalupe, was buried. So when I found them he was so happy. The first one I called was my mother, Caritina. And then mi abuelo, Fidel. I went to Mexico later that year, and I took copies of the certificates, and he said to me, 'You know, hijo, I can go in peace now. I know where my brother Guadalupe is, even if I don't see him, I know where he is buried.' So he was very pleased, and of course this made me happy. And then Guadalupe's wife, Micaela, my aunt, I went to see her too. And she cried and cried. And after that, every year that I went to Mexico she would ask me, 'Did you go visit the grave, hijo?'

And I'd say, 'Yes, of course, tía. Every year I go on Día de los Muertos.' And she would say, 'Don't forget, hijo.' And I would say, no, how am I going to forget? I didn't forget when I didn't know where they were, and now that I know, are you kidding? So, when I returned to Salinas, to my job, my supervisor asked me what I went to Fresno for, and so I told him the story, how my uncle and grandfather died in a plane crash many years ago. Then my supervisor looked at me, and he said, 'You know, I have a song, it was written about a plane crash in Los Gatos.' And I said to him, 'No kidding?' And he said, 'Yes, it's a very popular song.' So he gave me a tape. At the time I didn't know English like I do now, but I understood, not really the words of the song, but its sentimiento, of course. And I listened to that song, yes, a good song. I liked it. And that's the first time I ever heard the name Woody Guthrie—"

IV

THE POWER OF A SONG (ONE MORE NAME)

your gravestones now
rowuponrowuponrow
remind us
of all you gave for us . . .
and what of us?

—Martin Hoffman, "Driftwood"

41

PETE SEEGER

Beacon, New York
September 21, 2013

The road that winds through upstate New York toward the town of Beacon is a narrow labyrinth of turns and off-ramps that cuts through the lush emerald, north of Manhattan in late September. An hour outside of the city, we arrived at a gravelly incline that led into the woods. The small car we were in, driven by Pete's grandson Kitama, climbed deep into the thicket of trees until eventually it arrived at a clearing. There stood a quaint log cabin next to a two-story red house, with newly chopped firewood and vines strewn sloppily over a garden fence. The ninety-four-year-old folk icon appeared at the front door. To him it was just another ordinary day, but for me, hearing how the song came to be, from "the Master" himself, was a moment I never thought would happen.

The way it was told to me, on hearing of the plane crash over the radio, Woody Guthrie sat down at his kitchen table and penned a poem titled "Plane Wreck at Los Gatos (Deportee)." But nowhere is there evidence that Woody himself ever actually sang the poem. It was said that by the time the "worst plane crash in California's history" had occurred, Huntington's chorea had taken the better part of his musical abilities. Because of this, his poem would go untouched for nearly a decade. No voices to sing it. No ears to hear it. It wasn't until his closest friend, Pete Seeger, began playing the song in public concerts that the poem, and its message, finally gained traction. For me, learning the song's origins, and the people responsible for it, has always been crucial to the story. Had it not been for the song, I would've never known about the plane crash in the first place. The song, by all definitions, was the beacon.

Pete invited us into his home. It was a modest space. The living room cluttered with books and photos of family and friends. A red rug lay in the middle of the floor, next to a faded green couch, where a tired black-and-white collie named Mochi sat licking his paws. Through a triptych of long windows the Hudson River was visible, flowing just beyond the bluff. The light sifted through and illuminated the house.

The old musician pulled a wooden chair from the dining table. "Please, have a seat," he said, jumping right in. "Well, I'm ninety-four years old now and my memory's not so good. Now the song 'Deportee' was one of the most beautiful songs that Woody ever wrote. It's not always sung right though. Sometimes they make it too fast. I like to sing it like (sings) 'Goodbye to my Juan, goodbye Rosalita / Adios mis amigos, Jesus and Maria / You won't have a name when you ride that big airplane / All they will call you will be . . . deportee.' Make that last word, 'deportee,' stand out, you see? I pause a little bit here and there to make the words come out. The danger is, sometimes musicians are so eager to follow the music the way it's written. This often happens with singers. They're so busy thinking of the music and not thinking of the words. But Woody, he . . . uh, wrote that song . . . I guess he made up the tune . . . and, uh, I guess I learned it . . . directly from him—"

"The way I heard it, Pete, was that a man named Martin Hoffman played it for you."

"That's right, Marty! Yes, it was him. Marty Hoffman. He was a student at Colorado A&M, yes. And he said to me, 'Pete, do you think anybody would mind? I've, uh, made up a tune . . .' That's right, yes, that's where the tune came from . . . and I heard him play it, and I said, that's a perfect tune for that! That's it. Thank you for reminding me. Yes, of course. Woody didn't write the tune, it was Marty Hoffman who did—"

Martin's friend and Colorado A&M classmate Dick Barker would recall the moment with perfect clarity. "The way I remember it, in order to give the concert at Fort Collins, now this was around April of 1958, Pete Seeger flew in from Boston to Denver and was picked up by one of our Ballad Club members. We had this little group of musicians together, and anyway, one of us drives Pete to Fort Collins. That night he gives his concert, and then afterward joins a few of us club members at Marty's tiny house, while we college students sat around on the floor singing songs to 'the Master.' Well, the poor man was falling asleep on the couch, when at one point Marty says out loud, 'Hey, I've put music to one of Woody's poems.' Of course, Pete shakes himself awake to hear it, pulls his notepad out of his shirt pocket, and as Marty starts singing the song, Pete starts scribbling down the music. Some months later Marty received a letter from Harold Leventhal, Pete's agent at the time, saying that Pete had recorded the 'Plane Wreck at Los Gatos' and wanted Marty to get credit for the melody and to sign the accompanying form copy-written in Marty's name."

I told Pete this story, and he nodded his head. He became quiet, as if retreating to the memory of that day.

"Would you like to hear Marty sing that song again?" I asked.

"Do you have a recording of it?"

"I do. Martin first recorded the song in his living room in 1957, with his friend Dick, when they were students."

"Is that a recording machine?"

"It's an MP3 player; it holds the music," I replied, handing him a set of headphones. "Now what you're gonna hear is Marty's voice, and he's explaining to Dick how he came up with the song, and then he actually plays the song."

Pete put the headphones on and cupped his hands over his ears to listen. I pressed play. He shut his eyes and began mouthing the lyrics to the song. He did this the entire three minutes and fifty-six seconds. When the song ended, he tugged the headphones slowly off of his ears. "Extraordinary," he whispered. A long silence followed. It was clear that he was still scanning the files of his memory, perhaps searching for some clear recollection of Marty. He angled his gaze at me and cleared his throat to speak. "Years later, I believe Marty got a job as a teacher, and then . . . uh . . . well, something happened to him—"

42

ROUGH ROCK, ARIZONA, NAVAJO NATION

Lucy Moore: "Back in 1971, it was up to me as Apache County coroner to determine whether a non-Indian body died of natural causes or if it was foul play. So, uh, I got to the Rough Rock Demonstration School, and there were three Navajo policeman, and I remember they looked pretty grim. I pulled up in front of the house, and it was in the compound that went with the school. It was a very ordinary kind of plastered house on the outside, maybe twenty or thirty houses in that compound. The school was all by itself up by Black Mesa, a beautiful spot. So the police came out to meet me as I was getting out of my truck, and I said, 'What's going on?' And they said, 'We have a suicide.' I said, 'Well, I'd like a little preparation . . . how did he do it?'—"

Martin couldn't take his eyes away from the peaceful desert night. Standing at the front door of his house, he fixed his gaze past the baseball field and the water tower, out to where the purple silhouette of the Black Mesa stood guard over Rough Rock. He thought about his two children, so far away, somewhere in Los Angeles with their mother. He missed them terribly. Some nights, he would be consoled by his girlfriend, Sue, or his friends, Doug and John. Other nights, his only consolation was solitude. And music.

After a few minutes of staring out across the landscape, Martin retreated into his small house, fixed himself a Scotch on the rocks, and went and sat down in the living room.

Lucy: "Inside, it was a pretty simple house with not much furnishings. It didn't look terribly lived in. It didn't have a lot of personal things in it. It looked pretty functional. There wasn't a lot on the wall—a few things, a small Navajo rug, or pictures, gifts from students, stuff like that. And I remember there was a drink on the arm of the sofa, and there was a loneliness, you know. The house just had a very lonely feel—"

Martin placed his drink on the arm of the sofa, then picked up his guitar and strummed a few chords. Shunka, his black Labrador, went near his owner's feet and rested there. Martin addressed the dog. "Good boy," he said. And that was it. He petted Shunka on the head and went back to strumming. A moment later he stopped, took another a sip of Scotch, and then stared at the small painting of Canyon de Chelly hanging on his wall. He pictured himself lying down in the cool stream of White House Creek, staring up at the sky, like he so often did, connected with his surroundings. He plucked a few more strings before noticing a sensation of lightness in his chest. His body felt lithe, like the fluffs of cottonwood that danced across the canyon. At that moment, Martin stood up, guitar in hand, and drifted down the hallway. Shunka watched his owner disappear into the bedroom, shutting the door behind him.

In the room, Martin got down on his knees, let the guitar slip from his fingers, and then reached beneath his bed. He pulled his double-barreled shotgun out and held it in his still hands. While he sat on the floor, checking the gun's chamber, one thousand miles away, somewhere in Nashville, Tennessee, folk musician Joan Baez was in a recording studio, laying down Martin's melody to the song "Plane Wreck at Los Gatos (Deportee)." It would be featured in her upcoming album, *Blessed Are*... As Martin gripped the gun barrel with both hands, Baez gripped the neck of her guitar. While he was at the end of his life, the song was at the beginning of its life. While Baez leaned into a microphone and sang the words, "Goodbye to my Juan, goodbye Rosalita..." Martin folded his left leg beneath his right, and aimed the gun barrel directly at his face. He placed the gunstock near the heel of his right foot and wedged the barrel between his teeth. He could feel the hard-edged steel scrape against the soft palate of his mouth. He jammed his big toe into the trigger—

In the dreadful and silent days after, his friends and family tried to make sense of it all. His girlfriend Sue would discover: "The night before it happened, Martin had went to the homes of all his friends in Rough Rock, knocked on their doors and told them how much he appreciated each one of 'em. But that's just how he was; it was just Mart being his old self as far as they knew. So, of course, no one thought much of it. But later on, once they all got to talking and learned he'd been to each one of their houses the night before, they realized he'd come to a conclusion by that point. But that was the last thing Martin did, was say good-bye to his friends."

"I believe what touched Martin most about Woody's words was his own prevailing sense of loss," his cousin Margi ruminated. "It was the unresolved losses, you know. His parents, my grandparents, got divorced when Martin was eight, and he had some terrible experiences with that divorce as a young boy. At one point he had to, at his mother's request, get his father to leave the property with a shotgun. He'd gone through some real trying times, and it all just caught up with him. He was composing songs but he couldn't ever finish 'em. He would stop in the middle and then go on to something else. It was like his thoughts were coming too fast. But I believe it was that very real sense of loss, more than anything else, that attracted him to Woody's words."

43

THE FIRST RECORDING

May 22, 1957

It is a cool May afternoon in Fort Collins, Colorado. Martin and Dick have recently launched a group they call the Ballad Club, and as a part of their mission, they sing songs, host concerts and children's gatherings, and collect as many folk songs as they can get their hands on. When they're not busy organizing events, Dick carts around his reel-to-reel recording machine for whenever the two friends find themselves bored. Today is one of those days.

At Dick's small apartment they set up the recording equipment. Martin has a total of eighteen songs he's been working on. Some of them are short and sound almost like limericks culled from old Irish schoolbooks. A few of the songs are Woody Guthrie's. Among them, "This Land Is Your Land," "Ludlow Massacre," "The Car-Car Song," and "The Grand Coulee Dam." And then there is the second song listed on the sheet: "Deportees." Next to the song's title, it reads: "(1st recording) (Melody by MH)." Until this exact moment, no one has ever conceived a melody for the poem Woody wrote about the plane wreck at Los Gatos Canyon. What neither Dick nor Martin know in this moment is that they're about to capture what will become the only recording of Martin Hoffman singing the song, in his own voice, with his own original melody. It is the same melody he will go on to teach Pete Seeger.

The melody itself is a style of waltz that has roots in Mexico and is widely recognized by its three-four time signature. A "ranchera valseada," it's most often referred to by its informal name, *ranchera*. The ranchera was a style forged in the gunsmoke days of the Mexican Revolution. They were songs that typically told of peasant life in the farmlands of rural Mexico, in places like, where else, but Charco de Pantoja, La Estancia, and Jocotepec. The very song passenger Ramón Paredes sang to his wife, "La Valentina," was a ranchera. They are songs of sorrow, of loss and lamentation for what once was. Joan Baez, Dolly Parton, Johnny Cash, Arlo Guthrie, Bob Dylan, Judy Collins, Willie Nelson, Bruce Springsteen, Odetta, Kris Kristofferson, The Byrds, and Pete Seeger will all eventually go on to record their own version of this ranchera. No melody could've been more fitting for Woody's words than the ranchera, one of Mexico's musical pillars. And this is the melody that Martin Hoffman, a twenty-year-old college student who knew a thing or two about loss, carefully composed for this song.

There is no way either Dick or Martin can predict the historical significance of this moment. Nor that the impact of this one song would last seven decades, until it found the grandson of migrant farmworkers, moved by a question posed in the lyrics, "Who are these friends all scattered like dry leaves?" enough to go searching for the answer. Perhaps Woody knew, he must've—*A folk song is what's wrong and how to fix it.* On this day, as far as the two friends are concerned, their recording session is just one of dozens to be filed away.

Dick lifts the lid on the tape recorder and asks Martin if his guitar is tuned. Martin fiddles with the strings a moment. Dick checks on the reels. He plays some of their previous recordings, then fast-forwards the tape until he finds a silent spot on the reel. He taps the microphone, then gets up to shut the windows. It's spring in Fort Collins, and though the air is brisk, it sounds like everyone's out enjoying the sun. Martin sits in his chair and waits patiently. He scoots closer to the microphone stand. He pushes his blonde cowlick to one side and readies his guitar. Dick places the bulky headphones over his ears. He nods at his friend, as if to say, Ready? Martin nods back. Dick then presses the button and the reels begin to spin. Martin clears his throat and leans into the microphone. His voice is distinct. A tenor, his tone is middle to high range, almost translucent, airy. It comes through clear and has an almost innocent quality. The audio recording is so vivid you can hear Martin's callous fingers scrape against the ridges of each guitar string. A page turns over and the soft crackle sounds as if it's in your ear. He strums the guitar, and while strumming he speaks as if he's barely there. Listen close.

What you're about to hear is the only audio recording in existence of Martin Hoffman singing "Plane Wreck at Los Gatos (Deportee)." If you close your eyes and listen, you can actually hear him—

"This song, Dick, uh, the 'Plane Wreck at Los Gatos,' it was written by Woody Guthrie, and it seems that, um, the way Woody came to write it was that, uh, a plane went down carrying about twenty-eight Mexican migrant workers, deportees . . . uh, well, wetbacks, I guess you'd call 'em . . . uh . . . but they were flying back down to Mexico, and the plane went down over a canyon, near Coalinga, California, called Los Gatos Canyon, on the twenty-eighth of January 1948. . . . So I was sittin' one night and I had just the words and I was looking at it, thought it needed a tune to it, so, uh, here's what happened when I put the two together—"

(Guitar begins)

"The crops are all in and the peaches are rottnin' / The oranges are piled in yer creosote dumps / Yer flyin' em back to the Mexican border / To pay all their money to wade back again / Goodbye to my Juan, goodbye Rosalita / Adios mis amigos, Jesus y Maria / You won't have a name when you ride the big airplane / All they will call you will be . . . deportee.

Miguel Álvarez Negrete

Francisco Durán Llamas

Santiago Elizondo García

Rosalío Estrada Padilla

Bernabé García López

Tomás Gracia de Aviña

Salvador Hernández Sandoval

Severo Lara Medina

José Macías Rodríguez

Elías Macías Trujillo

Tomás Márquez Padilla

Luis Medina López

Manuel Merino Calderón

Luis Miranda Cuevas

Ignacio Navarro Pérez

Martín Navarro Razo

Ramón Ochoa Ochoa

Ramón Paredes González

Apolonio Placencia Ramírez

Guadalupe Ramírez Lara

Alberto Carlos Raygoza

Guadalupe Rodríguez Hernández

María Rodríguez Santana

Wenceslao Ruiz Flores

Juan Ruiz Valenzuela

José Sánchez Valdivia

Jesús Santos Meza

Baldomero Marcos Torres

V

FIELD NOTES (2012-2015)

. . . here, where the world is undone, and their bodies are remade, their spirits rise in star-flecked spirals. The pooling blood runs backwards, their splintered hearts come together. I know all their names. I will call them, and they will come . . .

—Ire'ne Lara Silva, "La Huesera"

Cemetery

NOTE -- ALLOW ONE LINE FOR EACH GRAVE.

DATE	NAME OF OWNER	RESIDENCE	~~GRAVES~~ Plot	~~PLOT~~ Grave
1-3148	Mexican National	Row I	Plot 1	1
	Mexican National			2
	Mexican National			3
	Mexican National			4
	Mexican National			5
	Mexican National			6
	Mexican National			7
	Mexican National			8
	Mexican National			9
	Mexican National			10
	Mexican National			11
	Mexican National			12
	Mexican National			13
	Mexican National			14
	Mexican National			15
	Mexican National			16
	Mexican National			17
	Mexican National			18
	Mexican National			19
	Mexican National			20
	Mexican National			21
	Mexican National			22
	Mexican National			23
	Mexican National			24
	Mexican National			25
	Mexican National			26
	Mexican National			27
	Mexican National			28

Holy Cross Cemetery catalogue. January 31, 1948

September 5, 2012

I called Holy Cross Cemetery yesterday and spoke to a man named Randy Giovannoni. He told me to try St. John's Cathedral, and I did but my calls were never returned. Tried the Hall of Records too, but the woman denied me info since I wasn't related to the victims. I should've lied and said I was. It's been two years now and I'm ready to give up. I tried St. John's again, but instead of calling the front desk I checked their website for a Latino surname. Carlos Rascon, Director of Cemeteries. I e-mailed him and he called me right back. Sounded nice enough. I told him the story and he said he'd check to see if they still had the "catalogue of names" for the people buried in what he referred to as "Section E, Plot 134 A."

September 17, 2012

Heard back from Rascon finally. "We do have the file for that plot," he said. "The problem is it doesn't show the names. In the column where the names typically go it only reads, 'Mexican National' twenty-eight times." He sent me a copy of the catalogue.

September 26, 2012

I met Rascon at the cemetery today. I showed him the list of names I found on the Internet, and he agrees that a lot of them look misspelled. He asked me if I've checked the Hall of Records, and I told him what they said. "Maybe you could approach them?" He said he would. "As the cemetery who buried these folks, we have official business." I was relieved to hear him say this. I thought about what Lance Canales and I had spoken about back in May—the idea of putting these names on a headstone. "If we can confirm the names, what would it take to put them on a headstone?" I asked. Rascon took his sunglasses off. "Good question. The bishop would have to approve, that's the first thing. Then it would just be about raising the money." He stood with both hands on his hips and glanced across the cemetery. "You know," he said, "regardless of things like politics, race, nationality, or social status, it's our business to see that the people we bury here have their names on a headstone. This is what we do for everyone; it's a basic service and human right that everyone has."

October 5, 2012

Rascon asked if I'd be willing to submit a proposal in writing to the Fresno diocese, something he could take to Bishop Ochoa, formalizing my effort to put the names of the deceased on a headstone. He asked that it be brief, but I couldn't help myself. It was four pages long. And then he said he wants to confirm a date for the headstone event, but I told him that's crazy because I don't have an accurate list of names yet. "The names will be confirmed at some point, and it'll be good to have the approval ready to go for when that day comes." The approval, okay, but setting a date? Maybe he has more faith in my search than I do.

November 4, 2012

I met Rascon at the gravesite, and he handed me a single sheet of paper. It was a new list of names. He'd been to the Hall of Records. "I gave the woman there my business card," he said, "and told her what I was looking for. From the card she could see that I was with the diocese, and I told her that we were trying to get clarification on some 'official matters.' I basically told her the story and said, 'I'm from the cemetery, I work there, I have people buried there, and I don't have their names, that's why I need the names.' And that's how they gave me the names." He continued. "And when the woman finally gave me the list, well, I had a kind of a mixed reaction because as I was reading the list I could see that some of the names were still not spelled correctly. I've never heard the last name 'Negroros,' but I have heard 'Negrete.' And you know, this is not the way you spell 'Ygnacio,' or you know, X, Y, Z. There were obvious errors. And according to this list there are three Mexican female passengers aboard, not one, like we originally thought. So now we have a lead, but it's not holding the weight we'd hoped. This list doesn't really clarify their names. We found a piece of the puzzle, but it doesn't necessarily fit yet. But at least this list has the first, middle, and last names for each passenger, so it feels like a milestone, doesn't it?"

February 7, 2013

Rascon called to tell me that Bishop Ochoa approved my proposal for the headstone. I called Lance to give him the good news—

"Rascon says it'll be a granite headstone with the names and story of the incident."

"How much money do we need to raise?"

"He says around ten thousand dollars."

A short pause.

"Let's get to work then."

February 21, 2013

I'm still not any closer to confirming names, much less finding any of the family members. When Rascon gave me the new list back in November I felt optimistic, but now the whole thing just feels fucking impossible. I've done everything I can think of. Even submitted a request to the Freedom of Information Act (I know I filled out the forms wrong). I've been trying the Department of Labor, but I can never get a real person on the line. I've been calling churches randomly all over Mexico, asking about birth certificates, but my Spanish sucks, and I sound like an idiot. And now Rascon tells me that the bishop set the headstone memorial date for September 2, six months away! That's impossible. I told him it's too risky. "I don't have the names yet!" I don't need this pressure.

March 2, 2013

Last night, I decided that I needed to start all over again, begin here at home. This morning I called my friend Juan Esparza, a local reporter for *Vida en el Valle*, the largest bilingual newspaper in central California. I told him the story, and that I was looking for the families. I asked if he'd be willing to write an article about my search. It's a long shot, but he said yes. It's a regional paper, which means that any relatives of the passengers would have to actually live in the San Joaquin Valley and have known about the plane crash in order for this to work. I mentioned this to Juan, but he thinks it's worth a shot.

March 13, 2013

The article appeared today.

Author Plunges into Deadly 1948 Crash for His Book

The first sentence: "Author/poet Tim Z. Hernandez wants more than just names. He wants faces and stories to go with the names . . ." It talks about the crash and my search for the families of the passengers, but the most important part is that it has my contact information. All I can do now is wait.

April 2, 2013

The issue of *Vida en el Valle* isn't on newsstands anymore. I give up. It's been three weeks and no word. Six decades is too long. The families are in Mexico. Or if they are in the United States, they're not in Fresno. I haven't slept much these past few days. Last week I made these paper strips with the names typed out on them and my phone number, and I've been passing them around everywhere. I spent a few days talking to this Ruiz family from South Texas, certain they're related to passenger Wenceslao Ruiz Flores. They were sure I had the wrong family, but I was insistent that it was them. They finally threatened to call the cops if I didn't stop "harassing" them. So I'm done looking. If Rascon and the diocese want to move forward with the headstone memorial, that's on them. I'll have to let him know tomorrow that I'm done looking for the names.

April 4, 2013

From: Ramírez_Jai@aol.com
Subject: Deportees
8:48 PM
Le escribo respecto al acidente del 28 de enero 1948 donde 28 mexicanos fallecieron. Mi nombre es Jaime Ramírez se algo de ese acidente por que ahi murio mi abuelito materno de nombre Ramon Paredes y un tio llamado Guadalupe Ramírez Lara, originarios del estado de Guanajuato. Yo cuando llege a Fresno me puse a investigar donde avian sido sepultados y di con el pantion del Cruz Sagrado. Si necesita informacion agamelo saber.

Jaime Ramírez

I am writing you in respect to the accident that occurred on January 28, 1948, where 28 Mexicans were killed. My name is Jaime Ramírez and I know about the accident because that's where my maternal grandfather named Ramon Paredes and an uncle named Guadalupe Ramírez Lara, originally from the state of Guanajuato, were killed. When I arrived in Fresno I investigated where they were buried and they said it was at Holy Cross Cemetery. If you need information just let me know.

Jaime Ramírez

I thought the e-mail was a prank. Mr. Ramírez told me that a friend had seen the article in *Vida en el Valle* weeks ago, but told him about it only yesterday. "It's my family's story," he said over the phone. He claimed it was a story he "knew well" and had "grown up hearing." I went to meet him at his restaurant a few days later. From the moment I walked in, I knew right off that Ramírez was the real thing. He was waiting for me with photos and documents of his family splayed across the table. He sat there, next to his brother Guillermo, both men with huge grins on their faces. It was as if they'd been waiting for this day. Their wait much longer than mine. I sat there stunned, as they shared story after story with me. The hours passed like seconds. Before I left Jaime showed me an old newspaper, *El Faro*. It has a complete list of all the passengers who died. Not only their names, but the names of their surviving family members, and the town in Mexico they're from. This is the third list, and based on everything I now know, it's the most accurate one. I'll call Rascon tomorrow to tell him the good news.

September 2, 2013

Day of the Memorial Headstone Celebration

Today was unlike anything I've ever been a part of. The weather was typical valley heat, brutal this late into the summer harvest. From the Highway 99 off-ramp onto Belmont Avenue, cars were bumper to bumper. The last time I'd seen anything similar was in '93, when my mom took my sister and I to Cesar Chavez's funeral procession in Delano. I was nineteen years old then. But it did something to me. Made me aware of myself and my own family, in a way I'd never considered. That was twenty years ago. Here I am, today, with my own children, wondering what impression all of this will leave on them twenty years from now. Over the past few months I managed to locate the families of Frank and Bobbie Atkinson, the Gaston family, and Martin Hoffman's family. They were all in attendance today. As for the Mexican passengers, I still only have the Ramírez family. Yesterday, I took everyone to visit the crash site. None of them had ever been. We started at the old Fresno road camp and made our way down to ground zero. It was an occasion of both beauty and pain, and we were silenced by the weight of it. At one point, Billy Atkinson (Frank Atkinson's nephew) embraced Guadalupe Ramírez (the nephew of passenger Guadalupe Ramírez), and everyone's spirits suddenly lifted. After that, we all stood together, arm in arm, on the bank of Los Gatos Canyon Creek, right where the nose of the plane was imbedded, and we took photos, and it felt as if none of us wanted to let go, and yet, that's exactly what we were there to do, let go. That energy carried over into today's ceremony. It felt like family. Everyone gathered under one big tent. Even when the seats filled, people stood in the glaring sun. "This is nothing compared to what it's like working in the fields," I overhead someone say. This sentiment was echoed throughout the day. At one point, a large brown SUV lumbered across the cemetery. It pulled as close to the tent as possible before the driver got out. It was Guillermo Ramírez. He hurried to the passenger side door to assist his mother. News crews swarmed to get footage as a seventy-seven-year-old Caritina Paredes Murillo climbed slowly out of the vehicle and held onto her son's arm. "It's the daughter of one of the passengers," people whispered, sneaking photos with their cell phones. Before Caritina could even take her seat she was already in tears. The child who had lost her father so long ago had risen to the surface, momentarily. "I don't know if these are tears of joy or tears of sadness," I heard her say, in Spanish, to one reporter. She wiped her eyes beneath her glasses and walked to her seat while everyone gazed at her. Surrounded by her children and grandchildren, she took her place beside the families of the other victims.

The grounds of Holy Cross Cemetery were pristine and the decorations photogenic. A sermon was given by Bishop Ochoa, and Carlos Rascon addressed the crowd of more than eight hundred people—at least double what the original funeral services attracted. A procession was led from the tent to the gravesite by traditional Aztec danzantes. They donned bright pink feathers and shells around their ankles; they burned copal and sage, honoring the dead as they would've five hundred years ago. As the people crowded around the memorial headstone, which had been blanketed with a Mexican zarape, Bishop Ochoa and priests from other congregations circled the headstone, sprinkling holy water. Crosses were presented to the family members, as they would have had they been present at the original funeral services.

And then came the moment. As we prepared to unveil the headstone, I took my corner of the zarape and clenched it between my fingers. Just like everyone else, I hadn't seen the headstone yet either. I was nervous, almost fearful, and I didn't know why. The feeling wasn't joy so much as being physically overwhelmed. I knew this was only the beginning. The fact that I've found the families of only four of the reported thirty-two passengers doesn't sit well with me. They should all be here. Every last one of them. As we lifted the zarape and people cheered and whistled, I stared at the names on the headstone. So many names. Each one represented months, perhaps years of work yet to be done. It was unsettling. While we celebrated, somewhere on this earth were the families of the other twenty-eight passengers, who had no idea that this was even taking place.

Standing before that wide slab of polished Italian granite, I thought about the story of the gravesite, and how it might be told one day: "Once upon a time it was a mass grave with no marker. Later, a small flat placard appeared, but without names. Today, it is a slab of Italian granite, four by eight feet in size, with the names and history inscribed." A compelling story, for sure, but still, a headstone is not people. Another thought occurred to me: because of the angle at which the headstone is mounted, it appears the names almost rise up from the earth. While the crowd cheered, I couldn't help but think that until the names rose completely out of the earth and had their stories told, the headstone alone would never be enough. Since the start of this all, people have asked me, "Have you found 'the names'?" "The names?" I ask them. "Yes," they say, "have you found the names?" I can now say, "Yes, I have found the names." But maybe I'll add, "Make no mistake, without the story, the names, just like the headstone, are only a symbol." The mariachi band kicked on and more cheers rose above the cemetery. Those who knew the words to the song clapped and sang along. It was the song requested by the Ramírez family, "México Lindo y Querido."

México Lindo y Querido	My beautiful, beloved Mexico
si muero lejos de ti	if I should die far from you
que digan que estoy dormido	tell them that I am sleeping
y que me traigan aquí . . .	and to bring me back to you . . .

January 28, 2015

Charco de Pantoja, Guanajuato, Mexico

Today is the sixty-seventh anniversary of the plane crash, and I'm standing in the wide rows of lush green garbanzo fields that once belonged to Guadalupe Ramírez Lara. The family still owns it, and they still refer to it as Don Guadalupe's parcel. The mesquite tree that Guadalupe planted as a young man is still standing, though now its branches seem to almost reach the clouds. I'm here with Guillermo, Don Leovardo, Don Fermin, and his grandson Fidel. It's a beautiful morning for what the family has in store. For their relatives who were unable to travel to the United States to attend the headstone memorial celebration almost two years ago, Guillermo and his sister-in-law, Dulce, have organized a gathering to take place this morning at the home that once belonged to Guadalupe. It now belongs to Don Fermin, who is seventy-two years old.

After the headstone memorial, my search continued. With Jaime Ramírez's newspaper clipping in hand, I've managed to find the families of three more passengers: Luis Miranda Cuevas, José Sánchez Valdivia, and Tomás Márquez Padilla. Three more families in a year and a half. At this rate it'll take a lifetime to find them all. My curiosity won't let me rest. Something is pulling me. This is what brought me here, to Mexico. I needed to physically knock on doors, dig deeper still. I've been here two weeks now, and I leave in a couple of days, not having located any more families. I'm exhausted of searching. But I know this pull will always remain.

Back at Don Fermin's house, the family has gathered. In honor of this day, the day Guadalupe and Ramón were killed, at exactly 10:40 this morning, the time of the plane crash, the descendants of both men, including their children, nieces, nephews, siblings, cousins, and great-great-grandchildren, circle up and together we observe a moment of silence. The air is mild and the sun is out. In the close distance we can hear dogs barking and tractors going about their daily work. A few chickens cluck about, and the smell of wet masa wafts from the nearby molino—the same one Caritina was at when as a child she first heard the news of her father's death. After the silence, we drink hot chocolate and eat pan dulce, while honoring Guadalupe and Ramón by sharing memories of them: firsthand accounts from the elders, and then stories passed down to the younger generations. Some tears are shed, but always they are accompanied by robust laughter.

This is when the family opens up and they begin asking me questions. They wonder about my research and the book that I'm working on. How will I write it if the memories are so spare and vague? they ask. How will I portray their loved ones? How will I portray Charco de Pantoja? Mexico? They're curious about the small recorder I carry with me everywhere, with its tiny red light flashing. But of all the questions they have, it seems they're mostly concerned with one in particular: How is it possible that my Spanish is so poor? I tell them that I'm the third generation born in the United States. The last relatives I had who were born in Mexico were my great-grandparents. "Mis bisabuelos," I say. They nod and commiserate among themselves. The chatter lasts a few seconds, until finally Don Fermin rises to his feet. Everyone quiets to hear him speak. He's the elder, and it's his house after all. He stands, slightly hunched, his gentle eyes glistening. He cocks his white cowboy hat back on his head and finishes chewing the bread in his mouth before speaking. "If I can interrupt," he says in Spanish. "In the days of the Mexican Revolution, there was a North American writer, a gringo, his name was John Reed. He wrote a book called *Mexico Insurgente*. It was about the time he spent with Francisco Villa and his troops. Reed told many stories of that time. He said he always carried with him four hundred dollars in his wallet, and not once did any of Villas's soldiers ever ask him for money. He said they were men of good will. He talked about their travels to Zacatecas, and when the battle began, he wrote about the rupture among the revolutionaries, and Obregón's involvement. Reed wrote about all those things that most of us all over Mexico could not possibly know about in those times, 1915. And well . . . here, we sometimes talk bad, or we tend to think bad about Norteamericanos, but the truth is, aside from the bad there is also good. Some of them care to learn about how we live in Mexico, about our lives, and our struggles. And this is a good thing. Especially when it is one of our own. They go away and we think they never come back, but they do. They do come back. Even if it takes a few generations. And they care to learn about Mexico, and write about who we are." The family nods in agreement. A few eyes glance in my direction. Don Fermin looks at their faces with a palpable love in his eyes. "And well, that's all I have to say for now—"

PHOTOGRAPHS

Original funeral services, January 31, 1948

Martin Hoffman, circa 1971, Navajo Nation

The author with the Ramírez and González families, Charco de Pantoja, Guanajuato

The author with (left to right) Leovardo Ramírez, Guadalupe Jáuregui, Celio Sánchez Valdivia, Guillermo Ramírez, and Armando Sierra Razo, La Estancia, Zacatecas

ACKNOWLEDGMENTS

First and foremost, a tremendous thank-you to the families who have entrusted me with the stories of their loved ones, and who throughout the research and writing of this book were willing to regress to that part of memory that stores the heart-matters. To them I am forever indebted. In the order in which they came into my life: thanks to June Leigh Gaston Austin and Larry Haws for inviting me to walk with them in their Los Gatos Canyon, to Bill and Diane Vigeant for making the most crucial of connections, to Margi Dunlap for her generosity and stories of Uncle Mart, to Sue Edelstein for regressing to those "hard-beautiful days" of Rough Rock and Martin, to Bill Spence for locating Martin's grave, to John Boomer and Doug Dunlap for sharing memories and for camping out with me in Rough Rock as we searched for remnants of Martin's past, to Lucy Moore for digging deep, to Glenn Streiff for permission to let his father's story be heard. My appreciation also goes to Lorraine Honie, Fred Bia, and the staff at Rough Rock Community School, and the community of Rough Rock, Arizona, for their generosity, to Dick Barker (RIP) and Barbara Barker, to Connie Ann Mart for sharing stories of Uncle Frank and for introducing me to Aunt Mary Lou Barry (RIP) and Aunt Helen Decker, to Jaime and Guillermo Ramírez and the entire Ramírez/Paredes/González/Lara family of Charco de Pantoja, with special thanks to Maribel Ramírez Baca for correspondence about family. Thank you to Ofelia D. Treviño and the Padilla Márquez family of San Julian, Jalisco, and to Yrene Navarro Miranda and the Miranda/Cuevas/Navarro family of Jocotepec, Jalisco, especially Casimira Navarro López for allowing me to intrude unexpectedly.

Thank you to the broader community of individuals whose support, encouragement, and conversation kept me focused. To Bea R. Franco (RIP), without whose light I would have never been led to this story, I am indebted. To Dolores Crabtree, Byron Aspaas—rising star, Joe Offer, the Mudcat Café, Jared Aldern, Tara Williams, Glenn Mitchell, and Don Howell for their dedication to preserving Coalinga's history. To Betty Jo Brenner for graphology expertise, David Shriner at Benitoite Mining for his generosity in giving me a landing pad in the canyon, Leza Junilla, resident geologist of Los Gatos Canyon, George Guerra and Bob Dockendorf at the War Eagles Museum in Santa Theresa, New Mexico, for opening the doors of a Douglas DC-3 to me, and Waldo Cavendar (RIP) and Steve Johnson, two generous pilots whom I consulted on the intricacies of the C-47/ Douglas DC-3—thank you. Also, thank you to family and friends who read this manuscript in various stages and offered detailed advice and critical feedback and pushed me to dig deeper: Jason F. McDonald, Lydia Z. Hernandez, Cindy Urrea, and especially Laurie Ann Guerrero for helping me iron out the kinks. Also, my sincere gratitude to my colleagues in the Creative Writing Department at the University of Texas at El Paso, and to my former colleagues at the Colorado Humanities and Center for the Book, and the California Council for the Humanities. I am also grateful to the following sources, which have been invaluable throughout: Three Rocks Research, Crabtree Corner, Ancestry.com, Libertyellisfoundation.org, the National Archives, the Fresno County Public Library, the Library of Congress, and the Coalinga Public Library.

The primary research for this book spanned five years. It began in December of 2010 and was completed, as much as any research can be completed, in January 2016. During this time, my travel included central California, Colorado, the Navajo reservation in Arizona, New York, San Francisco, Washington, D.C., El Paso, Texas, and central Mexico. In the first four years, in every aspect of the U.S. portion of this work, I had no financial backing whatsoever, despite my unsuccessful attempts to secure grants and other means of support. Had it not been for the generosity of numerous individuals in each of these places, this work would have been impossible to accomplish. To those individuals I'm greatly indebted: Bay Area artist Jane Oriel for donating her beautiful prints to the cause; Rollie Grandbois (RIP) for the corn offering and shelter; Adriana Dominguez for her support and generosity; my mother, Lydia Z. Hernandez, for research assistance; David "El Greñudo" Herrera; Tony Delfino; Nicole Henares; Juan Luis Guzman; Deana and Bill McCloud; Kate Blalack; the Woody Guthrie Center; Nora Guthrie; Anna Canoni; the Woody Guthrie Foundation; Arlo Guthrie; WGP and TRO; Poets & Writers Inc.; the California Center for the Book; Will Kaufman; Robin Wheeler; UC Berkeley's Bancroft Seminars on Latino and Borderlands Studies: David Montejano, Genaro

Padilla, and Theresa Salazar; the National Steinbeck Center; Mark "Silent Bear"; Kitama Cahill-Jackson; the incomparable Pete Seeger (RIP); the incomparable David Amram; Angela Mictlanxochitl Anderson Guerrero; Juan Felipe Herrera and Margarita Luna Robles; Mai Der Vang and Anthony Cody, who went with me to Pete Seeger's house; Joel and Lauren Rafael; Lance Canales for being in this with me from the beginning; Carlos Rodriguez for musical collaborations over the many years; Mike and Nori Naylor of Naylor Organic Farms; Todd Harvey at the National Library of Congress Folklife Center; Vani Kannan for research assistance on Martin Hoffman; Ken Leija, who followed me with his camera in the early stages; Valentin Sandoval for his willingness to film portions of this work and edit the footage; and Dayanna Sevilla for helping me with research assistance and translations, but mostly for enduring the magic and the impossible, all while giving our children a safe space to call home—Quetzani, Rumi, and Salvador, this one is for you, always for you.

For the research that occurred from the winter of 2014 through winter 2015, specifically my trek to Mexico, I had financial backing from the University of Texas at El Paso, and from donors who supported via an online fundraising campaign I coordinated in fall of 2014, as well as support from the community of Charco de Pantoja, Guanajuato, Mexico. Thank you to all those who contributed, especially my dear friends Wendy Lynn IP and Shelly Catterson, and my cousins Armida and Will Galaviz-Moreno. A tremendous thank-you goes to my brother, Guillermo Ramírez, for accompanying me in Mexico and assembling a vital research team that included Armando Sierra Razo (driver), Sandy Cano (videographer/photographer), and Don Leovardo Ramírez (story-gathering guru). Also, thanks to Mikel Miller and Maria Elena Martinez de la Torre for hosting us graciously while we were in Guadalajara. Thanks to the municipios across central Mexico for their generosity, especially the municipio of Nochistlán, Zacatecas, where Enrique Frias sent around a car mounted with a speaker on the roof into the neighborhoods that two of the passengers were from. Over the loudspeakers they told of the story and asked if there was anyone related to please come forth. Also, thank you to Ito Romo and the literary magazine *Arcadia* for publishing "Antropoema #1," an abbreviated poetic version of this story. And finally, thank you to the media outlets who have followed my search, especially Juan Esparza at *Vida en el Valle,* whose initial story was critical to this endeavor, Rebecca Plevin at KPCC 89.3 FM, Diana Marcum at the *Los Angeles Times*, Univision (Fresno), Jacqueline Santillan Beighley at Fusion TV (ABC/Disney/Univision), KGNU 88.5 FM in Boulder, Colorado, and the fine folks at National Public Radio. If I have left anyone out, I sincerely apologize. Rest assured, I will pay your generosity forward so that we may all flourish—all of us, no one excluded.

Acknowledgments of Books and Music

Throughout the research and making of this book I consulted several texts to which I am indebted, including the following: *Woody Guthrie, American Radical*, by Will Kaufman; *Merchants of Labor*, by Ernesto Galarza; *Photographing Farmworkers in California* and *Everyone Had Cameras*, both by Richard Steven Street; *Into the Canyon: Seven Years in Navajo Country*, by Lucy Moore; various works by Studs Terkel; various works by Elena Poniatowska; various works by Frank F. Latta; *Camera Lucida*, by Roland Barthes; *The New Journalism*, edited by Robert S. Boynton; *The Devil's Highway*, by Luis Alberto Urrea; *The Burden of Visual Truth: The Role of Photojournalism in Mediating Reality*, by Julianne H. Newton; *Mayan Drifter*, by Juan Felipe Herrera; *Akenfield: Portrait of an English Village*, by Ronald Blythe; *This Land Was Made for You and Me: The Life and Songs of Woody Guthrie*, by Elizabeth Partridge; *The Bracero Experience*, by Maria Herrera Sobek; *Mexico Insurgente*, by John Reed; *Ringside Seat to a Revolution*, by David Dorado Romo; and Rigoberto González's brilliant poem "Our Deportees." In the same way, I referred to a handful of singer-songwriters whose music provided the backdrop, soundscape, narrative, and inspiration as I wrote: Chavela Vargas, José Alfredo Jiménez, Lydia Mendoza, Buffy Sainte-Marie, Gustavo Santaolalla, Pete Seeger, Woody Guthrie, Lead Belly, Martin Hoffman, Los Lobos, Mississippi John Hurt, Lucinda Williams, Bruce Springsteen, Lance Canales & The Flood, Odetta, Joel Rafael, Carlos Rodriguez, Mezcal, 40 Watt Hype, Guadalupe Pineda, Jorge Negrete, Valerie June, and the Haunted Windchimes.

List of Memorial Headstone Donors (in random order)

Andre Yang, Joann Chacon Avila, Dayanna Sevilla, Lance and Samantha

Canales, Carlos Rascon and family, John McCutcheon, Felix and Lydia Hernandez, Jason and Delylah Elizondo-Hernandez, Lourdes Sevilla, David Quinday, Zak Parish, Conjunto Califas, Jemmy Bluestein, Abelino Bautista, Christine de la Hofer, Melanie Cervantes, Jesus Barraza, Malaquias Montoya, Jaime Montiel, Maceo Montoya, Carlos Francisco Jackson, Sylvia Savala, John Sierra, Shannon Johnson, Luis Bravo, Diego Monterrubio, Richard Juarez, Alejo Delgado, Ilan Stavans, Corrine Hales, Ester Hernandez, Berenice Guzman and students of Dinuba High School, Javier O. Huerta, Alex Espinoza and Kyle Behen, Lee Herrick Family, Arlene Biala Family, Jane Carter, Lucia Vazquez, Camille Taiara, Janigian Family, Mas Masumoto and Family, Everardo Pedraza Family, Matthew Espinoza Watson, Joseph Rios, Armstrong-Hagen Family, Ross Family, Shelly Catterson, Christopher Rosales, Bill and Diane Vigeant, Bruce Roberts, Kathleen Riley, Wayne and Deborah Petinak, Karasik-McCullough Family, Roth Crane, Saint Francis of Assisi Parish, Chuck McNally, Shubin Family, Berry Construction, Farrell Family, Ronald Scudder, Joseph Offer, Barbara Davis, Judith Major, Jacqueline Dwyer, Carol Giles-Straight, Michael Sands, Robert "V" Hansmann, Michael Fuller, Consuelo Romo, William Spence and Susan Edelstein, Richard Stone, Billey Adams, Joel and Lauren Rafael, Holly Hisamoto, Jonathan Segal, Daniel Sullivan, Beverly Nolan, Sue and Hansel Kern, Samuel and Maria Mercado, Gail Newel, Fulton 55, Danza Azteca, Jane Oriel, Douglas Dunlap, Todd Hara, Alene Campbell, Clare Anzoleaga, Rebecca Balcarcel, Lora Fike, Janet Webb, Anna Dresner, Emily Schmidlin, Richard Tellier, Merry Maisel, Henrique Reade, Mollie Weinert, K. A. Elias and S. Shena, Impress Printing, Christopher Bricker, Ken Larrey, Peter Alsop, St. Paul Council #8990, Victor Baca, Cordiero Vault, Paradise Pictures, Axiom Business Systems, Baloian Farms, Real People's Music, Hallowell Family, Holly Near, Charlie King, Donna Odierna, Olé Frijole Restaurant, Douglas-Larsson Family, Marshall Family, KNXT-TV, Janet Flores, Catherine Campbell, Thomas Quinn, Laurie A. Macallister, Manuel and Carmen Rosalez Zubiri, Richard Berquist, Cathy A. Fink, James and Marie Lambe, Marty Bocanegra, San Francisco Floral, Russell and Christine Thomas, Knights of Columbus, Donna R. Elliott, Helen and Paul Casares, Mary Jo Vernava, Grace Vernava, L. Liddle, Pamela and Paul Schramm, Hope Barnes, Vernon L. Tevriz, Louis Trivisonno, Richard Wheaton and Margaret Rivers, Gina Marie Cheeseman, Lena and Marino

Meacci, Frank and Delores Diaz, Oregon Memorials, Segel and Sapadin Family, Danforth Family, Kathleen L. Early, Nancy S. Erickson, Jane A. McCaleb, Glenda Garrick, Elise Witt, Bruce Fife, Cerniglia and Healy Family, Allan Hirsch, Charles L. Bernhardt, Clark B. Halker, Gerich Family, Robert Wilkinson, Nancy Tholen, F. Dennis Lynch, Kenneth P. Giles, Michelle Shocked, Carrol K. Allen, Carol E. Gay, Hedian-Woo Family, Jaroszynski-Hale Family, Cesar Chavez Foundation, Bennet E. Tousley, Linda M. Hamilton, Aileen Vance, Rani Arbo, Chuck Brodsky, James Durst, R. Howard Wooden, Local 1000 (Traveling Musicians Union), Kaplan-Lyman Family, Ted Warmbrand, Bell Memorials, Rosenberg Family, Nora and Kenneth Albert Family, Catholic Cemeteries of the West, Bezayiff Family, Kosch Family, Robin Wheeler, Beverly K. Grant, Michael and Janet Woodson, Michael and Carol O'Quin, and the Woody Guthrie Foundation.

PHOTO CREDITS

25 Photo of Luis Miranda Cuevas is the property of Teresa Miranda Navarro and is printed with permission of the Miranda Cuevas Navarro family.

43 Photo of Guadalupe Ramírez Lara is the property of Jaime Ramírez and is printed with permission of the Ramírez Lara family.

43 Photo of Ramón Paredes González is the property of Caritina Paredes Murillo and is printed with permission of the Paredes Murillo family.

69 Photo of a young Guadalupe Ramírez Lara is the property of Jaime Ramírez and is printed with permission of the Ramírez Lara family.

79 Photo of José Sánchez Valdivia is the property of Celio Sánchez Valdivia and is printed with permission of the Sánchez Valdivia family.

93 Photo of Frank and Bobbie Atkinson is the property of the Atkinson family and is printed with their permission.

202 Scanned image of the Holy Cross Cemetery catalogue is the property of the Roman Catholic Diocese of Fresno and is printed with their permission.

213 Photo of the original funeral services is taken from *The Register*, a newsletter published by the Catholic News Service, and is printed with their permission.

213 Photo of Martin Hoffman is the property of Glenn Streiff and is printed with his permission.

214 Photo of Tim Hernandez with families is printed with permission of Sandy Cano.

214 Photo of Tim Hernandez with men in La Estancia, Zacatecas, is printed with permission of Sandy Cano.

ABOUT THE AUTHOR

Tim Z. Hernandez was born and raised in California's San Joaquin Valley. An award-winning poet, novelist, and performer, he is a recipient of the American Book Award for poetry, the Colorado Book Award for poetry, the Premio Aztlán Literary Prize for fiction, and the International Latino Book Award for historical fiction. His books and research have been featured in the *Los Angeles Times,* the *New York Times,* CNN, Public Radio International, and National Public Radio. Hernandez holds a BA from Naropa University and an MFA from Bennington College. He continues to perform and speak across the United States and internationally, but he divides his time between Fresno and El Paso, where he is an assistant professor in the MFA Program in Creative Writing at the University of Texas, El Paso. You can find more information on his website, at www.timzhernandez.com.